DEATH DO THEY PART

J.D. WHITELAW

RED DOG
UK

Published by RED DOG PRESS 2022

Copyright © J.D Whitelaw 2022

J.D Whitelaw has asserted his right under the Copyright, Designs and Patents Act, 1988 to be identified as the author of this work

This book is sold subject to the condition that it shall not by way of trade or otherwise, be lent, resold, hired out, or otherwise circulated without the publisher's prior consent in any form of binding or cover other than that in which it is published and without a similar condition including this condition being imposed on the subsequent purchaser

First Edition

Paperback ISBN 978-1-914480-30-0
Ebook ISBN 978-1-914480-31-7

www.reddogpress.co.uk

For all the patience both Anne-Marie and Henry have always shown me.

One

THE THUMPING BASS of the nightclub speakers seemed to make everything rattle—including Martha's teeth. She already felt like a fossil—a hundred years old, with all the flesh on show. On more than one occasion, in then ten minutes she had been in the place, her jaw had almost hit the dancefloor.

Wave after wave of scantily clad young people washed past her. As if the thundering noise of the music wasn't bad enough, she had to put up with feeling like a complete dinosaur.

"Bloody hell," she said to herself.

"What?" yelled Helen beside her.

"Nothing," said Martha.

"What?" Helen shouted again.

The pulsing lights danced over her just long enough to show her face all screwed up. Martha sighed, not that anyone could hear it.

"I said 'nothing' Helen," she shouted.

"Nope, I can't hear a thing," said her sister. "This bloody place. How can anyone think this is enjoyable? I feel like my head is a bike tyre about to burst."

Just as she finished a huge roar went up from the crowd in the tightly packed room. Arms shot into the air and everyone danced that bit harder and faster to the new beat. Martha felt something wet on the back of her legs. She didn't want to look down to see what it was. She only hoped somebody had spilled their drink.

This was awful. She had to remind herself that they were there for work, not to have a good time. Which was probably for the best, all things considered. The last thing Martha Parker could do in a nightclub was have a good time.

"Where's Geri?" Helen nudged her in the ribs.

Martha felt a shove in her back. Then one in her front. The crowd was shifting, like a sleeping bear rolling from its back to its belly. She tried to protest but nobody could hear her. The music was far too loud.

She looked around the darkened room, across the dancefloor and over to the bar. What seemed like hundreds of different faces whizzed past, but none of them was her youngest sister. She wasn't sure if she should panic or not. Then she remembered who she was talking about. Geri Parker was a lot of things—fierce, feisty, her independence only matched by her intelligence. If she said she would be somewhere, she usually would turn up. Eventually.

"I don't know," said Martha, rolling with the ebb and flow of the heaving clubbers. "Come on, let's find a quiet place so I can think straight."

"What?" yelled Helen.

Martha grabbed her sister by the arm and tugged her over to the door. There was a small alcove just outside the main room. A cool breeze cleared the air out here. The music still blared and Martha was certain she'd have tinnitus for days after this. But at least it was quieter here. And she could breathe.

"Bloody hell fire," said Helen, buckling over and holding her knees. "Is this what nightclubs are like? I thought it would be more civilised. Not a flipping meat market."

"I don't know, Helen," said Martha. "I haven't been in one for about twenty years. The last time I set foot on a dancefloor, Kylie Minogue and EMF were in the charts. I don't think half the people we've seen in here were even *born* when that happened."

Right on cue, a gaggle of young lads strolled past, all dressed in identical outfits, creased, short-sleeve shirts and jeans so skinny it made their legs look like pipe cleaners. A waft of cologne followed them like the wake of a cruise liner. Martha stifled her impoliteness, Helen wasn't quite so measured.

"Yuck," she said, pinching her nose. "Those boys smell like open drains in the summer sun."

"Helen," Martha quietened her down. "Come on, pull it together. We need to meet Geri. Phone her, text her, find out where she is."

Helen tutted loudly. She unfastened her cardigan to reveal a waist bag, fastened tightly around her stomach. She unzipped it and pulled out her phone.

"What?" she asked, noticing Martha staring.

"That's very… fashionable Helen," Martha said. "I just… I just wasn't expecting to see something so *current* on your person."

"Hey, that's offensive," she said, wagging her finger. "I'm very current. I'll have you know that I have at least one other pair of sandals at home that have barely been worn."

She wriggled her toes in the sandals she was wearing. Martha laughed. How they'd made it past the bouncers on the door she still had no idea. But here they were, in the middle of a busy nightclub filled with children barely out of nappies.

A pang of panic snapped her back to the job in hand. They were there to work, they had a mission. They didn't need any distractions. Not tonight. They were very close.

"Come on, phone Geri, find out where she is."

"What do you think I'm doing?" asked Helen snootily.

A roar went up from the crowd in the room they had just left. Martha peered in to see what the fuss was about. She was none the wiser. Hands in the air, throbbing lights and pounding bass. Same scene, different song.

"Straight to answerphone," said Helen. "She must be in here somewhere."

"Damn," said Martha. "I hope she's alright."

"Martha, come on, it's Geri we're talking about here. Geri in a nightclub. That's about as alright as she's ever likely to get."

Martha nodded in agreement. "Come on then, let's check in here, we need to find her."

She walked around the narrow hall, past a long queue of people waiting to hand in their coats at the cloakroom. Helen trudged behind her, sandals slapping on the wet floor. Another room with a bar at the far side opened up in front of them. The music was just as loud in here, but the atmosphere was more subdued—less intense.

"There," said Helen, pointing over Martha's shoulder. "She's at the bar. Is that… is that who I think it is she's talking to?"

Martha gulped down a dry swallow. There was Geri, her sister, standing at the bar laughing and flirting with a tall, handsome looking man with slicked back hair and a sharp suit. They clinked shot glasses before downing the drinks. Then they congratulated each other, before he signalled over to the barmaid for more.

"Oh no," said Martha.

"Kevin McTrusty," said Helen. "The very man we're here to nab."

"Yeah," Martha said. "That's exactly who it is."

"But I thought the plan was just to take photos of him with his suspected mistress."

"Yeah, it was," said Martha with a sigh. "But you know our sister, Helen. She likes to take matters into her own hands at times."

"Oh, don't remind me," she rolled her eyes.

Geri and McTrusty downed another shot and burst out laughing. She clapped a hand on his shoulder, moving closer to him. He didn't seem to mind, welcoming the attention. Martha had suspected he might. Parkers Investigations specialised in people like Kevin McTrusty, you might even say they were their speciality. Good looking, confident and, most importantly, married.

"Right, bellies in," she said, tapping Helen on the shoulder.

They wandered over to Geri and McTrusty by the bar. When she saw them coming, the youngest Parker straightened up. The smile dropped from her face and her eyes widened. If Martha didn't know better, she would have thought Geri was surprised to see them.

"Good evening," she said.

"Hi," said Geri awkwardly.

"Hello," said McTrusty, wiping his mouth on the sleeve of his expensive looking suit. "Who are you?"

"We're friends of Geri's," said Martha.

"*Good* friends of Geri's, you might say," Helen added, rocking back and forward on her heels.

McTrusty eyed them both up and down. He sneered and reached for his bottle of beer that was waiting on the bar. The glare from his giant, designer watch almost blinded Martha, but she didn't let it show. She had an intense dislike for this man. Yes, she knew that his wife and young child were waiting at home until all hours, wondering what he did with his nights. Yes, she knew that he had been having at least three affairs with old school and college friends in the past month they'd been trailing him. And yes, she thought he was arrogant beyond all belief. Being in his company for the first time seemed to confirm everything she had learned from afar.

"Hi guys," said Geri, clearing her throat. "Good to see you."

"Geri," Martha nodded.

"Geri," Helen nodded too.

"I thought you guys weren't coming in until later?"

"We got her at the arranged time," said Helen, trying to sound businesslike. "Which is many, many hours past your bedtime young lady."

"Hey, back off yeah?" said McTrusty with an arrogant laugh. "You're not her mum, okay? We're just having a good time."

"Oh, is that so?" Helen lifted her nose high into the air.

"Helen," said Martha and Geri in unison.

"Yeah, that is so," said McTrusty.

He puffed out his chest and squared his shoulders, turning to face Helen straight on. "What are you going to do about it, eh?"

"What am *I* going to do?" Helen laughed. "I'll tell you what I'm going to do. I'm going to phone your wife and tell her where you are and what you're doing. How does that sound, eh?"

"Oh jeez," said Geri, clapping her hand to her forehead.

"Helen," said Martha, her toes curling in her boots.

McTrusty laughed. He took another swig from his beer and then looked the Parker sisters up and down again, Geri included this time. Something seemed to twig in the pit of his slightly drunken mind. Martha was certain she could see the penny dropping.

"Wait a minute," he said. "Wait a minute, here. Who are you three? Who are you?"

There was panic in his voice. Even in the sweltering heat and noise of the nightclub Martha could see it. She had confronted enough cheating partners down the years to know what guilt looked and sounded like. And Kevin McTrusty was sweating guilt by the bucketload.

"Is this a setup?" he shouted. "Are you three in cahoots or something? Did Angela send you? Are you fitting me up?"

"Kevin, calm down," said Martha, stepping forward. "We're more than happy to explain."

McTrusty leapt forward. His big, meaty hands thrust into Martha's chest with enough force, she felt like she'd been kicked by a horse. She tumbled backwards, Geri and Helen catching her before she hit the floor. McTrusty made off in the opposite direction, pushing and shoving his way towards the door.

"Oh no," said Martha, being helped to her feet. "I really hate it when they run."

The Parkers gave chase across the smaller dancefloor and out the door. They followed the noise of screams and shouts as McTrusty barrelled up the main stairwell that led to the exit. Martha, Helen and Geri weren't far behind, weaving into the gaps where eager clubbers had wisely ducked out of the way.

"Way to go Helen," panted Geri. "Another sterling success for Parkers Investigations."

"At least I wasn't trying to bed the target, Geri."

"Excuse me? I was trying to get him to cough up some evidence."

"Oh, is that what you call it these days."

"Quick," Martha shouted. "He's heading for the door."

McTrusty reached the exit before them, although they had made up plenty of space. He was wheezing and coughing by the time he reached the fashionable smokers huddled around the arched doorway of the converted church that now hosted the club. He staggered before trying to navigate the steps. His foot slipped and he tumbled forward, bouncing and thudding down the well-trodden stairs until he landed in a heap at the feet of the bouncers.

Martha, Helen and Geri reached the door in time to see him scramble to his feet. Dishevelled and filthy, he still carried an arrogance about him, even though he looked ridiculous. When he spied the sisters back at the door, he smirked. Tipping them a lazy salute, he laughed.

"Nice try ladies," he said. "But I'm too shrewd for that."

He tapped his temple and went to head past the security staff and off into the night. Martha panicked. This had been their chance to catch him in the act. It would bring the case to a close. If he got away then they wouldn't get another chance at him. He knew they were onto him and poor Angela, the forgotten wife, would never have closure.

Before she could scream in frustration, a loud whistle went up from beside her. Everyone outside the club seemed to stop what they were doing, including McTrusty. All eyes fell on Geri, her fingers in her mouth.

"Oi!" she shouted at the bouncers. "That bloke stole my purse."

She pointed at McTrusty, who looked dumbfounded. There was no time for him to react. The burly, broad chested bouncers, clad in black, pounced on him in an instant. He tried to resist, but it was futile. Before long he was wrestled to the ground and was cursing at anyone and everyone who would listen.

Martha let out a yelp of delight. Geri sauntered down the old church steps to the melee and produced her phone. Kneeling down beside McTrusty, she took a photo. The flash dazzled him before he started to struggle again.

"There we go, lovely stuff," she said, showing him the picture on her screen. "I think your wife will be delighted when we show her a picture of you fighting with bouncers at a trendy nightclub, don't you? Where was it you said you were again tonight? Work was it? Or helping out at a soup kitchen. I can't remember, you've told her so many lies Kevin, it almost doesn't matter anymore. We know them all, anyway. Still, nice of you to buy me that drink. I won't be taking you up on your other offer, and I won't mention it in front of these lovely gentlemen. I don't want them to tear you limb from limb."

"You cow," McTrusty snarled. "You little cow."

Geri laughed, as Martha and Helen joined her down the steps.

"Very good, Miss Parker," said Martha with a smile.

"Yes I suppose that was a good enough plan," Helen sniffed. "Not quite what we arranged, but it worked nonetheless."

"That's about as kind a compliment as I've ever had from you Helen, thank you," said Geri. She reached out and hugged both of her sisters as the bouncers led McTrusty away from the other guests. Geri sniffed the air.

"Oh," she said. "Do you smell that? Chips. Delicious."

"Chips it is then," said Martha.

"As long as you're buying," said Helen.

Martha smiled as they headed out onto the road. She felt her phone vibrating in her back pocket as they went, but she ignored it. Not now, not after this little victory. Another case closed. Not a happy ending, not this time. But justice was done. They could afford to celebrate. Or at least, that's what she thought.

Two

MARTHA STARED AT the hospital bed. It was empty, bare, and lifeless—the sheets and blanket folded back with expert, almost military precision. Stark lines of colour breaching the washed out white of the linen. Two pillows were propped up at the top, their duty done for the day. They'd been a great help of course, making things as easy as they could be, given the circumstances. Thoroughly cleaned and back on duty, they'd be helping someone else shortly, Martha didn't doubt that.

Her time here was at an end. And it was the worst possible outcome. Only a day had passed since they'd caught McTrusty. That fateful night in Glasgow's west end when everything seemed to be so full of promise, so full of *life*. It was a million miles away now, it felt like it had happened to someone else.

Now there was nothing. Everything was bleak. She stared down at a hospital bed where her mother had just spent her final few hours. Now there was nothing. The phrase kept going around and around in her sleep deprived, devastated mind. Martha wondered if there would ever be anything else in there ever again.

The door gently clicked open from behind her. She heard it but didn't react. She just sat there, staring numbly.

"You okay?" came a familiar voice.

Helen appeared beside her, hunkered down so she was at the same eye level. She looked awful, Martha thought. Her younger sister was clearly struggling just as badly.

"What do you think?" she sniffed, her voice broken.

"Yeah, I don't know why I asked that," said Helen. "Probably something to do with the amount of times I've been asked it in the last twenty-four hours. It's all I've been hearing. Are you okay? Are you okay? Like you say Mart, what the hell kind of answer is anyone expecting?"

"They're only being kind," she said softly, wiping her nose on the ragged tissue she'd been holding for the last hour. "People don't know what to say or do when this type of thing happens."

"Yeah," said Helen, her bottom lip trembling. "I guess… you're right."

She reached out and touched the edge of the bed, just before a sob escaped her. Martha took hold of her sister and pulled her in close to her. She hugged her, as they had done so many times in the past day. They just stood there for a moment, in the hospital room off the busy ward, close together but feeling alone.

Helen pulled away first. She rubbed her face, bright red blotches around her cheeks and above her eyebrows like a terrible superhero mask. She pushed back her long, frizzy hair and shook her head.

"I can't believe she's gone, Martha," she said. "I mean, she was an old woman and everything, I get that, I understand the logic. I just can't believe that she's away. This close to Christmas too."

"I know," said Martha. "I know Helen. I keep thinking this is some sort of strange dream. Or I've been spiked or something and it's one long, bad trip. I knew I shouldn't have gone to that nightclub."

Helen smiled at that. It was comforting to see her smile. Martha had quite forgotten how to do that. Much like she had forgotten to answer her phone that night. If only she had done, maybe they would have had longer with their mother, in her final hours. Ifs and buts, they went around and around in Martha's mind like the carriages of a Ferris wheel. Only they would never stop.

"Have the police spoken to you?" asked Helen.

The question caught Martha off guard. She was still thinking back to that night, that phone call, those hours that passed when she could have been by her mother's side after the accident.

"No, not since we came into the hospital," she said. "I haven't heard anything. Have you?"

"No," said Helen. "Although they're treating it as a hit-and-run."

"How do you know?"

Helen dragged her gaze from the empty bed. She reached into the pocket of her grubby cardigan and handed over her phone. Martha took it from her sister and looked down at the screen. A newspaper website was open, showing a street view of the road outside their mother's home. The headline made Martha's whole body stiffen.

OAP DIES AFTER HORROR WEST END HIT-AND-RUN
— COPS HUNT MANIAC DRIVER.

She wasn't sure what she was more bothered by—the idea that her mother had been killed by some maniac or that the whole country was now aware of the tragedy. She handed the phone back to Helen.

"Back in the headlines," she said quietly.

"We seem to be racking them up by the dozen these days," said Helen. "Although I suppose it's just standard procedure, no? Police have got to issue an appeal to try and catch that bastard."

The anger seemed to spark a bit of life into the room. Not that Martha could even think about revenge and justice at this stage. She was still grieving the loss of her mother. The woman who had raised her, who had always been there for her, who had taught her everything she knew. A hole that size couldn't just be filled in overnight. And no police investigation could even come *close* to it.

"You look exhausted," said Helen. "When was the last time you slept?"

"I'm fine," said Martha, shifting uncomfortably in her chair.

"You're not fine, Martha. You have to rest."

"I'm fine, Helen, stop fussing," she said. "There's too much to do, far too much to do. We need to organise the funeral, I need to let the extended family know, the cousins in Canada, all of that."

"We can do that, Martha. It's not fair that you shoulder all of it."

"You?" she laughed. "I appreciate the offer Helen, but I don't think I could ask that of you on your own."

The statement seemed to linger in the air between them. There was one noticeable absentee from the room. Martha and Helen had barely seen Geri since their mother had died. Neither had heard from her either.

"She'll be here," said Helen. "She's just in shock Martha."

"I know she is," said Martha. "We all are. But she should be here, with her family. Where else, or who else, could possibly be better company, better help or support than us at this time? We should be pulling together to sort everything out. Not sitting around wondering where one of us has gone."

She shook her head. Helen knew better than to argue back. Martha was glad that her younger sister was standing up and making excuses for their youngest sibling. There was a flash of loyalty there that money just couldn't buy. But it didn't gloss over Geri's absence. And that upset Martha.

A knock at the door interrupted her anger. They both turned around to meet a young nurse, face flushed.

"Martha Parker?" she said to neither of them in particular.

"Yes," said Martha nervously.

"We've just been given notice at the ward desk that you've been asked to go downstairs to meet with the police," said the nurse. "Now there's no rush, we understand that you've been put through the mill. But the police want to talk to you about your mum's accident."

Martha took a deep breath. She could feel that familiar burning in the back of her throat and behind her nose. She was about to cry. But something stopped her. She wasn't sure if it was a voice in the back of her head, or an emotional sledgehammer to her stomach. It was something. A force to be reckoned with.

She pushed herself up from the chair and nodded towards the nurse.

"Okay," she said, her voice now hardened.

"Martha, you can't, not in your state," said Helen.

"It's okay," she said, clasping her sister's hand tightly. "I've got this. It's okay. I have to. For mum."

Helen's eyes filled with tears. She smiled through her sadness.

"For mum."

Three

OF ALL THE interview rooms Martha had been in down the years, this was probably the most comfortable. A soft light made everything warmer, more hospitable. The chair she sat on was easy on her back and much more friendly than those on the ward. She had even been given a cup of tea for her trouble as she waited for the police.

The TV was on in the corner of the room—a quiz show Martha didn't recognise. The colours were bright, something to do with balls bouncing down a board. She realised then, as she sat looking at the screen, how utterly out of sync she felt with the world. Everything, even the TV schedule, felt like it had been turned upside down and onto its head. All with that final, fateful phone call she had finally answered.

Martha closed her eyes. She could still hear the breathlessness in her husband's voice on the other end of the line. She knew right away there was something wrong, something serious. There were only a few of those types of calls you would ever take in your life. She had been numb ever since.

Throw into the mix a police investigation, and it all felt very overwhelming. The road outside her mother's house had always been notorious for speeders. A thoroughfare between busy routes in the leafy west end of the city, too much traffic went up and down it on a daily basis. There was bound to be an accident sooner or later. If it hadn't been Martha's mother, the Parker's Matriarch, then it would be some other poor bugger.

The fact the driver hadn't stopped, however, was utterly scurrilous. To leave a pensioner lying hurt in the middle of the road was beyond forgiveness. And that was Martha being kind. When her mind started to work again properly, she might be able to muster some proper anger, some fighting rage. She would catch whoever did this and stare them down, look them in the eye and ask them one question. 'Why?'

"Martha."

The mention of her name startled her. She looked up from her chair to see a familiar face—Detective Sergeant Aileen Pope stood over her. The relentlessly severe cop creased her face into something vaguely resembling a smile.

"DS Pope," said Martha, standing up.

Before she knew what she was doing, she was hugging the policewoman. Pope was stiff as a board. She didn't reciprocate, instead making a sort of contained grunt that was both polite and clear enough that Martha should let her go.

"Sorry," she said. "I don't know what came over me. I think… I wasn't expecting to see you and it's really good to see you, actually. Does that make sense?"

"No, it doesn't," said Pope, moving over to the long sofa that stretched along the side wall. "But I've come to expect that from you and your sisters, Parker."

She switched off the TV set. Pulling the legs of her creased trousers up, and sat down, clasping her hands.

"How are you feeling?" the policewoman asked.

There was that question again, Martha thought. Helen had been right, it was getting annoying.

"I'm not really sure, to be perfectly honest with you," she said. "I've gone from being fairly happy and content to being an orphan woman in her mid-forties in less than two days. And that's before I even *think* about the fact my mother's killer is probably still driving around without a care in the world as we speak."

Martha felt better getting that off her chest. She wasn't trying to lay the blame at Pope's door. Far from it. She just needed somebody to vent to.

"Makes sense," said the DS, clearing her throat. "Losing your mother can't be a lot of fun. If it makes things any better, you're handling it a lot better than some of the folk I've seen down the years."

"I am?" asked Martha.

"Definitely. You're not smashing this place up, for starters. Nor have you gone on a drunken bender and ended up shooting gangsters. I'd say you're on the better end of the scale Parker. If there *is* a better end to the scale."

Martha smiled weakly. She could feel her chin puckering, the sadness only going for a split second. Thankfully she pulled it all back in and tried to focus.

"The nurse upstairs said that the police wanted to speak with me," she said. "Are you handling the case?"

"No," said Pope in her usual, hard, no-nonsense style. "I'm a murder detective Parker, this is a road traffic offence, or at the least that's what it is at the moment. If it turns out to be targeted then maybe I'll get it across my desk. But until then, I'm strictly here as a friendly observer with some skin in the game."

"I don't follow you," said Martha.

Pope leaned forward. She drummed her fingers on the back of her hands, thumbs poking up in the air like a pair of antennas. Martha could tell she was nervous. It was something she never associated with Aileen Pope. The hard edge, the sickly skin, the confrontational demeanour, this was the detective sergeant that Martha had come to know. Now she seemed almost human as she searched for the right words to say.

"I was in the parish," said the cop. "Some nasty business to do with gangsters that I won't bother you with. But I heard the name Parker to do with your mum's case and figured there might be a connection. Lo and behold, I see you're the next of kin and thought, well, you're going through enough of a time of it as it is, maybe you could do with being thrown a bone."

"Thrown a bone?"

"Yeah," said Pope. "Best to hear what's going on from me than some faceless CID moron two weeks into the job."

In typical Pope fashion, there was a friendliness there, but it was lost among the normal venom and less than passive aggressive spite.

"Thank you," said Martha.

She took a deep breath. Now that she was focussed, she started to feel nervous.

"What do you need from me?" she asked.

"I don't need anything," said Pope. "But the investigating team want you to know you'll have to wait."

"Wait for what?"

"Your mum's body to be released."

Martha began to shake. She clutched at her hands and tried to steady her nerves. There were certain phrases that you never, ever wanted to hear in your life. That had been one of them.

"I… I see," she managed to get the words past her teeth. "Why?"

"It's an ongoing investigation, Parker," said Pope, a slight warmth creeping into her voice. "There's going to have to be a post mortem. A report will need to be sent to the procurator fiscal too. And until we catch whoever it is that was driving when they hit your mother, this will remain an open case."

"No funeral yet, then," said Martha, sitting back in her chair.

"No, not yet," said Pope.

"I understand," she said.

This time, she couldn't hold back the tears. The first one trickled down her cheek and seemed to start the race for the others. She felt like she was sinking into the comfortable chair. Or something was dragging her down, backside first. The world around her melted away. She could see nothing, even though her eyes were wide open and, as far as she knew, were still working.

Thoughts about what to tell the family, what to tell Helen and Geri, flashed into her mind. Was this embarrassing? Was this something to be ashamed of? When would they be able to get some closure on all of this? Where would her mother's remains be kept?

"You okay there, Parker?" asked Pope.

The cop's croaky, stern voice cut through Martha's shock like a well-sharpened blade.

"Yes, yes, sorry," she said, sitting forward, making sure she wasn't stuck to the chair. "I'm sorry, this is all… this is all a *lot* to take in DS Pope. As I'm sure you can understand."

"Yeah, I can," she said.

"But thank you," she said. "Thank you for taking the time and the thought to speak with me. I appreciate that, a lot, as it happens."

Pope tried to smile again, but it came across as awkward and unsightly. She got to her feet and walked over to the door, past Martha. Before she opened it, she paused.

"I know how you're feeling Parker," she said. "Believe me I do. Losing a parent is the worst thing in the world. I've been there, I've done all of this. I know that it doesn't make anything any easier, being told how to suck eggs. But you need to get some rest. I'd wager you haven't slept since she passed away. Am I right?"

Martha didn't meet her eyeline. She just nodded.

"Thought so. Take it from me then, make sure you get some shut-eye. You'll thank yourself for it in the long run. That's my only advice. I'll try to keep an eye on things for you, but division will be all over this kind of thing. They're not great, but they'll do their best to catch the bastard who did this."

Martha nodded again. She rubbed her forehead and reached out for her tea. She sipped it. It was ice cold. It tasted stale and sour but it was something at least.

"Do you know how long the post mortem will take?" she asked Pope.

"No idea," was the answer. "Depends on how busy the boys and girls down at the morgue are. They'll look after your mum's remains though Parker, you don't need to worry about that."

"Thank you," Martha whispered.

Pope pulled the door open. The muted hubbub of the hospital seeped through the open door. Before she left, the detective sergeant stopped mid-stride.

"One last thing, Parker," she said, sounding serious.

Martha looked up at the policewoman.

"Don't go trying to be a hero with this," she said. "I know what you and those sisters of yours are like. There are professionals handling this, professionals who don't and *won't* make it personal. And that will mean there's a case, a *good* case, to put the scumbag who hit your mum behind bars. We can only do that if we have your promise that you won't interfere."

Martha couldn't help but feel like she was being told off for something she hadn't even done. The friendliness from Pope had been short-lived. She had come in, done her extra duty and was now leaving with, what Martha suspected, was the main reason she had called in to see her.

"Oh, and it's DI Pope now," she said. "Got a promotion a few weeks back. Not that I'm proud of it or anything."

"I give you my word DI Pope," she said. "We won't interfere, not with this one. It's too important."

Pope stared at her for a moment longer than needed. Martha felt like the cop was trying to read her mind. Chance would be a fine thing. Nobody, not even Martha herself, wanted to go sifting through that disaster zone right now. Eventually Pope relented. She nodded and headed out the door, closing it quietly behind her.

Martha waited for a moment to make sure she had been left alone. When nobody came in after the policewoman, she quietly and deliberately placed the cup of stale tea down on the table in front of her. Then she started to cry.

Four

GERI LAY STARING up at the ceiling. She had counted the cracks that stretched out from the side wall a thousand times. Damp, the landlord had told her, old damp. There was nothing to worry about—it had all been fixed. She didn't believe a word he said and had been meaning to pay for someone to come and have a look at it independently. The last thing she wanted, or needed for that matter, was Mrs Foley dropping through the ceiling midway through her Wednesday night bath. If for nothing else, Geri couldn't put up with the Gilbert and Sullivan concert that would accompany the bathing.

All of that seemed inconsequential now. They were only cracks after all. Geri had to learn to trust people, Martha and Helen had been telling her that for years. If her landlord said it had been fixed, then why wouldn't she believe it? He was an upstanding member of society, wasn't he? What would he have to gain if there was an accident? Stories she had heard from friends, vague acquaintances even, of coming home and there being no floor to stand on were few and far between. She had to trust that he was telling the truth. And Mrs Foley would stay firmly on her own level, scrubbing her back to the score of the HMS Pinafore.

She let out a long, painful sigh. Even in her thoughts, she was rambling. Her mind was getting away from her. Everything hurt. It was a pain she couldn't solve. Her very soul felt like it was searingly hot, burning her up from the inside and out. The hours had turned to days. Geri closed her eyes and felt the tears roll down her temples as she did her best not to make a sound.

A creak from beyond the end of the bed made her jump. She sat up, the duvet pulled all the way up to her chin. The door opened slowly.

"Are you awake?" came a whisper.

"I am," she said, rubbing her face. "Of course I am. I can't sleep."

Matt pushed the door open further with his bare shoulder. He was carrying two mugs, steam rising and curling from their lips. He raised them up and smiled at Geri sitting up in her bed.

"Breakfast in bed," he said.

"Breakfast?" she peered over at her watch lying among her clothes. "It's almost six."

"Dinner in bed then," he said. "What's twelve hours, eh?"

The thought made Geri's head hurt, literally. She rubbed at her forehead, feeling the pain yawn all the way back across her skull and wrap itself around the back. Matt hopped around the room, making sure his bare feet didn't stand on anything sharp, wet, sticky or squelchy. He stretched the short distance towards the bed and landed the springy mattress, wobbling around in an attempt to save the contents of his mug.

"Ladies' choice," he said. "We've got orange or we've got brown."

"Those aren't flavours Matt," said Geri.

"No, they're not," he sniffed the mugs. "But I don't think any actual ingredients were harmed in the making of the powder that this sumptuous feast came from. It's probably easier if we just call them colours, that way they won't get offended when we can't actually taste whatever flavours they're supposed to be."

He gave her a gawky smile. Geri, as sad as she was, smiled back. She grabbed the nearest mug and sipped down on some brown.

"That's disgusting, whatever it's supposed to be," she said. "And it's also boiling hot. My tongue has been vulcanised."

Matt glugged away at his own mug. He finished it in three swallows and wiped his mouth on the back of his arm. A little belch later, he lay back.

"That wasn't bad," he said. "Not great, but better than I was expecting. What did you say, Geri?"

"Nothing," she said.

She leaned down and put the mug among the others that had gathered in a small herd around the edge of her bed. She withdrew back under the duvet and hugged it about her, a cold shiver running over her.

"How are you holding up?" he asked her.

Geri didn't say anything. She just shrugged, staring into the middle distance at nothing in particular. She felt the corner of her mouth tugging to one side, a habit she found herself doing whenever she had too much to think about. Strangely, in the years she had been working with her sisters, it very rarely cropped up. Now that her mother was gone, she must have done it every half hour for the last few days.

"You know it's okay to grieve," he said, a sombreness about him. "You've lost your mum. That's a big thing. A huge thing. You only get one mum and it's sort of a rite of passage, if you will. It's okay to feel the way that you do and—"

"Matt," she held up a hand.

"What?"

"I know you're trying to help," she said. "Really, I know you are. And I love you for it. But I don't need some tinpot psychology lesson in coping with grief."

"Oh," he said.

He lay back, rolling away from her. Geri instantly felt dreadful. Even more dreadful than before. She looked over at him, watching his face turn from stoic to downtrodden with only a slight arch of his eyebrows. There was that burning again, hot and venomous, like a fire had been stoked with bellows.

"Matt, don't…" she said.

"Don't what?" he asked.

"Don't do that."

"Do what?"

"*That*," she nodded at him.

He looked up at the wall behind him then back to her.

"What?"

"*That* look. You know the one."

"I don't!"

"You do. It's the one where you look like a dog who's been caught chewing all the toilet roll and its owners are too entertained to chastise it."

"I have absolutely no idea what you're talking about," he said, sitting up. "This is just my normal face, the one God gave me. I can't help it if you think I'm some sort of master manipulator with my good looks."

Geri let out a loud laugh.

"Good looks is it? Chance would be a fine thing," she said.

"I beg your pardon, Ms Parker," he said.

"Ms Parker? That's my sister, who's old enough to be your mother I think you'll find. I'm *Miss* Parker."

"And you'll be a miss forever with that mouth of yours," he said, getting ready to leap.

"Good," she said, grabbing a pillow.

Matt sprung forward. Geri swung at him and caught him across the face with the pillow. He grabbed her and they both rolled over across the bed, entangled in the duvet and sheets. She leaned in and kissed him on the lips before burying her head in his neck. Matt wrapped his arms around her and they lay there panting. When they broke the hold, Geri wiped away more tears. She stayed perfectly still, listening to her boyfriend's heartbeat in his chest.

"Don't go," she said.

"I have to Geri," he said without moving. "I'm the only one on duty tonight. If I don't go then they can't open the doors. And you know what trouble that would bring."

She knew all too well. And she knew that she didn't mean what she had said. She just thought she would try.

"I know," she said.

She lifted her head and propped her chin on his chest. Staring up at him, he was looking at the ceiling.

"Four," she said.

"What?" he asked.

"Four cracks, across the ceiling. The landlord says there's nothing wrong, it's just a bit of old damp."

Matt sucked his tongue and whistled.

"And if you believe that, you'll believe anything Geri."

"I know," she said. "But you've got to have a bit of faith, don't you? That's what Martha and Helen always tell me. And they're the wisest people in the world."

"Now I know you're lying," he said, turning his attention to her. "Have you spoken to them?"

"No," she said curtly. "Not since we found out about mum."

"You should speak to them," he said. "They're your family, your sisters, your colleagues even."

"I can't," she said.

"Can't or won't?"

"A little of both," she said. "I just… I just can't right now. Not in this state of mind. I need to get my head together, get some breathing space away from the family, away from anyone who looks like my mum. Seriously man, the pair of them when I left them at the hospital, they had the same bloody face as the old lady. It was frightening."

"You're being cruel."

"I'm being serious."

She sat up. And it was true. After the doctors had told them of their mother's passing, they had all gone out for some fresh air. In the hard light of the streetlamps, Martha and Helen had looked more haggard and aged than Geri had ever seen them. Granted, she wasn't in much better shape. But it had been the last thing she had needed to see following the shock of the news.

"I can't tell you what to do," said Matt, reaching for her shoulder. "They're your family, your sisters. They'll be worried about you, like I am. You shouldn't ignore them Geri, not after everything you've told me. They're just looking out for you, that's all."

Geri knew he was right. She couldn't admit it though, not in her current mood. She shook her head and reached down for her soup.

"Bugger," said Matt. "I'm late."

He scrambled out of bed and started to dress, pulling his clothes from every corner of the room. The late evening light was still bright, shining with a steely greyness in through the window of her bedroom. Outside the birds chirped, dotted about the small courtyard to the back of the block of flats. Geri watched Matt dress, begging for time to stop or at least slow down with every sock, every button. It didn't, it wouldn't, and before she knew it, he was ready.

"What are you doing tonight?" he asked her, pulling on his jacket.

"Don't know," she said. "Might wash my hair. Might go up town and find a man who doesn't leave his grieving girlfriend on her own a matter of days after her mum died."

Matt's arms dropped to his side.

"Geri," he said. "That's not fair. You know it's only an internship and I need to be there before my shift, stay after, make a good impression, if I want to have a career and—"

"I was joking," she said.

"Oh," he said.

The relief was palpable. Colour flushed into his cheeks again and he paused. He reached down and kissed her once, gently, on her lips.

"Text me, when you're going to sleep," he said.

"Okay," she agreed, re-wrapping herself in the duvet. "Have a good shift. Say hello to all the cadavers for me."

He smiled and headed out of the door, waving. Geri sat still and waited until the front door had slammed closed. She sat and looked at nothing again. It felt like the natural thing to do, the *only* thing she *could* do. Then she felt her mouth tugging to the side again.

Rubbing her cheek, she rummaged around for her phone. The inevitable cavalcade of messages and missed calls were waiting for her as she expected. Top of the list was a dozen from Martha and three from Helen, all spaced out in neat ten minute intervals.

"Great," she said. "Just what I need."

She rolled back into bed and hit the call button on Martha's number. As she heard the rings she counted the cracks on the ceiling. There was a new one forming, only small.

"Blind faith," she said with an ironic laugh. "Who needs it?"

Five

THE HOUSE WAS quiet. Martha had never known it to be this quiet before. Even the floorboards beneath her feet felt muted.

Her mother had always been welcoming. The door was always open to everyone. It made for an interesting way to grow up. Maybe she had picked up some of that welcoming nature from her mother, she couldn't be sure. She always tried to see the positives in people. Being in her line of work, though, it put that faith to the test.

The thought of work made her shudder. There was a stack of files sitting on her desk that needed to be seen to. A growing profile—fame, if you wanted to call it that—had seen Parkers Investigations go from a tiny hobby in a draughty garage to a legitimate business. They even had social media profiles and followings, so Geri said. Martha still liked to keep a safe distance between herself and that side of things. The wrong thing said here or there and everything was topsy turvy. No, she would stick to the classic methods of investigation.

Not that she could concentrate on anything like that at the moment. She would have to sort out the endless paperwork another time and focus on organising a funeral for her mother. That was whenever the coroner's office released her body. And Pope's natural cynicism hadn't given Martha much hope for a quick outcome.

Walking through her mother's house now, with the encroaching darkness creeping up the main hall, was almost comforting. Everything in here was just as her mother had left it that fateful evening. Her glasses were still on the table beside the front door. A week of newspapers neatly stacked up below them, wrapped in string and ready to be recycled. Martha couldn't be certain, but she thought she could still smell her perfume lingering in the hallway.

It felt good to be back here. She had been worried about returning so soon after her mother's passing. But there was a comfort, a warmth about the house. Everything oozed memories. Her mother might be gone, but her memory was still very much alive here. She was glad.

"Pizza is on its way," said Helen, wandering into the hallway. "Says they're having a labour crisis and things will take longer than usual."

"Whoever heard of a fast food chain having a labour crisis."

"It's happening everywhere Martha, people are struggling to make ends meet out there. And we don't have to put up with the nonsense these big companies have put them through for decades."

"I have every sympathy for them," she said. "But I'm bloody starving."

"That's a good sign," said Helen. "Means you're starting to work through your grief."

Martha caught sight of a picture hanging on the wall near the stairs. It was of the whole family. Her mother and father standing with their chests pushed out, Mickey Mouse ears propped on their heads, Geri in their arms. Helen was wrapped around her mother's legs, acting bashful. And Martha was the moody teenager to one side.

"Do you remember this holiday?" she asked her sister.

Helen wandered over and laughed.

"I remember you complaining a lot," she said. "If it wasn't the heat, it was the number of people. You even seemed to moan when we met Mickey and Goofy and the rest of them. Totally ruined my childhood, of course."

"Stop it," said Martha. "That's not true."

"No, it's not," she said. "It was actually quite hilarious. There's nothing more entertaining than a teenager trying to rebel."

"You should know. You did it often enough when you were one," said Martha.

"It's your stonewall right as an acne riddled, hormone pumping pre-twenty-year-old to act like a complete and utter arsehole at all times, Martha. Didn't you get the memo."

"Some of us didn't stop at twenty."

"Cow," Helen smiled.

"That was the last holiday we ever went on as a family," said Martha wistfully. "I stopped coming away with you all the next summer."

"Probably for the best," said Helen with a sniff.

Martha looked around at her sister.

"Well, it's true," she said. "You were a teenager, you were growing up and listening to loud music and wanting to talk to boys. I just wanted to play on the swings and Geri was still at mother's breast. It was the best decision for all of us."

Martha went to complain, but found she had nothing. Helen was right. Being a teenager was hard, she knew that now as a mother herself. When her parents had told her she didn't need to go on holiday with them anymore, it had felt like such a victory, a relief. After all, she didn't want to traipse around theme parks, museums or other family haunts, when she could be off on her own. She regretted it all now of course. What she wouldn't give to have her parents back and to spend those precious moments together all over again.

"Moments lost in time," she said, touching the picture gently.

"Very prophetic," said Helen. "You know, if you're hungry, there is cereal in the kitchen cupboard. Mum didn't have any biscuits, or milk that was in date right enough. But you could just eat it raw, as it were."

"I'm good," said Martha. "I think I'll just wait until the pizza arrives."

"Ask and you shall receive," said Geri.

Martha and Helen almost jumped out of their skins. Geri had appeared from nowhere, standing at the far end of the hall, three large pizza boxes in her hands. She smiled through the growing gloom.

"Geri," said Martha, catching her breath.

"What?" the youngest Parker smiled.

"You blithering idiot, Geri," Helen blurted. "You could have given us a bloody heart attack. Where the hell did you come from?"

Geri opened the top box and fished a slice of pizza out. She took an unsightly large chomp and began to chew loudly.

"You know, for a pair of private investigators, you two are surprisingly unobservant," she said. "Firstly, I bumped into the delivery guy on my way in, he said he's been knocking on the front door with no answer for the last ten minutes."

"Ten minutes?" Martha asked.

"Cobblers," said Helen. "We've been in the hall looking at old pictures. We would have heard him."

"Not how he tells it," said Geri. "Secondly…"

"Oh there's more is there?" Helen sniffed.

"Secondly," Geri went on. "The side gate wasn't on its latch, so anyone or anything could just come wandering around into mum's garden. And as a bonus point, this pizza is really, *really* good. Turkey and ham, they should do this all year around and not just at Yuletide."

Helen scratched her head. Then she looked guilty.

"Okay, so I might have forgotten to lock the gate. Sue me," she shrugged.

"And lastly, the back door is open. Unlocked. So while you two were strolling down memory lane, you could have had an axe-wielding murderer come in here and lop your heads off, before you even knew what was going on."

"Well, that's extreme, is it not?" said Helen.

"I got in, didn't I?"

"You did, and you brought food, which is far more important and exciting than axe murderers," Helen snatched the boxes from her sister and scurried off into the kitchen.

That left Martha and Geri on their own in the hallway. They stood for an awkward moment, both unsure what to say or do. The past few days had been difficult for both of them. Martha knew that. She also knew that Geri was still young, in her early twenties. To lose her mother was bad enough, let alone in the way things had turned out. She had to keep reminding herself that this was her sister and that they shouldn't squabble.

"It's good to see you," she said, offering the first olive branch.

"Yeah, you too," said Geri, finishing off the crust. "Although I saw you like three days ago or something, didn't I?"

"Four," said Martha. "Four days, just after mum passed. You came outside with us and then vanished into the night, like a ghost."

"Ouch. Still a bit raw I see," said Geri.

"Just a bit," said Martha with a tired smile.

"I just needed some space, that's all, Mart. You go from having a mum to not having one in the space of a phone call and a day in the hospital. It's a proper mindbender and as you know, I like to handle these things in my own way."

"Yeah, I know," she said, dropping her head. "It's been hard though Geri, not having you around. Not just for me, for Helen too. Contrary to popular belief, she does actually miss you when you're not here."

A loud clank of plates and dishes emanated from the kitchen. Geri looked down the hallway and back to Martha, smiling.

"The only thing she misses is anything glaringly obvious," she said. "She's looking for a pizza slicer when it's already been cut up."

"Did mum have a pizza slicer?" shouted Helen from the kitchen.

Martha felt her face stretch into a broad smile and she started to laugh. And just like that, any lingering bitterness between the two was gone. She stepped forward and hugged her youngest sister. They stood there, in the dark of their mother's hallway, and enjoyed each other's embrace.

"We're a family, we stick together, through thick and thin," Martha said quietly.

"I know," said Geri. "I know that, Mart. I just miss her, that's all. She's only been dead a matter of days and already I miss her."

"I miss her too," she said, choking back tears. "But we'll get through this. We always do. We've had much deeper holes to burrow out of and we've got there in the end. We just have to stick together. We're always family, Geri. Always. That never changes."

"I know that," she nodded. "I know that, Mart. And it's good to see you, both of you, it really is. I can't remember the last time

I went more than twenty-four hours without being in your company. I guess I must have missed you."

Martha kissed her sister on the forehead and squeezed her shoulder. She was immensely proud of her, as always. And she was relieved to see her all in one piece. Fighting and confrontation weren't Martha Parker's style, no matter how often it happened. She certainly didn't want to fight with her sisters.

"Oh," cried Helen, emerging with the open boxes. "Turns out they were already sliced after all."

"Honestly," said Geri, rolling her eyes. "Remind me again how many degrees you have?"

"What's that got to do with it?"

"Never mind," said Geri, grabbing another slice.

The pizza was barely in her mouth when she snapped her fingers at Martha. The eldest Parker blinked, the smell of cheese and pepperoni making her mouth water.

"Yes?" she asked with trepidation.

"What's the next move, boss?" asked Geri.

"Yeah, what's the next move, moss," mumbled Helen, mouth stuffed.

"Move? What are you two talking about?" asked Martha.

"Our next move," said Geri again. "What's the plan?"

"Plan?"

"There's *always* a plan," said Helen. "That's why you're the oldest."

"The wisest," chimed Geri.

"The most sage of us all."

Martha didn't like where this was going. "I have no idea what you two are talking about," she said. "But if you're talking about what I *think* you're talking about, then the answer is a simple, but firm. no."

"Oh come on, Mart," said Geri. "You can't be serious."

"You can't be serious Martha," said Helen, now onto her second slice in as many minutes.

"This is mum we're talking about," Geri pressed. "We can't just let the scumbag who did this get away with it."

"No, absolutely not," said Martha. "I have my instructions."

"From who?"

"DI Pope."

Helen and Geri almost choked with laughter.

"And since when have we ever done anything that old wheezy has told us to?" scoffed Geri.

"Also, she's a DI now? When did that happen?"

"A few weeks ago apparently," said Martha.

"Blimey, they must be getting desperate," said Helen. "Clearly handing out promotions like sweets."

"Still, DI or DS, it doesn't really matter," said Geri. "She's not our boss, she's not our mentor and she's certainly not our mother. I say we press on."

Martha suddenly felt quite queasy. She really didn't like where this conversation was leading to. But her sisters had that all too familiar determination in their eyes.

"That way there be madness," was all she could manage.

Six

THE BIG LIGHT was on in the kitchen. Martha knew that sight all too well. Whenever there was trouble, whenever there was a problem, the big light over the kitchen table was turned on. And it wouldn't be switched off again until those problems had been resolved.

Mother Parker had always insisted on the kitchen for conferences. She had sworn it was the meeting place of the house. Everything and everyone passed through it at some point throughout the day. It was the giver of life, the provider of sustenance, support and everything in between. The kitchen, Martha had learned, was where family life started and finished.

It was hardly a surprise then that all three of the Parker sisters were huddled around the table, bathed in that same hard, oppressing light that had dominated their childhoods. Even in the summer, with the sunshine blazing outside, the big light still went on. And down sat backsides until the dealing was done.

They were much older now of course, all of them, even Geri. She might have only tagged along in the end days of the Big Light Summits, but she still knew what they were. That's why she had insisted they all sit around now, like patrons at a cheap seance. The light was hot and white, beaming down on them. Everything beyond its fluorescence was dark and black, the night having come down an hour ago as they finished their feast.

"So," said Geri, assuming the mistress of ceremonies role. "What are we going to do about this hit-and-run?"

"Nothing," said Martha.

She didn't believe for one moment that her negativity would be tolerated. She'd already failed on that front earlier when she insisted that the police were taking care of things.

"Wrong," said Helen, making a strange gargling noise with her throat.

"Seriously?" she said. "You too. You're going to break my back over this too?"

"So close, Martha, so close to the right answer," said Geri, her eyes closed tight. "But wrong nonetheless. The real answer, the *correct* answer, is that we're going to catch this absolute scumbag who ran over our mum and left her to die in the street."

"Oh," said Helen.

She shuddered in her chair. Martha and Geri looked at her expectantly.

"Sorry, I just, that just gave me shivers, that's all," she said. "I got all excited there."

"See, Helen gets it Martha," winked Geri. "She gets what we're all about."

Martha drew in a long breath.

"I told you, both of you," she said, still calm and measured. "That the police are dealing with it. I even had the pleasure of Aileen Pope telling me that was the case. And she thought it prudent enough to warn me, and us in general, that we weren't to go interfering with their investigation."

"And you think that's going to stop us?"

"She's right, Mart," said Helen. "We don't have a very good track record when it comes to doing what we're told by the police."

"Speak for yourselves," Martha blurted. "I *always* do what I'm told by the local constabulary. It's you two who have historically caused them and me nothing but grief."

"Historically being the right word," said Geri. "We've kept our noses clean for a good wee while recently."

"She's right, Mart," said Helen.

She *was* right. They had all been more than well behaved since the affair with the Steiners in London. Keeping a low profile had proven harder than before. But it had produced a steady flow of business into Parkers Investigations, and for that Martha was grateful. This, however, was on a different level. This was personal.

"This isn't like anything we've tackled before," she said. "We've got far too much skin in the game, I think is what people say. Geri, is that right?"

"Yes, it is Martha."

"We're too close to this, far too close. It's personal."

"You're damn right it's personal," said Helen, slamming her fist down on the table. "This bastard killed our mother."

Martha and Geri were equally surprised by Helen's sudden outburst.

"Sorry," she said. "I didn't mean to shout. And that table is *really* hard."

She rubbed at the edge of her fist where it had bashed the tabletop.

"My point remains the same though. There's somebody out there, probably driving about as we speak, who hit our mother, our own dear mum, outside her house and left her to… left her to die." She took a breath, almost as deep as Martha's. "It's too late for mum, we all know that. But it's not too late for somebody else's mother. Or father, or granny or grandad, auntie, uncle, brother, sister. How the hell would you feel if this maniac went out and did the same to somebody else's mum tonight Martha? How would that make you feel to know that there was another family out there who were feeling as bloody awful as we are right now?"

"Okay Helen, take it easy," said Geri, tugging at her cardigan. "Martha isn't the enemy here. You don't need to go off on one."

"Thank you, Geri," said Martha. "And in answer to your question Helen, I wouldn't feel at all happy. And I don't feel happy as it happens. To think that whoever did this to our mother is still walking free, is still able to get behind the wheel of a car and be on the road without a care in the world makes me sick to the pit of my stomach. Which is funny because I didn't think I was capable of feeling anything other than relentless grief after everything that's happened. But I gave Pope my word that we wouldn't do anything. We can't jeopardise a prosecution, especially if it turns out to be murder or culpable homicide."

"She's right too, Helen," said Geri. "Can you imagine if the cops nailed this dirt bag and his lawyers got him off because of something we had done to scupper the investigation? I don't think I would forgive myself. I know you two certainly wouldn't."

It didn't bear thinking about. Martha tried to push the thought from her mind as quickly as she could.

"Well, what the hell are we doing here then?" asked Helen, throwing her hands up into the air. "You're telling me that we sat around the big light just to talk about what we *can't* do? That's about as useful as a chocolate teapot."

"I didn't say that," said Geri. "I merely asked you both what we were going to do about what happened. Nobody mentioned snooping around, nobody mentioned interfering. And that's exactly what I'm suggesting we do. Or don't do, so to speak."

Martha was confused. Helen wasn't polite enough to keep her own confusion to herself.

"You what?" she asked bluntly.

Geri looked about the dark kitchen conspiratorially. She drew in closer, her sisters instinctively doing the same.

"We can't interfere in the investigation right?" she said. "But that doesn't stop us from taking look, does it?"

"A look?" asked Helen.

"A look?" asked Martha.

"A look," Geri repeated.

"A look at what?" asked Helen.

"Just a look," she shrugged. "A look about, get our ears to the ground, see what people are saying out there about what's gone on. You know, just a look."

"I don't like this, Geri," said Martha. "Pope told me personally to stay away. I don't want to jeopardize anything, you know this."

"I know, I know," she said. "I know and we won't. This is too important. Believe me, I know that. I'm just saying that we're in a unique position as a family, given what we do. We have contacts, people in shadows and dark places, down alleyways that regular folk fear to tread. What's the harm in asking a couple of questions to see if any of them know who it was who left our mother to die in the middle of the street just yards from her home."

"She's right, Mart," said Helen. "I mean, what harm could a look do? Just a teeny peek. Maybe not the barnstorming crusade of justice I was calling for. But something, anything. That's better than nothing, is it not?"

Martha shook her head.

"I don't know about this," she said. "It's exactly like I said, we're too close to this, far too close. We can't risk anything getting in the way of the proper channels of prosecution."

"But Martha," said Geri.

There was something in her tone that seemed to trigger Martha. She wasn't sure what it was. The pitch maybe? Or the persistence. Whatever it was, a red mist descended on her and she got up suddenly, the chair sliding back and away from the table.

"No," she shouted.

Her voice sounded strange, so loud in such a confined space. Even to her own ears it was odd. She didn't think she'd ever raised her voice before in this house. Everything was usually calm and sedate around her mother. It was a knack she had for bringing everyone together.

"What?" laughed Geri.

The red mist thickened. Martha leaned on the table.

"I said no Geri. You too Helen," she said. "I mean it this time. Seriously. I know we always have these little back and forths, and I eventually give in to your mad schemes and plans. Not this time, though. This time it's far too important, more important than anything we've ever done before. It's our mother we're talking about. Our own, dear old mum, who has… died. We can't risk *anything* that might see justice done, whatever that turns out to be. So, I'm saying it again, Geri. And to you too, Helen. There will be *no* questions. There will be *no* investigations. And, for God's sake, there will be absolutely *no* interfering with the police investigation. Do I make myself clear?"

She was shaking. She could feel her knees wobbling, struggling to hold her own weight. Geri and Helen looked back at her, their faces slack, pale under the big light.

"Well?" Martha coughed. "Do I make myself clear?"

"Crystal clear," said Helen, bowing her head.

"Geri?"

Geri kept her gaze locked on her oldest sister for a painful second longer than she needed to. If looks could kill, then

Martha would be disintegrated now. She thought, briefly, that she had made a terrible mistake. These were her sisters, her colleagues, they were accomplished detectives in their own right. If anyone could catch the driver then it was these two women.

Then she imagined herself back in a police station, being told that the investigation had fallen apart because of something *they* had done. The risk was too great. Even if it meant the pain was dragged out much longer than they were able to stand.

Martha remained firm. She straightened, fighting back tears and hoping her trembling lip wasn't obvious.

"Well Geri?" she pushed out.

"Fine," said the youngest Parker. "You're the boss, Martha. We do what you say, we always do. You're the one who signs the cheques, you're the one who knew mum the longest. If you say we stay out of it then that's what we do. Okay?"

Martha couldn't tell if her sister was being serious or this was one long jibe. She decided to move on. It had been a very long day.

"I'm going home," she said. "I need to rest. DI Pope told me it might help clear my head. We can start all over again in the morning."

"Sounds like a good plan," said Geri, getting up from the table.

They walked out the door, Helen lagging behind.

"Aren't you coming?" asked Geri.

"No, think I'll stay here tonight," said Helen, her eyes glassy in the darkness. "Think I'd like to sleep upstairs in Mum's room. Just… you know, to be about her a bit. As long as it's okay with you two."

Martha's heart ached.

"Of course it is," she said. "I'll come back in the morning and we can try and get things moving with plans. Hopefully the police will have an update on when Mum's post mortem is being carried out. Then, when they're finished, we can get her body back and have a funeral—a proper send off."

"Sounds like a plan," said Geri, pulling her jacket on.

There was a sense of urgency to leave from her now. The determination had changed, vanished. She had the same air of escape as the night when their mother had just passed away. Martha didn't like it.

"I'll lock up," said Helen. "Going to just sit here for a bit and get my head together, I reckon."

Martha and Geri wished her a goodnight and closed the front door behind them. They walked down the driveway, feet crunching on the grit and stones, weeds sprouting out between them. They got to the street and noticed a small bunch of flowers wrapped around the lamppost at the edge of the gate.

"There's no card," said Geri, stooping down to inspect the bouquet.

"It'll be one of the neighbours, they'll have read the story online or seen the ambulance or something," said Martha.

They stood quietly for a moment. The awkwardness they thought they had beaten was back. Martha didn't know what to say. And it made her feel awful.

"Do you want a lift home?" she asked. "The car is around the corner."

"No, it's okay," said Geri. avoiding looking at her. "I said I'd be back at mine for Matt coming home from his shift in the morning. Need to pick up a few things."

"You're still seeing him then?" asked Martha.

It sounded more pointed than she had meant.

"Yeah, I am," came the barbed answer.

"Is he still studying?"

"He's got an internship."

"Where?"

"At the coroner's office," said Geri.

Martha's tingles returned. The contacts, the investigations, the fears came flooding back instantly. It took all of her will to keep her mouth shut, to avoid urging Geri to keep him out of this whole mess. Geri in turn looked expectantly at her, obviously anticipating another lecture. In the end nothing was said.

"I'm heading this way," said the youngest sister, thumbing over her shoulder. "Let me know if the police call, won't you?"

"I will," said Martha. "Right away."

"Okay, cool."

Geri spun quickly, Doc Martens squeaking. She started on down the dark road, vanishing in and out of the shadows as she passed beneath the sickly orange glow of the streetlights.

"Geri," Martha called after her.

She didn't turn back around. She kept walking, too far to chase down now, until she was out of sight around the corner. Martha let her shoulders slump and her head drop.

"What a bloody nightmare," she said. "What an absolute, bloody, buggering, crap-filled nightmare this truly is."

Seven

MARTHA WOKE TO her phone vibrating on her chest. It was a small wonder that she could feel the device at all, given the thick blanket that had been laid over her. She craned her neck as she remembered she was in her armchair in the living room, not the big, comfortable bed upstairs.

A sticky note had been left on her phone. She lifted it up and read it aloud. "You looked so peaceful, I just left you there, kiss," she said, recognising her husband's handwriting.

She unfolded herself like a rusty accordion left to rot in some dusty attic and scooped up her phone.

"Hello," she said, not reading the number.

"Oh good, you're awake, I thought you might still be in your scratcher," said Helen.

She was excited. Martha could always tell when her sister had had too much coffee. The words would spill out of her mouth at the rate of a thousand a minute. She rarely touched caffeine, something about it being too exciting for her. So immediately, Martha was suspicious.

"Helen, calm down," she said. "You've been at that expensive export coffee mum had tucked away in the larder aren't you?"

"Yes, no, yes, no, no. I don't know what you're talking about Martha. Absolutely not, definitely not. What's a coffee anyway? Never heard of the stuff. Sounds nice though, might try it sometime when I get a minute."

"Helen, pull yourself together, woman," she said. "What's wrong, has something happened? Have the police called?"

There was silence from the other end of the phone. Martha panicked. She shot up from the armchair and stood on something soft. A screeching hiss made her jump as Toby, the overweight tomca,t shot off out the room like a bolt of lightning. It was the fastest she had seen him move in years and suspected he now had a very sore tail.

"Helen! Helen are you there?"

"What? Yes, sorry, I'm here," she sounded distracted.

"What's happening? What's going on? Are you okay? Has something happened at mum's house?"

"What? No, nothing like that," she said.

Martha was losing patience rapidly.

"Then what's wrong!"

"Have you seen the news this morning?" Helen asked.

"No, I haven't. You woke me up with this call. And seeing as I spent the night in a chair and have just taken at least five of Toby's nine lives away, I'm somewhat behind the times at the moment."

"Stick the TV on, quickly, you'll just catch it," said Helen.

Martha sighed loudly. She pinched the bridge of her nose.

"Helen, I really don't have time for this," she said. "We've got so much to do with Mum. I have to see about making sure everyone in the family knows. I need to stop all of her direct debits and bills and—"

"Just stick the TV on now, put the news on, you're going to miss it."

Martha gritted her teeth. She could already see she wasn't going to get anywhere with her sister until she did as she was asked. She dug around the cushions until she found the TV remote. It flickered into life and she turned it over to the news.

A smart-looking woman stood at a tall table. The huge screen behind her showed the unmistakable shape of the Glasgow morgue, police cars and officers standing guard at its doors.

"What's going on?"

"Are you listening?"

"Hold on," she said, turning up the volume.

"Police remain at the scene first thing this morning, following the break-in at the city's morgue last night," said the smart newsreader. "Detectives say that they are working with the coroner's office to establish what happened and to pinpoint exactly when the burglary took place. Nobody was hurt. What was stolen from the property has not been confirmed by police. However, it's understood that a large HGV was involved in the incident overnight."

The screen cut to a wide shot of the back of the morgue. The whole rear wall was a crumbling mess, debris strewn across the street where more cops were standing guard.

"Bloody hell," said Martha.

"I know, right?" said Helen. "You can see all the way inside the place. It's mad. The robbers must have smashed their way in."

"Ssshhhh," Martha quietened her sister.

"Members of the public are being urged to come forward if they have any information that might help in catching the thieves," said the newsreader. "The investigation is ongoing and local traffic disruption is expected in the area as the clean-up operation gets underway."

The newsreader moved on to another story and Martha turned away from the screen.

"That's insane," she said. "Who the hell would want to break into a morgue? It's morbid."

"It gets better," said Helen, sounding giddy.

Martha's phone pinged in her hand. She pulled it from her ear and checked the screen. A message from Helen.

"Open that up," said her sister through the speaker.

Martha opened the attachment. It was a link to a story on a news site. The headline blazed back at her in huge letters.

'CADAVERS STOLEN' IN MIDNIGHT RAID ON CITY MORGUE — COPS HUNT BODYSNATCHERS

"What is going on?" she asked.

"Just read the story," said Helen.

"I'm totally lost, Helen. What's happening? I was sound asleep two minutes ago."

"Essentially there's a rumour doing the rounds that there have been bodies stolen from the morgue in this robbery," said Helen. "That's why it's on TV. Have you seen the damage? It looks like a flipping bomb has gone off."

"Yes, I saw it. I can see it in this story too," she said, scrolling down the page.

The words were all jumbled up, scrambled in Martha's freshly woken brain. Normally she was wide awake instantly. It was a testimony, then, to just how out of it she had been in the armchair.

She blinked a few times, trying to jumpstart her brain. It seemed to do the trick. A clarity came over her. She could think straight and she began to consume the news story in front of her. Then it struck Martha.

"Helen," she said, the phone almost dropping from her hands. "Mum."

"What?" said Helen. "What about Mum?"

"Mum's body," said Martha, the blood pumping faster now than it ever had. "Mum's body, it was being taken away for a post mortem."

"You mean… it could have been in the morgue?"

"I… I don't know, maybe," said Martha. "I don't see why it wouldn't, that's where these sorts of things take place isn't it?"

"We have to get down there."

Martha heard Helen rustling around down the other end of the phone. She hunted around the living room for her boots. Two glistening eyes met her under the sofa, Toby come to make amends then.

"I'll get you down there," said Helen, still on the line. "It's quicker if we head there separately, you don't need to pick me up."

"Okay," said Martha. "I'll drive, I can be there in less than fifteen minutes."

"Good," she said. "What about Geri?"

Their younger sister's name stung in Martha's ear. She tried to ignore the bitterness between them.

"I'll call her," she said. "Just get down to that morgue as quickly as you can Helen. We need to get some answers."

"Here, Martha," said Helen.

"What is it?" she asked, finding her boots bundled beneath the armchair where she had spent the night.

"Does this mean we're back?"

"Back?"

"Yeah," said Helen. "You know, back in business."

Martha let out a long groan. She wasn't ready for any of this. Why, she thought, why would something like this happen to them? Were the fates playing some sort of cruel trick on her? Why couldn't something as tragic and personal as the death of her mother go without a hitch? What had she done so wrong in this life or another one that meant she must be punished so?

"Just get down there," she said.

"Wilko," and the line went dead.

Martha pulled on her boots and snatched her keys and purse from the coffee table in the centre of the room. She went to turn the TV off when another shot of the huge, gaping hole in the side of the morgue appeared again. The newscaster was speaking and she turned up the volume.

"Once again, police are appealing for witnesses and information on a robbery at Glasgow's morgue overnight," she said. "Officers remain on the scene this morning and are conducting door-to-door inquiries as their investigations continue. Forensic teams have been scouring the area since dawn. Police won't confirm what has been stolen, only that there had been a robbery at the scene. Anyone with information is urged to get in contact immediately."

Martha turned off the screen. She felt sick. Her stomach churned at the thought of what was going on, what she had seen so early that morning. The idea that her mother might be involved in some way was almost too much for her to handle. First the hit-and-run, now this. Was she cursed? Had she broken a mirror and forgotten all about it? Surely this couldn't be happening, not now, after only a few days. Why wasn't she allowed to grieve in peace?

She hurried out of the front door, pulling her long coat on as she jumped into her car. She started it up and immediately dialled Geri's number. The dial tone sounded out all around her as the new-fangled hands free system she'd had installed kicked into action.

Drone after drone it went. On and on. Martha was halfway down the street, darting through amber lights just turning to red when Geri's answer machine finally kicked in.

"You've reached the voicemail of Geri Parker. Please leave a message after the tone."

She gritted her teeth and hung up, immediately redialling. The south side of the city rolled past in a blur as she pressed on through the early morning rush hour. Darting and weaving between lanes, she didn't come close to the speed limit once as she headed towards the morgue on the banks of the Clyde.

"You've reached the voicemail of Geri Parker. Please leave a message after the tone."

"Damn it!" Martha punched the steering wheel with her open palm. "Where *are* you Geri?"

The looming, imposing shape of Glasgow's old High Court building came into view across the river. Martha had grown up seeing that building and wondering just how it worked, where and why people went in and out. The brilliantly high colonnades that fronted the listed structure were filthier now, tarred and scarred from centuries of pollution from the main road that ran in front of it. The new building was tucked around the corner and had none of the mesmerising history of its predecessor. Wedged neatly between them was the city morgue, now half-destroyed.

Martha made her way over the Albert Bridge but was quickly met with a police cordon. Squad cars and vans with their lights still flashing were dotted across the Saltmarket. Officers in bright yellow hi-vis vests peppered the spaces between the roadblock. A crowd of fire engines were parked up on the pavement close to the entrance to the nearby park. Police were directing traffic back around and over the bridge but Martha ignored them. She pressed on and swung the car around the corner, parking up and getting out.

The noise was immense. The clanking of heavy machinery drifted up and over the court building, carried by the unusually cold wind that snaked through the city and down along the river. She pulled her coat about her tightly, phone still in hand. There was no sign of Helen so she tried Geri again. Still no answer, just her voicemail.

Martha wasn't sure what she was angry about. The truce with her youngest sister had been altogether far too short. There was something else at play between them, something off that didn't quite add up. She had no idea where it had come from, their mother's death the trigger perhaps. Since that fateful evening when they'd all learned what had happened, it had felt like the pair were butting heads over everything. Even Geri's new boyfriend wasn't immune from Martha's wrath. And she really didn't mean it.

"Martha," shouted Helen.

The middle Parker came bounding over the Albert Bridge, out of breath, cardigan flailing in the wind behind her like a scruffy, woollen cape.

"I saw you overtake my bus," she gasped, joining her sister. "I don't think I've ever seen you drive so fast."

"Have you heard from Geri?" she asked Helen.

"No," was the answer. "I tried her when I sat down but it went to her answering machine thingy. You?"

"Same," said Martha, her brow lowering.

"You two aren't seeing eye-to-eye at the moment, are you?"

"You could say that," said Martha. "But that's for another time. Come on, we need some answers."

She ushered Helen around the corner and they marched towards the police barricade. A gaggle of reporters and photographers were hustling what looked like a senior officer. He was holding his hands up, trying to hold them back. The two uniforms on either side of him weren't offering much support. Stoic and statue-like, they appeared to be happy to let their superior take all the flack.

"You've all had the press release," he was saying, as Martha and Helen approached. "I can't tell you anything else. Any questions need to be directed to our media office who will tell you everything we know."

"What about the bodies?" asked one journo from the back of the herd. "Is it true that bodies were stolen from the morgue last night?"

"I cannot comment on what has been stolen," said the senior officer, the tendons in his neck tense.

Martha didn't believe him. She had a terrible feeling, a horrible sinking sensation in the pit of her stomach, that they weren't going to be happy with what they found out here.

"He's not going to be much use, is he?" whispered Helen.

"No," agreed Martha. "He's not."

Martha Parker then did what she had never done before. Maybe it was the stress, or perhaps all the worry she had been put under over the past few days. But the prospect of arguing with another police officer and getting nowhere slowly didn't appeal much to her. In fact, the thought made her feel worse than she already did.

So she took action. Stepping away from the press pack, she checked quickly to see what the senior officer and his cronies were doing. They were all distracted, preoccupied by the rabid journalists, photographers and camera crews who wanted answers and wanted them now.

Satisfied, Martha lifted the tape that had been strung up across the width of the street. She ducked underneath it, eyes locked on the cops up ahead.

"Martha?" asked Helen. "What on earth are you doing? This is very unlike you."

"Are you coming?" she said. "Because if we're going in we've got to go now, while those policemen are fighting with the press. So it's move it or lose it time, toots."

"Wow," said Helen. "Who are you and what have you done with my sister?"

She ducked beneath the police tape and joined Martha. They hurried away from the huddle, unseen. Sticking close to the outer wall of the old High Court, they passed undetected, like two mice scurrying across a kitchen. When they reached the morgue, both Martha and Helen stopped. Breathless, they took in the sheer scale of the devastation.

"Bloody hell," gasped Helen.

"Bloody hell is right," said Martha.

The gaping hole in the side of the building was as big as a house. Forensic cops in white suits looked like ants scurrying over a picnic as they sifted through the rubble and debris. The TV cameras hadn't done the scale of damage justice. And all the two Parker sisters could do was stare.

"This is serious," said Helen. "Really serious."

"Yeah," said Martha. "I hope Mum is okay."

Eight

FOR THE SECOND time this week, Geri sat in a hospital waiting room staring at the ceiling. To add insult to injury, it wasn't even the *same* hospital. There were more ceiling tiles to count, more squares of carpet to pick at with the edge of her shoe. More time to waste waiting for a stressed-out doctor to come and deliver more bad news to her.

She sat back in the uncomfortable chair. The waiting room in accident and emergency was full, packed from wall to wall. There were all kinds of injuries, some obvious, others not so. A TV was on in the far corner, infuriatingly too small to enjoy from where Geri was sitting. Not that she could concentrate on anything at the moment.

She spun her phone over and over in her hand. She'd given up ignoring messages and calls from Martha, Helen and everyone else. She'd put the device on mute and was happy for it to be an expensive paperweight for a while. It seemed that it only brought bad news these days. Better to leave it silent. Ignorance was, after all, bliss.

A thought struck her then. And it was quite breathtaking. Here she was, sat in A&E for hours on end, waiting for her boyfriend. It made her shudder. How times had changed in such a short period. Who did she think she was anyway? Some sort of normal person? Geri Parker, sat on her own, surrounded by the sick and needy, all because of a boy? That wasn't the Geri Parker she had grown to love over the years. Geri Parker cared for nobody but herself, especially when it came to men. They were disposable playthings, used to get whatever she wanted and when. What would that Geri Parker think of the one sitting in A&E right now?

It made her laugh. The couple who sat beside her gave her a dirty look. Geri sneered back at them. She nodded down to the man's arm, hand stuck in an ornamental teapot.

"Think there was gold in there or something?" she asked, sarcastically.

They grunted and turned away from her. Geri laughed to herself and folded her arms, phone still dead. She had always hated hospitals, waiting rooms especially. They felt like there was some unknown, unspoken hierarchy going on that she wasn't privy to. Being in her early-twenties was clearly some sort of prejudice that meant she was at the bottom of the pile. And being in a fit and able condition, as she clearly looked, wasn't helping her either.

It had been the same earlier in the week when she had rushed to a different hospital across the city after news of her mother's accident. The whole journey in that taxi had seemed like some drunken dream. She hadn't even been sure she had heard Martha correctly—that Mum was in hospital having been run over. This was the sort of thing that happened on TV to other people. Sure, they were private investigators, they should be used to these sorts of scurrilous acts. But all of those years spent dealing with underhand crooks and villains hadn't prepared her for something as shocking as this. Her own mother, left to die, in the middle of the street, yards from her front door.

The thought made the blood in her veins chill. She gave a shudder, the couple beside her now completely ignoring anything and everything she did. The man sat stroking the antique teapot like a cat. His partner stared off into space with a sour look etched into her wrinkly, older-than-her-years face. Geri had a sudden panic that she would end up the same. Was this what being in a long term relationship was all about? Total, unabating misery?

Her own imagination frightened her. She thought about getting up, running for the door and not looking back. In less than three minutes, she could be speeding away from the hospital, and everything else it brought with it. Her old life was just that close. She could have it all back. All she had to do was stand up, walk calmly towards the big, wide, sliding doors of A&E and she'd be gone.

Then Matt appeared, a nurse helping him, gently easing him through a set of double doors and out into the waiting area. He had two black eyes—big, thick bruises stretching out across his cheeks from a heavy impact. His lip was burst too, a nasty, dark red gash right in its middle. He was puffy and uneasy on his feet, the nurse making sure he didn't collapse. When he saw Geri he smiled, a big gap in his teeth where one or two of them used to be. He waved a trembling hand and she knew she couldn't leave, not now. What was worse, she didn't want to. All those thoughts of misery, and escape, vanished in an instant. Maybe it was pity for her boyfriend and the state he was in. Or maybe it was something else. She didn't want to think about that now.

"Blimey," she said, getting up to meet him. "You look absolutely terrible."

The nurse gave her a shocked look, still hovering at Matt's elbow.

"Thanks," he said. "You, on the other hand, look as wonderful as ever."

He puckered his lips and leaned in, expecting a kiss. Geri felt her cheeks flush hot with embarrassment. The nurse's eyes burrowed into her expectantly, so she caved in. She kissed his big, swollen bottom lip with as little contact as possible, and felt her toes curl with embarrassment. Public displays of affection were *not* in Geri Parker's repertoire. It was a common thread among all three sisters.

"How are you?" she asked.

"He's been through a lot," said the nurse sharply.

"That's an understatement," said Geri. "Are you allowed to go home?"

"Yes," said the nurse, cutting Matt off again. "He's got painkillers he'll need to take regularly for the next week or so. And the doctors want him to come back in for a check-up. Are you his next of kin?"

Geri wasn't sure what to say. Of course she wasn't, it should have been an easy answer. But the way Matt looked at her, even with his eyes bloodshot and nearly closed over from the swelling, she couldn't help but pity him.

"Yeah, sort of," she said.

"Sort of? You either are or you're not."

Geri spied a white paper bag in the nurse's hands. She pointed down to it, desperate to change the subject.

"Are those the drugs?" she asked.

"Yes," said the nurse.

Geri snatched the bag. This nurse was starting to get on her nerves. She wanted to get out of there as quickly as she could. Her patience had run its course.

"I'll look after him," she assured the nurse.

Before she could answer, Geri took Matt by the hand and led him through the waiting room and out into the car park. The fresh air was welcome in Geri's lungs, just as soon as they cleared the huddled smokers choking up the outside of the entranceway.

"Thanks," said Matt.

"What for?" asked Geri.

"For waiting for me. For getting me away from that nurse. For saying you'd look after me."

"Yeah, well, I couldn't very well just leave you, could I?" She waved down a taxi. It pulled up and they climbed into the back. When they were far enough from the hospital, Geri handed him the paper bag.

"Did you speak to the police?" she asked.

"Yes," said Matt, wincing as he pulled on his seatbelt. "Not that they'll be much use, I don't suppose. I didn't see much before I was buried under the rubble. The doctors said I was lucky to get away with just the cuts, bruises and other aches I've got. Otherwise it might have been serious."

"Well it looks pretty serious," said Geri.

"I'm a serious kind of guy Geri, you know that," he smiled at her.

"Yeah, I guess you are."

The taxi pulled on to the motorway and began speeding back towards the city centre. Geri felt like a half-closed knife. She was neither here, nor there. She didn't know what she wanted, where she wanted to be. Everything inside her screamed at her, telling her to get out of the taxi and move on. And yet, at the same time, there was nowhere else she would rather be than with Matt, heading back to her flat, for some rest and recuperation.

That was her answer, she supposed.

"You're welcome," she eventually said.

"What for?" asked Matt, prodding gently at his swollen nose and face.

"For looking after you. That's what I'm here for. That's what I'll *always* be here for."

He stopped poking and touching his face. Looking at her, he reached out and touched her cheek, caressing it gently. She closed her eyes, leaning in to him and they just sat there, watching as the city came into view through the front of the cab.

"Take it you won't be going to work tonight then?" she asked him.

"No," laughed Matt. "No, I think there might be a problem with the front door or something like that. Maybe I'll just stay in with you and eat junk food."

"Yeah," said Geri. "That sounds good to me."

Nine

A FOUL SMELL lingered in the air around the rubble of the mortuary. Martha had smelled it before. The last time she had been in this building, it had been in very different circumstances. Cramped and stuffed into a cupboard to avoid the authorities, she still remembered that stench. Formaldehyde. The chemical used to preserve corpses. It was everywhere, hanging in the air like a ghost. The closer they got to the broken wall, the worse the smell became.

"Bloody hell," coughed Helen, wiping tears from her eyes. "That's some stink."

"The burglars must have smashed up the morgue's supply or something," said Martha. "It really is awful though, isn't it?"

As the sisters neared the massive hole gauged out of the building, they stopped.

"What exactly are we looking for here Mart?" said Helen. "I don't know if I can handle this stench for much longer."

"We need to find out what's happened to Mum," said Martha, covering her mouth and nose with her sleeve. "If they've taken her body, then we have a right to know. And I'm not sitting about on my backside, waiting for some bureaucrat to send me a letter two weeks later explaining what's happened. This is too important, too personal."

"Wow," said Helen. "That's impressive."

"What is?"

"You," she said, sounding surprised. "I don't think I've ever known you to be so direct, so focussed."

"Should I take that as a compliment?" asked Martha.

"I'm not sure, I don't know," Helen said. "I've noticed it over the last couple of days, it's like you're changing or something. There's something different about you."

"Nonsense," said Martha. "I'm just tired, that's all. Everything that's been going on, I've barely stopped. I fell asleep in an armchair last night, Helen. My neck feels like it's been put through a mincer."

"No, that's not it," said Helen. "I know when you're tired, you're much… quieter. This is something else."

Martha felt her fists clench and tighten. Her breaths grew shorter too.

"Whatever it is, it's probably what's causing you to fight with Geri all the time," she said.

"I'm not fighting with Geri," Martha lied.

"You are," said Helen. "All of the time. Ever since mum died, the pair of you have been at each other's throats."

"We're *not* at each other's throats Helen," she shouted.

Helen smirked.

"There, see what I mean," she pointed at her sister. "That. That's what I'm talking about. When would you *ever* snap at me like that, Mart? Never, that's when. You're always the cool head, the sensible one. It's usually you telling me or Geri, or both of us, to stop bickering. But the last few days you've been just as bad."

"Can you blame me?" she blurted. "After everything that's going on? Look at us, Helen. We're sneaking about a morgue looking to see if our mother's body has been stolen, all while her killer is still out there on the loose. Can you blame me for being snippy?"

"No," said Helen flatly. "But Geri is our sister Mart and she's much younger than both of us. She's lost her mum too. And maybe you should try to remember that."

"Remember? I can hardly forget, can I?"

"I know," said Helen, much more sympathetically this time. "It's hard, I know it is. And this whole thing isn't helping. But we've all got to stick together."

"Yeah," said Martha, snorting. "Stick together. That's why you and I are here, and Geri isn't even answering her bloomin' phone. Real, proper togetherness."

Helen had no answer. She wiped tears from her eyes and blinked hard, the stench getting to her.

"I've said my piece," she said. "This probably isn't the time or the place. It never is with us. We should get moving."

Martha was relieved. She couldn't argue with anything her sister had said. That didn't make it any easier to swallow though.

"Come on," she said.

They moved around the building towards the mountain of rubble. The place was empty. Martha checked her watch, it was presumably the construction workers' tea break. They had to move fast.

"Where are we going?" asked Helen.

"Up there, into the hole," said Martha.

She looked about the scene. Taking their chance, they climbed up the broken masonry and bricks that had been strewn across the street. At the top of the rubble hill was an examining room, the smell the strongest it had been so far. Martha and Helen coughed as they pushed on through, past a wall of storage units, some doors hanging ajar. They splashed through clear liquid spilled across the floor.

Martha shouldered a door open, Helen close behind her. The smell wasn't so bad in the corridor beyond the examining room.

Martha could still feel the rawness in her throat. As she bent down, she could still smell the formaldehyde coming from her feet.

"I think that was the preservation liquid we just walked through," she said, sniffing and wiping her eyes. "It's disgusting."

"I don't think anyone in those fridges is complaining," said Helen. "Nor would you if the alternative was having bits of you fall off."

"Bloody hell," she breathed.

The narrow corridor stretched off in both directions from the door. The place was quiet, almost eerie. The pale light of the morning flooded in through tall, frosted glass windows, distorting everything just enough to make them unsettled. Martha tried to remember the last time she was here.

"Which direction then?" asked Helen. "Do you think there will be anyone here?"

"I hope so," said Martha. "We've broken into a crime scene, it had better be worth it."

She looked up and down the corridor, no wiser as to which way to go. In the end, it hardly mattered. She nodded down the way and Helen followed her.

"Should we get our story straight then," she asked.

"Story?" asked Martha.

"Yeah, why we're here."

"I don't think we need a story Helen," she said. "We want to know what's happened to our mother's body. It's as simple as that."

"You sure?" she asked. "Don't you think we should cook up some better excuse? Like you said, we've just broken into a crime scene."

"An unguarded crime scene," said Martha. "We have a right to know."

"You're the boss," Helen shrugged.

They continued down the hallway. At the end were two large doors. Martha pushed one of them open and it swung with a creak. She hesitated as the sound of voices drifted towards them. A tingle went up her spine as the hairs on the back of her neck stood on end. She recognised one of the voices.

"Is that…" whispered Helen. "Sounds like DI Pope."

The detective who had warned Martha not to interfere was speaking just out of view, somewhere in the next room. If the Parkers needed any more convincing, they had their evidence when she started coughing uncontrollably, the distinctive click and suck of an inhaler following closely behind.

"It is," said Martha. She tried to angle herself better to see who the cop was speaking to.

It was bright in the next room and the crack in the door didn't offer much by way of a vantage point. They were too far away to make out any detail.

"She doesn't sound happy," said Helen. "Whatever it is she's saying."

"Sssshhhh," whispered Martha.

Footsteps started and the sisters recoiled. Pope's voice grew louder as she neared them.

"How the hell did those vultures in the newspapers find out about the bodies?" growled Pope. "If you've got a leak in your operation Vass then you need to plug it and quickly. This place is going to be crawling with journalists for the next week. I can't have my investigation hampered by loudmouth morgue workers out to make a quick couple of quid on the side."

"I can assure you detective inspector, there is *no* leak in my team," came another woman's voice, the Vass Pope was speaking to, Martha assumed.

"Well somebody tipped them off," said the cop.

"Have you gone through your own ranks with a fine tooth comb?"

"I'll pretend I didn't hear that, Vass," said Pope angrily. "My officers are nothing but professional. Which is more than can be said about this shambles."

The two women passed by the door where Martha and Helen lingered. The sisters waited for a moment, holding their breath, until the conversation continued.

"Do you have final numbers for me?" asked the detective.

"We think two have been taken," said Vass. "Although we can't be certain of that number until they clear up that mess outside. There's a chance that cadavers could be among the debris."

"Good God," sighed Pope. "That's bloody grim, even in this line of work."

"It is," said Vass.

"The two who are missing, do you have identification of them?"

"We do."

Martha's whole body stiffened again. She felt Helen nudging her in the back.

There was a rustling of paper. Then it was Vass' turn to sigh.

"I have the names here," said Vass out of view. "The first one is a Gary Millar, thirty-four, motorbike accident, came to us two days ago."

"And the other?" asked Pope.

Martha could barely breathe. She stared, wide-eyed through the gap in the door, not looking at anything in particular. The whiteness of the room next door seemed to brighten, burning her eyes.

She had never known a sensation like this. Utter dread and expectation all at once. In her line of work she had grown accustomed to bad news. Unfortunately she was usually the one who was delivering it. These past few days had been like no other in her entire life. Time and time again she had been given the worst information. At every turn, events had gotten more grim and harder to handle. Now, as she hunched over, eavesdropping on DI Pope and whoever this Vass woman was, she didn't know what she wanted them to say next. Would it be better if her mother wasn't the other missing cadaver? Would she feel any better? She couldn't tell.

"Miriam Parker," said Vass.

Her voice sliced through Martha like a sharpened needle piercing her ear canal. It was too much for her to handle and she stumbled forward, Helen tripping up behind her. They both fell through the door.

Pope spun around. Her grey complexion seemed to fade paler as she realised who had just appeared in front of her. Vass stood beside her, much shorter and sharper, her long lab coat much too big for her and almost dragging on the floor.

Martha was shaking. She grabbed hold of Helen who was trying to keep them both from falling flat on the floor.

"I… I…" she kept saying.

"Parker," Pope shouted, her voice breaking. "What the bloody hell are you doing here? This is a crime scene. How did you get past the guards?"

"Nothing but professional officers, eh Detective Inspector?" smirked Vass.

"I… I…" Martha kept saying, the shock taking hold. "I'm sorry."

"Sorry? You're sorry? This is a crime scene Parker, I told you not to interfere with police business. You can't be here." Pope was growing angrier by the second. "Get out of here, before I have you both nicked."

"Mum," said Martha. "Our mum. Miriam Parker. You just said her body has been stolen."

With that, Pope's fury evaporated. The look of anger on her pasty complexion instantly changed to one of panic and regret. All four women stood silently, unsure what to say or do next. This, Martha thought, was a mess.

Ten

HELEN WASN'T QUITE sure how she was still going. Was this what athletes called 'pushing through the wall'? She'd never have described herself as an athlete. Far from it, in fact. But this pumping adrenaline that was keeping her standing, keeping her awake, keeping her fighting, was probably as close as she was ever going to get.

She paced about the small room, hands behind her back, flapping back and forth. Occasionally she would look over at Martha to make sure she hadn't keeled over. She was worried about her older sister. The strain was starting to show. For the woman who had looked after them all for so long to be put under such strain all at once wasn't healthy. Helen knew that Martha would never admit this. And that could cause all kinds of problems. She didn't want to lose her too, not so soon after their mother had gone.

Maybe that was why she was being so pragmatic, so level-headed. Somebody had to pick up the slack. How did the old idiom go again? Cometh the hour, cometh the man? While she didn't agree with the sexist overtones, Helen felt that perhaps this was her own time to shine. With everything they had been through over the past few years, maybe this was her chance to step up and become a leader.

The thought made her feel better. She felt compelled to do better, to keep going. She could be the rock that Martha could confide in, the shoulder to cry on. And for Geri, wherever she was, the new role model, a younger role model, on which to base her life and beliefs. Yes, Helen Parker liked the sound of that. And she knew she could do it. Not just for herself, or her selfish ambitions. But for the others too. She would grasp the bull by the horns, grab it with both hands and press on as the new focal point of Parkers Investigations.

"This is out of your hands now ladies," said DI Pope, breaking her chain of thought.

"Pardon?" spluttered Helen, not having heard the detective come into the room while she had been lost in her delusion of grandeur.

"I can't even begin to describe how much of a shambles this all is," said Pope. "And believe me, it's the absolute *last* thing I wanted to happen to anyone. Especially you guys."

Helen had no cause to disbelieve the stressed out policewoman. When everyone's initial shock had settled, Pope had led her and Martha out of the crumbling morgue and straight to an unmarked police car. They had been sped across the city to the main headquarters in the west end and left in the cramped room. Pope had seemed apologetic for the whole journey. Although Helen had noted that nobody had, as of yet, said sorry for what had happened.

Now the disgruntled, ashen policewoman paced in front of them. Helen wondered if it was just a natural instinct to do something like that in a situation like this.

"How are you both holding up?" she asked, finally decided on what she was going to say.

"How do you think we're holding up?" asked Helen.

They both looked down at Martha. She was rocking back and forth slightly, her arms wrapped tightly about her, like her insides would fall out if she didn't hold them in.

"Yeah, stupid question, sorry," said Pope.

"At last," Helen sighed.

"I don't follow you," said the cop.

"An apology. I've been wondering how long it would take before somebody said sorry for this whole rotten mess."

"I wasn't… I wasn't apologising for *that*," said Pope.

"Excuse me?" sniffed Helen.

"I was saying sorry for my stupid question."

"So you're *not* sorry then?"

"What?"

"You know, for losing our mother's body? The body that was entrusted into you and Her Majesty's constabulary's care while you found the person who killed her? You're not sorry for that."

"No," said Pope. "I was talking about something else."

"Unbelievable," she threw her hands up in the air.

"It's… complicated," said Pope.

"Complicated?" Helen's voice broke at the end. "You can bet your bottom dollar it's complicated. And it'll get a whole lot more complicated when we get our lawyers involved."

Helen impressed herself, not that she showed it. She wasn't sure where that had come from. Maybe it was the adrenaline sharpening her senses. Maybe it was the newfound leadership. Maybe it was all of these things. She liked it. She sounded professional, like she knew what she was talking about.

"Okay, you need to calm down," said the detective. "You've had a big shock, you all have… wait a minute. There are only two of you."

"Astute detective work there," Helen snorted.

"Where's the other one, the youngest sister?"

"Her name is Geri, Detective Inspector. And we don't know where she is."

She made the admission with such authority it still sounded good. She added a set of folded arms to hammer home her point.

"Whatever," said Pope. "Now let's all just take a deep breath and calm down, shall we? Like I said, this is the last thing any of us wanted. And we don't want to be making threats that we won't follow through on, okay?"

"What's going to happen now?" Martha's voice was hoarse and quiet. Everything in the room felt like it had frozen.

Helen and Pope were drawn to her like an apparition appearing in the corner. Suddenly Helen didn't feel like she was in charge anymore.

"We have a top team from the Serious Crimes Unit working on the break-in as we speak," said Pope.

"What does that actually mean?" Martha sounded weak.

Her face was haggard and tired. She looked like she was struggling to keep her head up, weak from the weight of it. Helen went to give her a hug, but Pope's frosty ambivalence returned.

"We're professionals Parker, we know what we're doing," she said. "We're working on what's happened, drawing up a list of suspects, touching base with colleagues up and down the country who might have more experience in this sort of thing."

"What sort of thing? Body snatching you mean?" Helen blurted. "Because that's what it is, Pope. There's a giant hole in a mortuary and two bodies missing from inside, one of which was our pensioner mother who, I might add, was the victim of a hit and run. Oh by the way, any further forward on that investigation, now that we have your ear?"

Pope straightened. She looked like a skeleton trussed up in a cheap suit. Her short hair appeared to be greying by the moment. She was doing her very best to stay stoic. The pulsing in her temples, the tendons in her neck, however, dictated a different tone.

"We're doing our best," she said. "I know that's not what you want to hear. And I know that it's all the more difficult with me being a part of things, given our past history. But you have to trust me and you have to trust the process. I'm going to overlook the fact that you know all about this because you effectively broke into a crime scene."

"Cup runneth over," scoffed Helen.

"But I *won't* overlook any further amateur investigations on your part. And that goes for your sister too. I know you three have a burgeoning reputation as private eyes or whatever. This, however, is serious. Very serious in fact. You're too close to what's going on."

"Maybe we can help," said Martha

It surprised Helen to hear her sister.

"We can?" she asked.

"I don't know," said Martha, losing confidence. "Maybe instead of being this nuisance to you Aileen, maybe we can help. Not in any official way, obviously, but *some* way. We shouldn't have gone to the morgue, that was my fault. I've just been so frustrated with everything that's been going on. I felt like I, we, needed to do *something*. So let us, please."

Pope puffed out her cheeks. She scratched at her chin, clearly thinking on the best way to put what she was about to say.

"I appreciate your understanding," she started. "I really do. And it's not often we get victims' families offering to help out with an investigation. Especially not in these circumstances."

She looked about the room in the depths of the station.

"I'll level with both of you," she said. "And this is strictly confidential. Nothing I say here can *ever* be repeated outside of these four walls. Do I make myself clear?"

Helen felt her knees wobble. No matter how many investigations she was a part of, how many stakeouts or snooping behind closed doors, when a police officer was so candid it was still a cause for excitement. She leaned in closer to Pope.

"We think this might be a professional hit," said the detective.

"Professional?" asked Helen. "What, you mean... like gangsters? The mob?"

Pope said nothing.

"I said, was it gangsters?" Helen shouted.

"Would you shut up?" Pope yelled back. "These walls are paper thin. I could lose my job just telling you this, you moron."

"Sorry," whispered Helen.

"What would gangsters want with our mother's body?" asked Martha.

"I don't know," said the cop pragmatically. "But the manner, the equipment used to pull this hit off. It's organised, well thought out, planned. Police work isn't the easy part ladies. Working out of the who, what, where and the when, those are simple. The why, now that's a completely different story. Once you crack that, then you're onto something and everything usually falls into place. We're not there yet, that's why I'm asking you to be patient."

"So you're saying you can't let us help," said Helen.

"Officially, we would not be allowing members of the public to help in any investigations, no matter how famous and renowned they are becoming," said the cop. "Unofficially, you guys don't want any part in this, believe me. If this is organised crime then you don't mess around with those sorts of people. Having you find out the way you did, under the current circumstances with the open investigation, that's bad enough. I couldn't and won't have something terrible happening to you by some gangland nutter with nothing to get up for tomorrow. My conscience is dirty enough without living with that. Do you understand?"

Helen's confidence was gone. Her leadership of Parkers Investigations had been short lived—ten minutes, fifteen if you were being generous. Instead of being decisive and making a stand, she'd buckled. She looked to Martha for the response.

"It's not what we want to hear," she said. "Of course it's not. We just want our mum back and we're willing to do whatever it takes. You're asking an awful lot of us Aileen. An awful lot."

Pope nodded, her lips puckered.

"I know," she said. "But this is my job. And I have to do it in the best, most professional manner possible. For what it's worth, this shambles has taken the wind out of my sails. I don't appreciate you guys interfering and hanging around me like a bad smell. That doesn't mean I don't think what's happened here isn't the worst anyone could ever put up with. I just need you to know that I'm working on it. And you'll be the first to know as soon as there are any developments."

An uneasy, but inevitable silence fell between the three women. Helen felt a knot of frustration beginning to grow in the pit of her stomach. She suddenly had the urge to punch or kick something or someone really hard. Martha was too easy a target. And Pope would probably fight back. So she kept it to herself.

"Thank you," said Martha, getting to her feet.

Pope opened the door for them. They walked slowly out of the room. The DI guided them to a back door where another unmarked police car was waiting for them. A uniformed officer opened the door and they climbed into the back. He was just about to close it when Pope stopped him.

"Thank you," she said.

"What for?" asked Helen.

"For being understanding. I know what's happened is hell. I just need you all to trust me and my team. We'll catch whoever did this, I promise you."

The words were said with genuine warmth, but they felt hollow to Helen. She nodded and the door closed. The officer climbed in the front and they pulled off out of the small courtyard and off into the night.

"Well that was a waste of time," she said.

"Have you heard from Geri?" asked Martha.

Helen pulled out her phone. No surprise—there were no notifications.

"No," she said. "Shall I try her again? Where could she be?"

"I don't know," said Martha, staring ahead.

"I mean it's not like she's got work to go to or anything."

She felt her sister shudder beside her. Helen panicked, thinking something was wrong.

"Martha?" she said. "Are you alright?"

"Work," said Martha. "Work. Geri said work."

"Work? Geri? Those two things don't mix, you know that."

"No," she said. "No, not Geri. Her new boyfriend. Mark, Mack, Matt, that's it. Matt."

"What about him?"

"Matt. She told me she was going home, he was working, last night. She was going to wait for him coming home in the morning."

"Yes, so what, plenty of couples do that?"

Martha looked around at Helen.

"No, Helen, don't you see," she said, a wild look in her eyes. "Matt, he's an intern. At the morgue."

Helen's mouth hung open. It wasn't often she missed something so blindingly obvious. And immediately she felt like a complete buffoon.

"Bloody Nora!" she said, slapping her forehead. "How did I forget that?"

"We have to go round there," said Martha, leaning forward to the driver. "A quick change of plan please officer. We've got to go check on our sister."

Eleven

"I DON'T CARE what anyone says. The Americans know how to make a good ice cream."

"Do people say otherwise?" asked Geri, licking her spoon.

"Oh yeah," said Matt, scooping the last of the tub out with his finger. "You see it all the time online. Italian ice cream versus American. It's a whole subculture on social media."

"Everything is a subculture on social media, Matt," she said. "If it's not debating how bad the Star Wars sequels were, it's the latest conspiracy theory about the flat Earth and why we don't all fall off the edge."

"Don't forget the Kirk versus Picard war that's been raging for thirty years."

"Ah yes, how could I forget," said Geri. "That's what the internet was invented for wasn't it? To boldly go where no spotty-faced dork had ever gone before and decide once and for all who was better—one fictional space captain or another."

"It's not the *only* thing it was invented for."

He lifted his eyebrows up and down and flashed a devilish smile.

"Oh shut up," said Geri, hitting him with a cushion.

"Ow," he yelped. "That's my sore side."

"Sorry," she said. "I forgot."

"I'm an injured hero, I'll have you know," he said. "I should be treated with the same respect that all heroes are given. Unashamed and unabashed reverence."

"If you think you're going to get *that* from me then you've clearly had a bump on the head. I don't think in all the time we've known each other I've ever suggested I was capable of reverence."

"No, this is true," he said, letting his head rest on the sofa. "Clearly I'm so traumatised from my experience that I'm losing my marbles."

Geri laughed. Despite the week she had been having, this had been a very pleasant, comfortable evening. They had returned to her flat, locked the door and watched bad movies all afternoon, eating ice cream and drinking cheap wine. A blanket had been added to the equation when the sun had disappeared and things had grown chilly. She had, contrary to her better judgement, even let Matt sit with his arm around her shoulders.

They had barely spoken all afternoon and it had been wonderful. She knew how he felt, without ever having to say it. Geri Parker had never felt so close to someone like this. Someone not in her family. She had never rested, never stayed still long enough to let something like this happen before. Now that it had, she couldn't deny that she was happy. The distant, fleeting Geri was fast becoming a thing of memory. The new Geri liked sitting and fussing over her boyfriend as they watched Groundhog Day for the umpteenth time.

As if the universe had been listening in to her thoughts, the credits started to roll on the TV. Another film was at an end. That meant she had to get up.

"How are you feeling?" she asked Matt.

His eyelids were heavy. He looked perfectly at peace. The bruising around his eyes and across his face was still angry. But he was happy.

"Like I'm more ice cream than man," he said, patting his belly.

"Now we both know that wouldn't be hard, would it, darling?" she clapped his hand. "Tea?"

"That would be lovely," he said, closing his eyes.

A big, silly grin made its way across his face. Geri got up, gathering their spoons and the empty tubs. She walked quietly over to the doorway and looked back at the living room of her flat. Everything seemed to be glowing. It was healthy, happy, content. Sure, things were pretty awful outside. Not within these four walls though. In here, everything was as it should be. She could have stayed there forever. Only a draught from the hall making her shiver brought her back down to reality.

She wandered through to the kitchen, flipped on the light and reached for the kettle. Geri felt her ears prick up. She stopped and popped her head out of the kitchen doorway. She had always had a keen sense of hearing. The slightest sound, no matter how far away, she could pick it up like a shark on the prowl in the depths of the ocean. She stood still, looking through the darkness at the front door. It stood looking back at her, unmoving, unflinching, quiet.

"I must be losing it," she said to herself, still not entirely convinced that she hadn't heard *something*.

The kettle clicked as steam billowed from its spout. Geri was just about to grab the handle when the doorbell went. She paused, hand in mid-air above the kettle. She really, really hated being right.

The doorbell went again, much angrier this time, more urgent. It was followed by a barrage of bangs on the old wood of the door itself. Geri didn't move. She thought maybe, just maybe, if she had been good enough and had welcomed enough nice karma, that whoever it was would just go away. She would be left alone in peace with her boyfriend and, after one of the most stressful weeks of her life, she could just enjoy an evening of junk food and rotten TV.

The banging and ringing continued unabated. If anything they were getting louder, more furious.

"Who the bloody hell is that?" asked Matt.

He was at the kitchen door behind her, hobbling. Geri spun to face him. She touched his arm and smiled weakly. She didn't want to tell him that she knew *exactly* who it was. She didn't want to break his heart the way that hers was currently going. Even if it was only for a few more seconds. Just let him live in the wonderful fantasy that their evening wasn't about to be totally ruined.

In the end, she couldn't hold off the inevitable.

"I'll get it," she said sadly.

She pushed past Matt and walked with heavy limbs down the hallway towards the front door. Every thump and every ring seemed to cut her that bit deeper. The louder they grew, the angrier she became. She grabbed the snib and pulled it open with a flourish. On the other side, bathed in the pallid light of the hallway, her two sisters stood gasping for air.

"What's this? Avon? What a wonderful service you guys have nowadays. I'd like to buy one of everything you're selling please. Especially that perfume old ladies wear that make them smell like litter boxes."

"Geri, thank God," said Martha. "Where have you been?"

"We've been trying to get a hold of you all day," said Helen. "You won't believe what's been going on."

"I think I've got a fair idea," Geri sucked her gums.

Martha appeared to step forward, like she was going for a hug. But something stopped her. She sort of floated for a moment, halfway between the landing and the lobby. Geri let her linger longer than she needed to before giving way.

"You'll want to come in then," she said.

Martha plodded into the hallway, Helen following close behind.

"Geri, where the bloody hell have you been, we've been trying to…" Martha trailed off when she spotted Matt.

"Hi," he said, cradling a mug of tea.

"Hi," said Martha, looking between him and her youngest sister.

"Hi, Matt," said Helen. "I don't think we've met before, but Geri has told me everything about you."

"No I haven't," Geri sneered.

"I'm her good looking sister, Helen," she said, marching towards him. "So good to finally put a face to a name and reputation. Although it looks like you've been through the wars."

She recoiled. Matt rubbed the back of his head, awkward and embarrassed.

"Yeah, sorry about this," he pointed at his bruising. "There was a bit of an incident at work."

"Of course, yes," said Helen, snapping her fingers. "That's right. You work at the mortuary don't you. What a terrible business that is, eh? You didn't happen to see who made off with the bodies did you?"

"Helen!" Martha barked.

"What?" she said, shrugging. "I'm only asking."

"Wait, what?" asked Geri. "Bodies? What are you babbling on about Helen? Has she been on the sauce or something?"

"No, she's not," said Martha, tight lipped. "She doesn't have that excuse I'm afraid."

She took Geri's arm. Even in the dull light of the hallway, Geri could see her oldest sister looked tired and weak. The unspoken animosity between them was still there, she could feel it, like an invisible block separating them at chest height.

"Geri, we need to speak to you, privately and right now," said Martha.

"Go for it," said Geri. "What's wrong?"

Martha couldn't conceal the strain. She looked over at Matt and then back to her sister.

"I think we should maybe go into another room, just for a moment," she said.

"Why?" Geri dug her heels in. "Because Matt's here? What's that got to do with anything? Whatever you've got to say to me, you can say to Matt too, he won't mind."

"Geri, please," said Martha quietly.

"No, I'm serious, Mart," she said, pulling her arm away. "Whatever you've got to say, just get on with it. I'm not hiding anything from him."

"Hey, maybe I should go," said Matt from the kitchen.

"No, you stay put," said Geri. "You were here before they were, and I'm serious. Come on you two, whatever it is, out with it before I lose my temper."

Martha sighed. She shook her head.

"Fine," she said. "I don't have the energy to fight with you, Geri. I'm utterly devastated and all I'm trying to do is do right by everyone. If that makes me such a bad person then fine, nail me to the cross. I'm only trying to think of you."

"Mum's body has been stolen," said Helen. "By gangsters."

Geri blinked once. She squared her shoulders and stiffened her back.

"Okay, wow, blimey," she said. "That's an awful lot to take in. I didn't know so few words could feel like being run over by an eighteen wheeler."

"Your mum's body has been stolen?" Matt repeated, walking over to them. "Stolen like thieved stolen."

"Yes Matt, stolen like thieved stolen," said Helen. "Is there any other kind of stealing?"

"Bloody hell," he said. "Bloody hell, bloody hell, bloody hell. That's… that's horrible. I'm so sorry."

"Yeah, well, it's not your fault," said Helen. "Stuff like this happens right?"

"No, Helen, it *really* doesn't!" Geri yelled. "What do you two know? I mean, what's going on? Are the police on the case?"

"They don't know a lot," said Martha. "They know nothing actually, it's all speculation at this point. Just that two corpses were taken from the city mortuary last night after the raid. And that one of them was Mum."

Geri ran a hand through her short hair. She stared down at the floor, her throat feeling like it was closing up.

"This is… this is madness," she said. "I'm having a bad trip or something. I mean, this is… what is this? Mum's body has been *stolen*? She was only in there because of the hit-and-run. That's the only reason she was in the morgue in the first place."

"We know Geri, thanks for the update," Helen rolled her eyes.

"Helen" said Martha sharply.

Geri backed into the wall and slid down it. She felt like her chest had been compressed in a vice, like there were a hundred elephants sitting down on it, crushing the air from her lungs. The ice cream and movies seemed like a thousand years ago. The fact she could still hear the music from the end credits made everything feel almost dream-like. Although she knew this wasn't a dream, or a nightmare. It was reality.

"I can't handle this," she said. "I mean, I know we get ourselves into some scrapes. But this… body snatching, our mum's body snatched from under our noses. That's a whole new level of messed up."

"We tried to tell you," said Helen. "But your phone's been off all day."

It took the words an extra moment or two to sink in. Geri could hear Helen's voice but she was distant, like she was behind a partition or screen.

"Yeah," she said. "Yeah, I know. I know, I turned it off when I was waiting for Matt to be released by the doctors."

All eyes fell on Matt, the mug still in his hands, less steam drifting up from its rim. He looked intimidated, put out by everyone looking at him.

"Did you know about this?" Geri asked him. "Did you know and not tell me?"

"What? No! Of course not Geri!" he yelled. "How could I know something like that and *not* tell you."

"Then what happened?" asked Martha. "What happened last night, Matt? What the hell happened and who did this? Who would steal a body from a mortuary?"

Matt cleared his throat. He looked at each of the Parkers in turn, finally settling on Geri. She stared at him, unsure what she wanted him to say next. Did she want to know? Did she think he was lying? Did she want this perfect image she had cooked up in her head of how they were together to be a lie? Whatever he said next could change everything she had grown to feel for him. It had better be good, she thought. It had better be damn good.

"You'd better come in and sit down," he said. "I'll tell you everything I know."

Twelve

MARTHA COULD, QUITE easily and without any doubt whatsoever, say that today had been the worst in her life. It wasn't an accolade that she particularly wanted to celebrate. The notion that she could celebrate *anything* ever again was totally lost to her.

Between her sadness, her sense of loss, her anger and her anxiety, it felt like there was a cloud all around her head. She couldn't think straight, could barely string two words together. Everything was foggy and dull around the edges. Her whole body ached, but not from any physical ailment. Her hands felt like they were weighed down by lead, her feet the same. Staying upright was a challenge, keeping her eyes open almost impossible.

To be sitting now, in her youngest sister's living room, interrogating her boyfriend about the theft of her mother's remains seemed almost comical. She might have laughed on another day. Or cried. Sobbing uncontrollably was the latest weapon in her arsenal and one she took no pleasure in. And above all else she was fighting with one of her closest, dearest friends in the whole world.

Geri sat on the opposite side of the room. The huge bay windows of the flat framed her perfectly, the dark night and ethereal glow of the sulphurous street lamps lifting up behind her like a neon cape. She didn't meet Martha's eye, instead looking down at the coffee table, chewing on her bottom lip and thinking. Always thinking. She was smart, so smart, Martha knew that. She needed that sharpness and intelligence now, more than ever. While she was in the mire of misery, Geri might see something, know something, that could help them out of this terrible situation.

Helen was pacing, again. She marched back and forth in front of the fireplace, regular as clockwork never going any more than three or four paces before turning back around. She was the constant in all of their lives. Nothing seemed to phase her, even all of this. She was energetic, arrogant, and gabby. She was just Helen.

Then there was Matt. Martha barely knew him. She didn't even know his surname. Such was the fleeting nature of their acquaintance. She had met him just once before, almost by accident. Geri had been dropping something off at the office, Matt having given her a lift to the leafy suburbs. After a lot of persuasion and coaxing, her youngest sister had finally agreed to introduce her new beau. He seemed like a nice enough guy, Martha thought. Clean shaven, tall, broad shouldered. He was nothing like Geri's previous boyfriends—if you could even call them that. Boyfriend, Martha had always believed, involved more than just a casual fling and two weeks of infatuation. Geri wasn't known to keep anyone around for very long. And Martha had made peace that day with never seeing Matt again.

Yet here he was. Sitting on the sofa, his knees bobbing up and down, looking very nervous about being stuck in the same room as all three Parker sisters. Martha couldn't blame him for being on edge in that sort of situation. She was hardly at ease herself.

She was exhausted. All the good her long sleep the night before had done was completely undone. She had so many thoughts, so many worries piling up in her mind, she didn't know where to begin. At no other point in her life had she felt such terrible strain. And she knew she couldn't carry on like this. Something was going to have to give. Otherwise she'd become very unwell.

"Thank you, Matt, for staying," she said, feeling it was only right to try and make him feel at ease. "I don't imagine the last twenty-four hours have been easy for you. And it seems that, like us, you've been put through the ringer."

"Yeah, it's appreciated, mate," said Helen.

Matt nodded politely. Geri was close to him, trying to protect him, it seemed. Martha went on.

"I don't think I ever imagined I'd be sat in a room with my sisters talking about something like this," she said. "I know that our lives have taken a turn of late. But this is way beyond my imagination. And I think we need to decide what we're going to do next."

"I agree," said Helen. "We need a battleplan, a strategy, something we can all get behind and focus on. Good thinking Martha."

"Oh please," Geri rolled her eyes. "She says jump and you say how high, Helen. Give it a rest."

"What's that supposed to mean?" Helen stopped her pacing.

"It's fairly self-explanatory Helen. You two are clearly pulling rank in all of this. If we'd done what I suggested in the first place, we might not be sitting here right now with our thumbs up our ar—"

"Geri, please," Martha interrupted her. "We're not going down this route. Nobody, absolutely *nobody* could have predicted what was going to happen to Mum. Not you, me, Helen or Nostradamus. This is a bizarre and unique problem we're facing. And we all have to be on the same side, no matter what's going on elsewhere."

"What's going on elsewhere? What's that supposed to mean Martha?" said Geri.

Martha was about to retaliate. But she stopped herself. She had to keep remembering that Geri was grieving too. This spikey insolence was nothing more than a coping mechanism for her. It had to be. They were too close to be feuding. Weren't they?

"We need to think about what we're going to do next," she pressed on. "And I was hoping you'd be able to help us out with that, Matt."

Matt sat up, on edge. His knees picked up pace, bobbing up and down enough that the floorboards started to creak.

"Eh… yeah, sure," he said, nervously.

"Wait, hold on," said Geri, getting up from his side. "This has got nothing to do with Matt. We don't have to drag him into this."

"He works at the morgue Geri," said Helen. "He was working last night. Look at him, he was there, in the thick of it."

"I know that, Helen," said Geri scornfully. "I was the one who sat in A&E for hours waiting for him to be released. I know all too well, and better than you two, how deep he's into this. But that doesn't change anything."

"We just want to know what happened," said Martha, trying to calm things down. "That's all."

"He's got nothing to do with Mum's body vanishing, Martha," she said.

"I know that, Geri."

"So he doesn't need to get tied up in all of this. He could lose his job, haven't you thought about that?"

"Don't you want to find Mum's body Geri?" Helen blurted.

"What kind of question is that to ask me, Helen?" she spat back. "Of course I do. I don't want anything more in this world. But I also don't want Matt being forced to compromise his career, his *life*, because you two have lucked out and found an eyewitness."

"It's okay Geri."

The three sisters stopped their warring to all look over at Matt. His nervous knee bobbing had stopped. He was wearing a weak smile.

"It's alright, honestly," he said. "I'm happy to talk about it. I'm happy to tell you everything I know. I want your mum's body back, I want all the bodies back. It's not right what's been going on in there. Something has to be done."

Martha felt a prick somewhere behind her chest. She felt her cheek twitch as she quickly went back over what Matt had just said.

"Wait a minute," said Helen, stepping forward. "You mean this isn't the first time something like this has happened?"

"What?" asked Geri, just as perplexed

Matt bowed his head.

"What I'm about to tell you can't go anywhere, do you understand?" he said, his voice low. "I reckon I'd probably be fired just for talking about it. I don't know. But there's something rotten going on down there and it's been happening for months."

"The mortuary," said Martha.

"Yes," Matt nodded. "Nobody is talking about it, but everyone knows. The staff, I mean. Some of the senior management, they're convinced it's an inside job. But I don't know, I've not been there very long."

"What's an inside job?" asked Helen. "Body snatching?"

Matt took a dry gulp. Geri sat down beside him and rubbed his arm.

"You don't need to talk about this," she said. "I don't want you doing anything you don't want to do."

"No, it's fine," he clapped her hand with his own. "It's actually quite good to talk about it."

"Only if you're sure Matt," said Martha. "Only if you're sure."

"I'm sure," he nodded.

He took a long, deep breath, wincing as he sat forward. The others listened closely, unsure of what was about to be said.

"I've been doing this job for about six months now," he started. "It's a good job, I don't do anything on my own, I'm always shadowing somebody. I'm grateful for it, really I am. I graduated a couple of years ago and trying to get into this sort of work is a bit of a nightmare. So when I saw that the procurator fiscal was offering this sort of internship program, I thought great, excellent, that's ideal. I don't mind admitting to you guys that the first day I was sick. It wasn't at the sight of a body or anything, it's the smell."

"The formaldehyde," said Martha.

"Yes we know that stench all too well, Matt," she said, sniffing at her sleeve.

"You get used to it after a while, though. That was fine, I carried on, keeping my head down, trying to make a good impression and not doing anything stupid like tip a body onto the floor or anything."

"How long is the internship?" asked Martha.

"A year," he said. "Maybe more if there are any jobs at the end of it. I help out with the bookkeeping, the cleaning of the tools and carting the cadavers around the building. It's grunt work but occasionally they'll let me into a PM."

"PM?" asked Helen.

"Post mortem," said Matt. "I don't do anything obviously. I just observe and clean up when and where they ask me. Classic intern stuff. Anyway, that's fine, the first month flies, and I stop throwing up every morning when I turn up for work."

"He really wasn't well," said Geri, rubbing his back. "Our first date he told me all of this pretty much as soon as my bum was on the seat."

"How romantic," Helen rolled her eyes.

"What's happened, Matt? Go on," said Martha.

He cleared his throat. Shifting on his seat, he clicked his knuckles.

"Yeah, about a month in, I started noticing a couple of things wrong with paperwork I was being given," he said. "They're sticklers for accuracy, as you can imagine. Everything has to be catalogued, where bodies are kept, if they've had organs removed, results of PMs, all of that stuff. It's data entry at its very worst, but it's important, obviously. Some of the information in these forms can lead to criminal convictions and the like. Usually I help out with entering the stuff into the main database, it saves some of the others from having to do it. And the pathologists aren't interested in that kind of bureaucracy. I guess you've got other things on your mind when you're up to your elbows in someone's innards all day."

"Lovely," Helen snorted.

"What was wrong with the information?" asked Martha.

"It wasn't that it was wrong as such, more that it didn't make sense," he said. "We were seeing a lot of John and Jane Does, you know, the name given to somebody who hasn't been identified. Again, it's not unheard of, but for it to be *every* person who came in through the doors, something didn't seem to add up to me."

"Why?"

"If a body isn't identified, it essentially belongs to the state," he said. "There won't be a funeral or anything, and essentially it's just taken care of quietly, the cadaver cremated and the ashes disposed of. It's really sad, of course, and a lot of it happens to old people with no relatives or homeless folk who are alone. But for pretty much all of my second and third months at the place, *every* body coming in was a John or Jane. It didn't make any sense to me. How could everyone coming in not have any next of kin or not be identified? Surely it was a mistake?"

"Did you raise it with anyone?" asked Helen.

"Yeah, I did," he said. "I didn't want to be the one who messed up, especially if it meant families weren't getting their bodies back. Can you imagine the scandal?"

"And what happened?" asked Geri.

"Nothing," he said, flatly. "Well, actually that's not true. There was a steady drop off of John and Janes coming through the system. First it was every second body, then every third, then only one or two a week, which I reckon was probably more accurate."

Martha shook her head. The more she heard, the worse it sounded.

"Do you have evidence of this, Matt?" she asked. "Any sort of record of the drop offs?"

"Not on me," he jokingly patted his chest. "But I could get it for you."

"What happens to John and Jane Doe bodies that aren't claimed?" asked Geri, tapping her chin with her finger.

"See, this is where it gets a bit creepy," he said. "I don't know."

"What do you mean?" asked Helen, leaning on the fireplace.

"I don't know what happens to these bodies," he said. "They belong to the state, right? If they haven't been claimed after a certain amount of time, a week, maybe two, depending on circumstance around their death, they fall into that category I told you about. Only nobody ever seemed to see them go out the door. I don't know who collects them, or when they're picked up, nothing. I work different shifts, all around the clock, and I've *never* seen or heard of who it is that does the pick-ups or, more importantly, where they go."

"That doesn't mean they're being stolen though," said Martha. "It might just be a coincidence that you've never seen what happens to them."

"Nobody talks about it though," he said.

"Have you asked?"

"A couple of times," he said. "But it's always non-committal answers I get back. It's easy to brush off the intern, though, right?"

Martha rubbed her temples. She could feel a migraine coming on. Or maybe it was just gaining strength. She felt like her head was fit to burst all of the time these days.

"You said you think these bodies are being stolen, not going missing," she said. "That's a pretty big difference Matt."

"Why else would they vanish?" he asked. "I mean, if somebody wants cadavers, for whatever reason, it's a steady supply if you just doctor the way they're clerked in. As soon as they're not claimed then they're essentially just things that fall between the cracks of society. And when it comes to something like the dead, it's super sensitive so not a lot of questions are asked."

"What about the people who *do* know the bodies?" asked Geri. "Wouldn't they be kicking up a fuss? It's not like you can just misplace something like that and get away with it. Grieving families want their loved ones back."

"Like us," said Helen.

"Like us," Geri repeated quietly.

"I don't know," said Matt. "Like I said, I don't get to see everything behind the curtain. And I reckon with all my question-asking that whoever is involved has closed ranks. That's what I mean by saying it's an open secret in the place. Nobody wants to rock the boat or ask any questions. It's a heads down, just get on with it kind of place."

"What does this have to do with last night then?" asked Helen. "I mean stealing bodies subversively is one thing. Driving a digger into the mortuary is something on a whole other level."

Matt's jollier demeanour seemed to slip away. He had come around to the conversation as he'd been talking to them. But a darkness fell over him now.

"I don't know, I don't remember much," he said. "I was only in work an hour or so when the lights started to flicker. You always notice that sort of thing when there are bodies about. Next thing I know, there's a loud bang and everything goes dark. I was covered in God know what. It felt like being buried alive actually, or how I imagine it feels like. Really horrible, dust choking you, plaster and all kinds of crap up your nose. I was lucky though, I've been discharged and spoken to the police already. Couple of my colleagues are still in hospital being checked over."

Geri put her arm around his shoulders. She hugged him close as he looked at Helen and Martha.

"Dreadful stuff," said Helen.

"I'm glad you're okay Matt," said Martha. "I really am. And thank you for talking to us. It's food for thought."

"I take it the police don't know about these John and Jane Does that have gone unaccounted for?" asked Helen.

"Not that I know of. I'm an intern though, I know nothing and get told nothing. They know that I've got to keep my nose clean and not upset the applecart. So I'm an easy target for being kept in the dark. But I tell you this, something isn't right down there. And Shirley Vass knows it."

"Vass," said Martha.

"Vass," repeated Helen. "That's who Pope was talking to when we were down at the morgue."

"She's the boss," said Matt. "She's the chief pathologist, but she also manages the whole operation for the city. I think she gets two cheques that way. She's a real viper, a proper power woman who doesn't take any nonsense from anyone."

"We know the sort," said Geri.

"Ain't that the truth," tutted Helen.

"If anyone knows what's going on, it'll be her. In fact, I wouldn't be surprised if she had something to do with it all," he said.

"What makes you think that?" asked Geri.

"Access," he wriggled his fingers. "Nobody has any greater access to files and the whole running of the set up than her. She'll know *exactly* who is collecting bodies and from where and at what time."

Martha was aware that Matt had been put through terrible strain. She still had questions, but her conscience dictated she couldn't go on. It was getting late too, she needed to go home, needed to be with her family. If only for a few hours until the new day and it all started over again.

"Thank you, Matt," she said again.

"I haven't really done anything," he said. "And you're no closer to finding out what happened to your mum. I just wish I did more last night."

"Rubbish," said Geri. "What were you supposed to do? You were under six feet of rubble."

"And by all accounts the people who pulled off that job aren't to be trifled with," said Helen.

"Pope said they were probably gangsters."

"Then I imagine that's who's involved with the other bodies too."

Martha nodded. She stood up, the interrogation over. Everyone seemed to breathe easier.

"We should be going," she said. "Come on Helen."

"Wait, aren't we going to decide what we're doing next? A battle plan?" asked Helen.

"Not tonight," said Martha. "Let's just call time on it all and get some rest. We need to be able to think straight before we make a move. There's too much at risk."

"But…"

"Helen, come on," she beckoned her sister towards the door.

"Fine," she sulked.

Martha had expected Geri to see them out. But the youngest Parker didn't move from beside Matt. She was rubbing his shoulders, draped across him. Martha felt suddenly embarrassed as she headed for the door.

"One last thing, Matt," she said, pausing. "How many bodies do you think have gone missing since you started?"

Matt blew out his cheeks.

"I don't know," he said. "It's hard to say. But if I had to put a rough estimate on it, I'd say at least three dozen."

"Bloody hell," said Helen. "That's unbelievable."

"It's a scandal," he said. "And it's going on under everyone's noses. The dead can't talk, after all. And they can't defend themselves either."

"No," said Martha. "They certainly can't."

She turned and headed for the front door. Helen was close behind her as they skipped down the stairs of the building and out into the night. She looked up at the bay windows of Geri's flat, hoping to see her sister. There was nothing, all the windows empty. They walked along the pavement towards the car.

"This is getting worse with every twist, Mart," said Helen, huddling beside her. "It's like something from Burke and Hare."

"They were caught and hanged," said Martha. "I'd like the same to happen to the bastard who has Mum's body too."

"Hear hear," she said. "Do you know what we're going to do yet?"

Martha mulled the question over for a moment. She had been hoping to sleep on it and, in the morning, try to involve Geri more. But it was becoming ever clearer that their young sister wasn't interested.

"Yes," she said eventually, as they reached the car. "Yes I think I do."

Thirteen

THE PHONE RINGING woke Martha. That was twice in two days she had been caught short. She sat upright with a startle, trying to remember when she'd fallen asleep. Hours, minutes, it was all the same. She had no idea how long she had been there. Only that she was still dressed in her clothes from the night before.

"Hello," she said, answering the call without looking at the screen.

"Oh good, you're awake," came Helen's voice on the other end. "I didn't wake you, did I?"

"You did," said Martha. "But it's alright, I can live with it. Or, at least, I'll be able to when I remember who I am, what I'm doing, and why I slept another night in the living room and not my bed."

"Do you think you could put a pin in all of those things for a moment," said Helen, sounding excited. "I have some news."

Martha's fogginess was getting harder and harder to shake. She groaned as she stretched out her legs and back, the sofa no place for a woman of her vintage to sleep. Students and those with good chiropractors were the *only* market for these sleeping arrangements.

"What's happened now?" she asked. "Has Mum's house burned to the ground? What about Buckingham Palace, the Queen abducted by aliens perhaps?"

"What? No, nothing like that? What makes you think something like that has happened?"

"Helen, it was a joke," she rubbed her eyes. "I haven't slept well in a month. I have a hundred and one things to be getting on with. And on top of it all, our mother's body has been stolen by the mob. Do you want to cut me a bit of slack or will I just go back to being utterly bewildered at how strange life can be?"

"You can do," said Helen chirpily. "I should probably tell you my news first though."

Martha found the remote and turned on the TV. There was a cyclical, almost monotonous similarity to how this day was unfolding already. Only when she spotted the clock in the corner of the news screen did she perk up.

"It's not even six in the morning yet Helen," she blurted. "I know I'm an early riser and all of that. But we can't have been home more than a few hours."

"Yeah, so what?" asked her sister. "That's what coffee and energy drinks are for Martha. Didn't you ever pull an all-nighter before you became a private dick?"

"I can barely remember the day of the week, let alone what life was like before all of this started," she said. "What's your news?"

"Right, okay, the news," Helen said, focussing. "So, I started doing some digging when you dropped me off."

"Digging into what?" Martha was almost too afraid to ask.

"This disappearing body act," she said. "Something didn't add up to me about what Matt was saying. If there's somebody in the morgue writing off bodies as being unidentified to do God knows what with them, people are going to notice. We live in an uncaring society, I know that as much as anyone. People who are genuine John and Jane Does are completely forgotten about. But the number of cadavers Matt was talking about, surely somebody is going to kick up some noise about that. Aunties, uncles, grannies, grandads, husbands and wives all vanishing. That's going to cause some ripples, no?"

Martha hadn't been able to properly digest everything that Matt had told them. It all seemed too fresh, too raw still to sit down and work out. The haze that was clouding her was reaching into every corner of her mind. She felt like she was trying to catch up with the running pack, but she was wading through toffee.

"I suppose you're right," she said, pinching the bridge of her nose. "So what have you found?"

"The internet is a wonderful thing, I mean really, it is, when you think about it," said Helen. "It's just this great big mixing pot of every piece of human knowledge that's ever existed. Even stuff that *doesn't* exist yet, it's in there."

"Helen," Martha said. "Focus, please, I'm at my wit's end."

"Yeah, sure, sorry," she said. "I get carried away. Anyway, the internet, yes. You know how I said that bodies going missing wouldn't go unnoticed. Well, it's not."

"It's not?"

"No," said Helen. "There are forums, yes forums, remember those, in the deepest, darkest corners of the internet that still attract communities who share everything. And I mean everything."

"I don't like where this is going," Martha gulped. "You're not joining an underground cult or anything are you?"

"What? No, absolutely not," Helen protested. "What I'm saying is, it seems that the grateful dead of Glasgow upping sticks and moving without anyone knowing has attracted some attention. People are talking about it, online."

"What people?" she asked.

"Oh you know, conspiracy theorists, angry loners, people with nothing else better to do."

"Helen," Martha moaned. "I can't be going down a dirt track of one of your conspiracy theory games. We need proof, real proof that can get our mother's body back. Not bring-your-own-tinfoil-hat parties."

"If you'd let me finish," Helen snipped. "You're right. A lot of it is noise, people looking for things that aren't there. But there are one or two who seem to be legit. I'm not saying they're upstanding members of society. I don't know who they are. But there's a chance, just a chance, that what's happened to them could lead us on the right path towards catching whoever did this to Mum and, more importantly, get her back."

Martha didn't know what to say. She wasn't sure there *was* anything she could say. The world had felt like it was darker than before. A light had been switched off in the upper rooms and its shadow was spreading over her every hour.

"You're intrigued," said Helen.

"What? No," Martha said.

"Yes you are, I can tell."

"How can you tell?"

"You're silent. You haven't told me to get my head out of the clouds. You're hooked."

"I'm *not* hooked!"

Martha smiled. It felt good, even if it was only briefly.

"You are," said Helen. "I've dangled that carrot in front of you and now you want a bite."

"Helen, please, I'm not a donkey," she said. "And I don't know if I have the energy for this kind of thing, not at the moment. Maybe we should just take a back seat with all of this and let the police do their jobs."

"Pope and her cronies? We'll be lucky if we ever see *her* again. You know they're hopeless, Martha. They mean well, especially DI Pope. But they're constrained by rules and regulations."

"The law, you mean," she said.

"Yes, if you like," Helen pressed on. "Come on, we've got a chance here, it's slim to nothing. But it's something the cops wouldn't entertain. We owe it to Mum, don't we? To at least check it out."

Martha could feel her energy sapping already. She wasn't ready for this. She wasn't sure *any* of them were ready for this sort of thing. It felt like an investigation, a case, work. Martha didn't want to think about it. She wanted to stick her head in the sand and hope it all went away. That, however, would have seen her do something the total opposite of what she'd done her whole life. She'd never backed away from a challenge, never turned her back on something because it was too hard. Maybe this was her chance to put her grief behind her. Maybe this was the relief she'd been praying for these past few days.

"Okay," she breathed, the word too heavy to fight with.

"Seriously?" asked Helen. "You're up for this?"

"Yes," said Martha. "Although I have no idea why I listen to you. Maybe it's because Geri isn't here to talk some sense into the both of us."

"Do you want me to call her? To give her the chance to talk some sense into us."

"No," said Martha, without having to think. "No, I think she's happy to fly solo on this one."

"I see," said her sister. "Well I'm certainly glad you're on board, Martha, it'll be a big help today."

Martha felt her legs go numb.

"What do you mean, today?" she asked.

"Actually, I mean this morning," said Helen. "You've got about twenty minutes to get ready and to pick me up before we're meeting him."

"Meeting him. Who's him?"

"Our contact," Helen was smiling on the other end of the line, Martha could tell. "He's very kindly offered to show us what he's got. And I said we'd be around to his by eight, before he goes to work. So come on, chop, chop. We're heading to the country."

"The country?" Martha asked. "Are you serious?"

"I'm *always* serious double-oh seven."

"I don't get it."

"I'll explain in the car."

Helen hung up. Martha was left standing there, staring into space, the line dead, her phone still at her ear. She let her arm drop and the screen went dark.

"Just that easy," she said aloud to the empty room. "We're back."

Fourteen

THE SQUAT, GRANITE grey buildings rose up from the concrete like tombstones in a giant cemetery. The weather wasn't helping, the sky almost as dull and bland as the flats and semi-detached houses that surrounded them. The sixties had been famous for its colour, its liberation, its free spirit. All of that seemed to be amiss in this decaying council estate on the fringes of the city.

Martha thought she spotted some rolling green hills between two of the taller structures. Although they were quickly gobbled up again by the relentless brutalism of this place.

"Not very nice, is it?" asked Helen, peering out the windows. "Would it have killed them to have some trees or bushes or something."

Martha hadn't noticed until now but there was no greenery. Only grey and black, tarmac and concrete, everything natural paved over for parking spaces and the four-storey high flats overcrowded and bursting at the seams. Long cracks ran up the outer cladding, the numbers of the buildings bolted over the splits as if they were holding everything together. Martha spotted the one they were after and parked up close to the main entrance.

"They were built for practicality," she said. "Places like this are pretty common across Lanarkshire and heading out towards Edinburgh. We learned about them in school, New Towns they were called. It was hoped they'd take the strain off the slums in the inner city after the war. Give people a bit more room to live and breathe and stretch their legs. But it broke up a whole load of communities, generations of families that had lived next door to each other spread across the four corners of the city and beyond. Kind of sad when you think about it that way."

"Not an excuse for it to be so bloody gloomy though is it?" asked Helen. "The countryside feels like a long way away from here. But I'll bet it's only a stone's throw away beyond those flats."

She pointed down the street. Martha agreed. She tapped the steering wheel and took a deep breath.

"Anyway," she said. "We're not here for a social science lecture. We can talk about the slum clearances of Glasgow to your heart's content when we don't have a meeting."

"Oh, yeah," Helen scratched her mop of frizzy hair. "I almost forgot about that. I'll text him."

"Does *he* have a name?"

"Hamish," said Helen, concentrating on her phone.

"Hamish what"

"Just Hamish."

"Helen," said Martha.

"Alright Hamish the Horrible four-four-two, that's his username."

"His username?"

"Yes, okay, I don't know his real name, just the name he uses on the forum," she said.

"Look, do you want results or do you want to know his full name? It's the most boring part of a person anyway Martha, you don't even get to choose it after all. What does it matter if I don't know it?"

"It matters a great deal when we're about to walk into his house," Martha protested. "He could be *anyone* Helen. Didn't you think of that?"

"It's a risk we'll just have to take. Besides, we're not alone, are we, we've got each other."

"That's not the point."

"Come on, Martha, lighten up. This could be a breakthrough. You've got to take risks now and then, you know that as well as I do."

Martha went to answer back. Then she realised there was no point. Her haziness was still lingering, she felt the uncontrollable desire to just close her eyes and sleep. She shook her head and they sat in silence.

The minutes passed and nothing from Hamish. Martha almost didn't mind. She kind of hoped that he wouldn't answer, that this had been nothing more than a wasted trip to the countryside—albeit covered in tarmac. On the other hand she was curious. Helen had been right, she was hooked, her curiosity whetted. Only the last time that had happened she had been given the devastating news that her mother's body had gone. Surely something like that couldn't happen again.

"He's late," she said. "Ten minutes."

"Hardly the end of the world," said Helen. "I'm later than that for most things. You know that."

"True," Martha nodded.

She looked about the street. It was empty. No cars coming or going, nobody heading to work or coming home. Desolate and grey, the way it had probably been for sixty years. And would remain for the next six decades. If the buildings lasted that long.

A loud bang jolted both sisters to attention. They looked up at the roof as a figure appeared at the driver's side. A huge, wide, moon-like face dropped down to the window to peer in. Breath smoked the glass before a mighty hand wiped it away. A man smiled back at Martha and Helen, dirty ginger beard clinging to his chin and jawline, no matching moustache above it. He was wearing a filthy anorak, zipped all the way up to his neck. His big hands lingered on the window, fingers drumming slowly on the glass.

"You the Parkers?" he asked, roughly.

"Oh God," said Martha.

"Hamish?" asked Helen, smiling.

"Aye," said the big man. "You Helen."

"That's me," she said. "And this is my sister Martha."

"Pleased to meet you both," he said, stepping back from the window. "Sorry for the delay. I had to make sure you weren't being followed."

"No, no," laughed Helen. "Just us, like I said it would be."

"Good," he sniffed. "Well, come on in then, kettle is boiling. I don't have long, need to get to work. You've been having a bit of bother with dead bodies then."

"Yes, we have," said Helen, getting out of the car.

"Helen," said Martha, grabbing her by the arm. "Are you sure you want to do this? I mean, are you *sure* you want to do *this*?"

She nodded back at Hamish as he rounded the front of the car.

"What? Yes, of course, come on Mart, it's fine. He's making us tea."

She climbed out of the car. Martha, not wanting to leave her sister alone for a second, quickly followed. Hamish led them around the corner, past the door they had pulled up beside.

"Wait," said Martha. "I thought you stayed at number seven."

"No, I only told you that," said Hamish. "I couldn't be sure you two were on the level. Still can't, right enough. I'm around here at eleven. Got to be security conscious these days, a lot of funny people about."

"There really are," agreed Helen.

Martha didn't like this one bit. They were out of view of the main street now. And at least a ten, maybe fifteen second sprint from the car. She was on edge, her fuzziness retreating. It felt good but at the same time terrifying too.

Number eleven came into view and Hamish fished out his keys. He opened the front door and the smell of stale urine came tumbling out.

"Aye, sorry about the stench," he said. "Upstairs have this old dog you see. It's harmless enough, but the bloody thing pishes all over the place. The old dear who owns it can't smell it. God knows what her carpet is like."

"Lovely," said Martha.

"Here we go."

Hamish shouldered open the door closest to the main entrance. At least they were on the bottom floor, Martha thought. Less time required to escape. Before they followed Hamish in, she stopped Helen.

"Are you sure about this?" she asked her sister.

"Of course," said Helen. "What's not to be sure of. He's going to help us."

"So you say. But he seems a bit… unique."

"He hangs around on internet forums Mart, what did you think he was going to look like? Tom Cruise? Yeah, because all the good looking ones spend their waking hours online talking about body snatching in the West of Scotland."

Martha couldn't deny the logic. It didn't make her feel any better, though. Reluctantly she let Helen go and they followed Hamish into his flat.

Much to Martha's surprise, the place was spotlessly clean. The walls were a crisp white, the carpet shaded where a vacuum had gone over it. She closed the door and locked out the stench of urine, only to be met with a fragrant hint of fabric conditioner.

"In here," Hamish called.

They followed his voice into the kitchen. The big man stood over his kettle, pouring it into an ornate teapot with beautifully painted flowers around the spout. Martha had to stop and take stock of what was going on.

"You've got a lovely place Hamish," said Helen.

"Aye, thank you," he said with a big smile. "It's a bit of a hobby of mine, DIY. I like to try and keep things up to date and modern like. You know all those stories you read about online how folk transform their houses for like fifty pence. I've got them all beat. You see that worktop over there? It's Italian marble, shipped in specially on a bulk order. See, a mate of mine works for this big DIY chain online and he gets me all the best stuff at cost. I reckon this is about a hundred grand's worth of a kitchen. But I didn't pay that, no chance. Good ain't it?"

Martha was dumbfounded. She had pictured Hamish's habitat before she set foot in the place. Now that she was there, she never wanted to leave.

"Stunning," she said.

"You're very kind. Here."

Hamish handed Martha a mug of tea. A rich, biscuity smell wafted up into her nostrils. She sipped at it, thinking there and then that this was the single best cup of tea she had ever had. She was speechless.

"You're not here for a social call, ladies, I know that much," he said, leaning against his expensive worktop.

"No, we're not," said Helen. "I've been explaining to Martha about your posts on the forums, about how there are bodies vanishing from all over the city."

"Aye, that's right," he said. "Grim business, so it is. Proper Victorian times stuff, grave robbing and the like. Makes your teeth itch just thinking about it."

"It does," agreed Helen. "We won't mess you around Hamish, we know you're busy and time is marching on. Our mother's body is missing and we'd very much like to catch whoever is responsible. The police are a bit hopeless, and you said online that you think you've got a lead."

"I don't think, Helen. I *do* have a lead," he said proudly.

"May we know what that is?" asked Martha.

"That depends," he said.

Here it was, Martha thought. Of course, there would be a catch, something terrible, something awful. The house, his kindness, it was all just a ruse. She had known it all along. She wondered if her tea was still hot enough to scald him if she threw it in his face. Anything to buy some time to get out of there when it inevitably went awry.

"Depends on what?" asked Helen.

"Depends on who you're working for," he said.

"Oh, that's an easy one," she said. "Nobody. We work for ourselves."

"You sure about that?" he smiled wryly.

"Yes, fairly sure we know who we work for, Hamish. What are you getting at?"

He reached into his back pocket and pulled out his phone. It was the biggest device Martha had ever seen. He flipped the screen to face them, showing the landing page of the Parkers Investigations site. There they were, Martha, Helen and Geri smiling out at her.

"See, I did a bit of digging," he said. "That's why you shouldn't use your real name online Helen Parker. Too easy to do a trace and find your digital footprint."

"We've got nothing to hide," said Martha, piping up. "We're just looking for answers, Hamish, if that is your real name. We just want to get our mum back."

"Aye, I understand," he said. "But, I don't deal with private investigators, they're as good as the police. And, like you say, the police are hopeless. Worse than hopeless, they'll nick you for stuff you haven't even done."

"We know a few of them," said Helen. "We're genuine, Hamish, we only want to find our mum."

"Aye, so you say," he sniffed. "But as soon as you're out of here you call nine nine nine and I'm hauled in front of a magistrate for spying."

"Spying?" asked Martha. "Spying on what? Or who?"

"See, there you go," he pointed at her. "Asking all these questions."

"If you knew who we were, why did you let us in?" asked Helen. "Why waste our time like this?"

Hamish's smile dropped. Martha tensed. The tea was cooling with every passing second. And she was starting to panic.

"I'm not sure, maybe a moment of weakness," he said sadly. "It's not been the same around here since my dad died."

"Your dad?" asked Helen. "What happened to him? Is his body missing too? Is that why you've been on the forums for the last few weeks?"

Hamish's whole mood seemed to change in an instant. His big frame deflated in front of them both. His eyes went glassy as he looked down at his phone.

"I think you two might have to go," he said. "This was a bad idea. I shouldn't... I shouldn't have led you on like this. I'm sorry. Please, please just go."

He ushered them out of the kitchen. For a brief moment, Martha was relieved. That relief turned quickly to anger. This had been a waste of time. He knew something, and they deserved to know what.

"No," she said, stopping in the hallway. "No, I'm not going."

"What?" Hamish and Helen said at the same time.

"Do you know what kind of agony I've been in for the past few days? Do you have any idea what it's been like to live through this total horror of having your mother killed in a road traffic accident, only to find out her body has been stolen from the morgue? Do you have even the slightest inkling of what that feels like to be put through?"

Her voice filled every corner of the flat.

"Because I think you do, Hamish," she said, thinking quickly. "I think you know all too well what that feels like. And I think that's why you invited us here, even though you discovered we're private investigators. I think you want answers. And I think you're worried that we'll shop you to the police.

Hamish stood fidgeting in the hallway behind them. He was panicking, Martha could sense it, feel it radiating off him like a bad smell. He picked at his shabby ginger beard, scratching at his neck.

"Please," he said. "I'm sorry, I made a mistake. You should go."

"Not until you tell us what you know," Martha said, standing firm. "Maybe we can help you. Maybe we can get you the answers you're looking for. But for that to happen you have to help us, now."

"She's right," said Helen. "You need to tell us what you know, Hamish. If your dad's missing then we might be able to find him. It could be the same people who have our mum."

Hamish wobbled a moment. For a split second Martha thought he was going to faint. Then he burst out crying. He sobbed and wailed like a child who had fallen off their bike. Martha looked at Helen, not sure what to do. In the end, she followed her sister's lead and consoled the big man.

"I'm sorry," he said. "I just miss him so much."

"We know," said Martha, feeling a sudden pity for him. "But we might have a chance to put things right. You just have to help us to help you."

"Okay," said Hamish, drooling. "Okay."

Fifteen

"I DIDN'T WANT any of this to happen," said Hamish, perched on the end of his bed, holding a picture. "I didn't want it to be like this. No funeral, no rest for him. He was supposed to go in beside my mum and they'd be together forever, inseparable, like they were when she was alive. Now there's nothing."

He looked down at the photo. It showed the whole family, the three of them, waving football scarves, their faces painted in the team colours. Everyone smiling. Martha saw the resemblance between Hamish and his mother, the same round face, the same ginger hair. His father was much slimmer, more severe looking. She noticed his kind eyes, though, a warm glow about them shining out from the deep sockets perched either side of a beaky nose.

"Heart attack," Hamish went on. "He'd always had a bad heart, said he got it from his Uncle Joey. He'd died young, but he'd been a smoker and a drinker too. Dad was nothing like that. He had a pint on a Saturday afternoon when he went out to watch the footie. He never smoked though, can you imagine? A man of his generation never touching tobacco. He said he always used to get pelters from his pals over it, like it made him less of a man or something. But he never caved to peer pressure. I learned that from him at least. Something I never do is cave. Until now I suppose."

He bowed his head in shame. Helen, sat beside him, rubbed his shoulders.

"This isn't peer pressure," she said. "You're helping out with something that's important. You're giving yourself a chance at closure. This is you fighting back."

"Aye, maybe," he said. "Something like that."

Martha looked about the bedroom. It was full of strange ornaments and what she could only describe as toys. Action figures, models, of different shapes and sizes. Some of them she recognised from old TV shows and films. Others were completely new to her. Her chair swivelled at the desk near the bed, a huge computer processor mounted on the top. It glowed—a brilliant green shining through the vents and grill of the device. Again, Martha had never seen a computer like it. She wasn't quite sure what to make of it all. The room was half teenage angst, half hi-tech bolthole. She wouldn't be surprised if it was lead-lined to stop satellites from spying on what was going on.

"What happened to his body?" she asked, pulling herself away from the analysis.

"I don't really know, to be honest with you," he said with a deep breath. "The doctors phoned me up in the middle of a shift to say he'd been brought in. He'd keeled over while out at the library and they'd called an ambulance. Twenty minutes later he was gone. Just like that. Massive heart attack. They tried to console me with the fact that even if I had wanted to, I wouldn't have been able to be with him in the end, it was just so quick. I guess it's a blessing in a way, he didn't suffer, not like some of these other poor souls you see when you go to hospital. Or a care home or the like."

"And what happened to his body?" asked Helen.

Hamish's face tightened. His brow pulled in on itself as he thought hard about what he was about to say.

"I never got to see his body," he said. "The doctors told me that because it all happened in a public place, the council library, that the coroner's office would have to get involved. Something about health and safety and writing up a report or some such. To be honest with you, I didn't know if it was Shrove Tuesday or Sheffield Wednesday. I was numb, I'd just been made an orphan, technically. My head was up my backside and I nodded along with everything they said. It wasn't until I got a call, about a fortnight later, to say there had been an issue at the mortuary and that they weren't able to release dad's body, that I started to think something was wrong."

"Who did the call come from?" asked Martha.

"I can't remember," he said, rubbing his eyes. "It was a woman, she told me her name too. I've spent the past month and a half trying to remember and it's *really* bugging me."

"What did they say exactly?" asked Helen. "Did they try to make an excuse?"

"Hell no," Hamish sniffed. "They just told me outright that they'd lost my dad's body. Simple as that. So I was like, what? How the hell do you *lose* a body? It's not like they can get up and walk out the front door in the middle of the night. That's literally the *last* thing they can do, right?"

"You'd hope so," said Helen with a smirk.

"And what did they say to that?" asked Martha.

"They didn't really say anything," he said. "They were pretty blunt, very matter-of-fact. They asked that I be discreet, that discretion would be advised and recommended, given the sensitive nature of what had happened. Oh, and that the council would be in touch in due course about compensation."

"Money?" Martha's ears pricked up. "They offered you money? To stay quiet?"

"They haven't offered me *anything*," said Hamish. "That was about six or seven weeks ago, and I'm still no closer to knowing what happened to dad. Or if I'm being compensated. It's an absolute scandal."

"So what have you done about it?" asked Martha.

"Ask your sister," Hamish smiled.

She looked at Helen.

"Hamish has been on those forums I was telling you about," she said. "And it seems that this has happened to a good few folk already. The same line from the coroner, the same promise of compensation, the same plea for silence."

"We're thinking about going to the press," he said with pride. "Me and a couple of the others online. The newspapers would absolutely *love* this sort of thing, especially with what's been going on the last few nights. They're onto the bodies going missing. Imagine what they'd say when we came forward."

"And why haven't you before now?" asked Martha.

"Evidence," said Hamish. "You need evidence if you're going to uncover a scandal. And we just haven't had enough of it. Until now."

He got up from the edge of the bed. Putting the picture down carefully on the desk, he nudged past Martha and turned on the screen of his computer. He rattled the keys, a host of encrypted boxes and files appearing from nowhere. Hamish started opening the icons, revealing blurry pictures.

"And here it is," he said, standing back from the screen.

Martha and Helen looked at the images. They tilted their heads, unsure what to make of the grainy grey and black shapes that were being presented to them.

"Hamish," said Helen. "I don't want to sound unappreciative. But just what exactly are we looking at here?"

"You're no serious?" he laughed. "Look. Look, right there, in front of your noses. Can't you see it?"

"No," said Martha bluntly.

"It's a van," he traced his finger around one of the darker blobs. "It's a van, in the dead of night, picking up bodies from the back of the morgue in town. I took these pictures myself, about three in the morning. It was bloody freezing too, I was huddled up in a doorway across the street. It's quiet, really quiet around that part of the town at that time. It's close to the park, so there's a whole empty space where nobody will be looking. This big van pulls up at about three, like I said. Then these two blokes get out and open up the back doors. A few minutes later, the door in the back of the morgue opens up and out come the trollies, five, maybe six at a time. The van gets closed up and it drives off, gone, fast as lightning, down across the river and away. No sirens, no markings, nothing. It's like it's never been there at all. Only it has and I've got the proof."

Martha squinted at the pictures. Now she knew what she was looking at, she thought she could just about make out some dark figures moving about near the back of the van. Although it was impossible to identify exactly what was going on. She felt her stomach sinking. Her bubble had been burst. This was nothing useful.

"Well?" asked Hamish expectantly. "What do you think? Water tight, eh?"

"It's something," said Martha, trying to be polite. "Although, I don't know if it shows anything really happening."

"What do you mean?" he asked. "I told you what happened. That's it there, happening in front of me."

"Yes, I know you said that, Hamish. But it doesn't really explain what's happened with the bodies. I mean, what makes you think these are something sinister? It could just be the normal practice for bodies at the mortuary. For all any of us know, it's just two people going about their regular work."

"Martha's right," Helen agreed. "I don't know what I was expecting. But this wasn't it."

"Helen," said Martha.

Subtlety didn't run in the family, she knew that. Still, Helen didn't need to be so blunt.

"But... but it's there, happening on the screen. You can see it, clear as day," he said. "They're stealing the bodies, taking them away somewhere for some reason and leaving us without our bloody family members. Leaving us unable to give them a proper send off, let them rest in peace."

He was starting to get emotional again. Martha's pity flared. She couldn't blame him, he was just as broken, just as hurt as they were. Martha had never taken her detective skills for granted. They were a talent she had honed over the years she had been working as a PI. It was all too easy to forget that not everyone could do what she did. Especially those who were hurt.

"Have you got print outs of these?" she said.

"Print outs? What for Mart?" asked Helen.

She ignored her sister.

"If you've got print outs, I'd like to take them away with me, to look them over and see what we can do," she said.

"You sure?" asked Hamish. "Not sure about print outs. I could maybe email them to you. Better quality, digital back-ups and that kind of thing. Plus I don't want you leaving these things on the bus for any old Tom, Dick or Harry to take a look at."

"Fine," said Martha. "You've got Helen's address, could you send them to her?"

"Of course."

He bent over the computer and started to send the files. Helen rolled her eyes silently behind his back. Martha shook her head slightly, trying to appease her sister.

"Done, they should be with you now Helen."

"Great," she said.

"Now you won't show them to the police will you?" Hamish said, panicked. "I don't want them knocking on my door asking why I'm out at all hours spying on the morgue. They'll lock me up. I'd lose my job and... bugger. I'm late!"

He closed his computer down. Hurrying out of the bedroom, they heard pots and pans clatter, cupboard doors slamming shut.

"I guess that's our curtain call," said Helen, slapping her thighs as she stood up.

"Really sorry to do this to you both," he said, hurrying them out the front door. "But if I'm late, I'll get grief from my gaffer. And I can't lose this job. It's been the only thing keeping me going through all of this. This and the forum and the community. I don't know what I'd do without them."

Hamish locked the door of his flat. It was raining, spray-like droplets filling the air. He pulled the hood of his big coat up over his head and offered his hand to Helen first, and then Martha.

"Lovely to meet you Hamish," she said.

"Yeah, good to put a face to a username," said Helen.

"Be seeing you," he said, with a lazy salute.

He hurried down the path, big tree-trunk legs pumping like the pistons of a huge ship. Martha and Helen watched him disappear around the corner of the flats before making their way back towards the car.

"Bloody hell," said Helen, puffing out her cheeks. "Sorry about that, Martha. What a wild, bloody goose chase that turned out to be. That's the last time I trust anyone I meet on the internet."

They climbed into the car. Martha locked the doors and turned on the ignition. She was about to reverse out of the space but stopped. She stared blankly out of the windscreen, thinking.

"What's the matter?" asked Helen, sniffing loudly.

"What if we're being too cynical," she said. "What if we're so jaded and paranoid with all the low lives and the cheaters that we deal with that we can't see the wood for the trees?"

"What are you getting at?" asked Helen. "Hamish is a conspiracy theorist, I sort of knew that before we came here today. I just thought he might, *might* have something we can use. Not the Rorschach tests we've come away with. Which reminds me, I should delete that email account. I don't like the idea of him having it to hand."

She started scrolling through her phone. Martha put a hand out to stop her.

"That's my point," she said.

"I'm not following you," said Helen.

"My point is you led us here with good intentions," she said. "You came here thinking it might be a lead. Now what if, and you have to bear with me, what if Hamish isn't the total dead end we've thought he is? What if we're so used to sticking so rigidly to the clear, cut and dried evidence we get with clients, that we can't see this is an opportunity? Literally sitting in our laps."

For the first time in ages, Martha could feel her mind whirring over at a productive speed. The dreariness that had plagued her, the misery, had lifted. She knew it wouldn't last, but she had to make as much of the opportunity as she could.

"You can't be serious, Mart," said Helen. "Those pictures Hamish took, you couldn't present them to anyone and think they would fly. They don't show anything. What's worse, the nothing they show is in a really low resolution. It's garbage Martha, total garbage."

"On their own they're not great," she said. "But, if you combine them with our story, Matt's story, Hamish's story and the others online, you've got something."

"The police already know about the missing bodies," she said.

"I'm not talking about the police," said Martha.

Helen's face dropped. A sudden paranoia crept over her. She checked her phone was locked and not dialling anyone. Then she checked again.

"Martha," she whispered. "You're not thinking what I think you're thinking."

Martha nodded silently. The idea had been germinating in her mind ever since Hamish had mentioned it in his flat. The press. They were on to the vanishing bodies already. Martha had seen the pack of journalists at the crime scene yesterday. There was a good story there, something huge, something that could break a few wheels if told properly.

Her misery was hardening. She hadn't been able to place the feeling, but for the past few hours she had been growing slowly angrier. What had happened to their mother was a scandal. If Matt was to be believed, and she had no reason to doubt him, there was clearly something rotten at the coroner's office. She just didn't know what. Now, with Hamish and the others he spoke of, she might, *might*, just have enough to take some action.

"That's a dangerous game to play," said Helen. "The press don't take any prisoners Martha, you know that. If one place gets a sniff of a story then the others are all over you like a rash. You know this. It's why we try to keep our dealings with journalists to a minimum. Less fuss. Less attention."

"We can hardly dodge attention these days," Martha said with a sigh. "Think about it, Helen. We've got enough already to take to a newspaper. Pictures, reports of shady goings-on in the dead of night. Even what Matt said. He could be our whistleblower, anonymous obviously. He's seen it first-hand. He's seen where the chain breaks down and he's not allowed beyond a certain level. And he was there the other night, a direct witness. The papers would be tripping over themselves for something like that. It's dynamite."

"It is," said Helen. "Have you thought about Matt? Or Geri for that matter, what it could mean for them?"

Martha had grown tired of worrying about Geri. Not that she said that of course. She kept her mouth firmly shut.

"I don't know, Mart" said Helen. "It's giving me shivers just thinking about it. It's kicking a hornets' nest and then some. What would Pope think if she saw our faces all over the papers blabbing about missing bodies? She'd have our guts for garters. And she said she would look over us breaking into the morgue. That was a favour."

"Favour," Martha laughed. "A real favour would be to call me and tell me our mother's body had been found so we could give her a funeral. She didn't deserve this Helen, you know that. I just want her back."

"I know, me too," said Helen.

They both sat in sad silence for a long moment. The engine idled away, the only sound in the entire estate as the mid-morning sun shone a hard, unforgiving light on the brutal architecture.

"I think it's our only option at this stage," said Martha at length.

"Are you sure?" asked Helen. "There's nothing else, nothing else you can think of, we could do right now?"

Martha shook her head. Helen took a deep breath.

"We should tell Pope, before we do it," she said with a nod.

"What? Why?"

"It's the right thing to do," she said. "She might try to stop us. And that's fine, we can only expect that. But what if she's got news for us and we go and shout from the rooftops. It might scupper her investigation."

"And what if she doesn't Helen? What if we're still sat here in a month's time, two months, like poor Hamish, none the wiser and the trail even colder than it is now? What then? The papers won't be interested. If we do this, we have to do it now, this week, while the iron is hot."

Helen bit her nails. She was nervous, Martha could tell. Her already pasty skin was even whiter than usual. She didn't blame her sister. She was terrified too. She knew what the consequences would be if this all blew up in their faces. But she had to do something, *anything*.

"We should at least give her a chance," said Helen. "It's a dealbreaker for me Mart. We go to Pope and ask for an update. If there's nothing, then we go straight to the press. It's a compromise, a halfway house. At least then we can say that we tried."

Martha agreed. She offered her hand and Helen shook it. She kicked the car into gear and started reversing. Bringing up Pope's number on the hands-free controls, it started to ring.

"Parker," came a croaking DI Pope on the other end. "This better be good."

"Do you have five minutes to see Helen and myself, Detective Inspector?" Martha asked.

Pope hesitated, sighed loudly, papers shuffling in the background. "What for? I'm very busy you know?"

"We'd rather speak to you in person, if that's okay?" Martha said firmly.

She glanced over at Helen. There was no confidence there, she was shrinking into the passenger seat.

"Fine," said Pope after a moment. "Come to the station in the next hour, I'll give you five minutes, but no longer."

"Make it the pub around the corner," said Martha. "We'll be waiting for you."

"This better not be a prank Parker," said Pope. "You know my general feelings towards japes."

"It's no joke," she said, a hardness creeping into her voice. "Be there in an hour."

With that, Martha hung up. As she drove on she tried to stay calm. But it was tough. She had to stay strong, stay confident. This, she thought, was the test of her mettle. She had to be sure.

Sixteen

THE PUB SMELLED really bad. Martha had decided that this was clearly going to be a case of odours. A lingering scent of stale beer and cigarette smoke hung in the cloudy air. The place was the definition of an old man's pub. In fact, it even came with a pair of old geezers who propped each other up at the far end of the bar.

It was dark, too. Glasgow wasn't quite enjoying a glowing run-in to Christmas. But for this time of the day, it felt like everything should have been lighter. Even the glow of the fruit machine in the corner seemed faded and sad.

"You know how to pick 'em, don't you, Mart," said Helen, turning her nose up. "How the hell do you even know about this place?"

Martha didn't want to say. Not now that she had seen how run-down it had become. In its glory, *The White Horse* had been among the most popular pubs in the city. Set right in the heart of the action, the whole world could pass in and out of its doors on any given day. As time had moved on, the city with it, the pub had clearly stayed exactly the same. And was looking rather worse for wear.

Martha was glad her mother couldn't see it like this. It was, after all, where she had met the Parker sisters' father. In the halcyon summer of 1975, when flares were as wide as sails and hair was long and lush. Now the only thing lush about *The White Horse* was the mould growing under the tables.

"Can you see Pope?" she asked, moving the conversation on.

"No, I can barely see the end of my nose in this dump," said Helen. "Maybe she's had the good sense to not be seen dead in a place like this and is waiting outside."

"We would have passed her," said Martha. "Go take a seat, keep an eye out."

"Where are you going?" she asked, almost frightened.

"To get a drink."

Helen reluctantly agreed and disappeared off into the back. Martha looked about again just to be sure the DI hadn't snuck in before them. It was empty, all bar the two old men at the far end.

She tried to imagine this place as something other than the ramshackle it was now. There were hints of a much more sophisticated past. The lamps that protruded from the pillars at the bar were ornate and intricately carved, frosted glass hiding and dampening the lightbulb within. The bar itself was nothing short of a work of art—long, curving wood as dark as the night sky. The floor, all cracked and broken now, looked like it once may have been marble and not just for walking and stumbling on. The whole pub felt tired and worn down, like its best days were long behind it. Martha knew exactly how it felt.

"What'll it be love?" asked the hoarse barmaid. She coughed, wiping her sour mouth on the back of her hand.

"Two colas please," said Martha. "Diet, in glasses and a bit of ice."

The barmaid's already dour demeanour seemed to get worse. She sniffed hastily, as if Martha was doing her job for her. Or maybe it was the lack of alcohol that was upsetting her. That was one thing *The White Horse* wasn't short of. Row after row of booze bottles lined the far wall behind the bar. All kinds of alcohol, some Martha didn't even recognise, stood proudly to attention like soldiers on parade. The place might be falling apart. But at least you could get a drink.

The barmaid returned with two ice cold cans and glasses as requested. Martha handed over a rolled up ten pound note and was surprised when most of it came back in change. She thanked the barmaid and tried to work out how she could carry it all over to Helen in the back of the pub. Balancing drinks had never been Martha's strong point. She'd always worried that she'd drop everything in a big mess, making a frightfully embarrassing scene.

She settled on jamming the cans into the tops of the glasses and carrying them separately. It was efficient and would work. Hopefully. Using all of her concentration, she picked up the glasses and turned around, only to be given a fright.

"These for me," snorted Pope.

In her terror, Martha dropped the glasses. They slipped from her hands and were smashed at her feet before she knew what was going on. All of her nightmares rolled into one. Not that there were many there to see it. That didn't make it easier.

"Sack the juggler," said the barmaid, laughing loudly.

"Bugger," said Martha. "Sorry. I just… I wasn't expecting…"

"It's fine," said Pope. "I'm trying to cut down on caffeine as it is anyway. The last thing I need is some of that junk going in me."

"They weren't for…"

"What did you want to see me about Parker?" the cop pressed. "I don't have much time. And, by much, I mean any."

Martha composed herself. She felt the tinge of embarrassment start to wane. She had to remember what she was there for, why she was bending Pope's ear.

"You better come into the back," she said. "Helen has us a seat."

"Oh good. I was worried there for a moment," said Pope looking about the empty bar. "Thought we might have to stand."

They walked into the deserted back area of the pub. Helen was lying flat across a long row of dusty looking seats that lined the back wall. Her eyes were closed and her hands clasped across her chest.

"I'd wash your hair when you get home, Helen," said Pope, startling her. "Those seats haven't been cleaned since the early nineties. And this place still gets a bit tasty on a Saturday night, if you catch my drift."

"Eww," said Helen, scrambling to her feet. "That's disgusting."

"Hey, I didn't pick the venue, that was your sister, blame her," said the DI. "So what's this all about then?"

Martha sat down beside Helen. Pope remained standing, towering over both of them. She put her hands on her hips as she waited expectantly.

"Well?" she asked.

Martha looked over at Helen. She shrugged. Was this a good idea? Was she really going to try and stiff-arm the police into giving her answers? It didn't seem right now. None of this did. But something had to be done.

"We know," she said at length.

"Know what?" asked Pope.

"We know about the bodies vanishing from the morgue," said Helen, butting in. "We know that there's some sort of scam happening, something that's not just our mum and that other body that vanished the other night there. We know that the city's dead are disappearing. And that you guys need to do something about it. Otherwise…"

"Otherwise what?" asked Pope, her pallid features even more ill-looking in this light.

"Otherwise we're going to the press," said Martha.

She didn't really know what reaction to expect from DI Aileen Pope. In the years they had known each other, there hadn't ever really been a moment of proper anger. Nor had there been resolute calm between them either. Pope was a strange character to reckon with, Martha had always thought. A career woman, dedicated to her job. Surely hearing something like this would tip her over the edge.

Instead the Detective Inspector remained perfectly stoic. Her face was blank, eyes darting between the two sisters sat in her presence. The only sign of emotion was a slightly raised eyebrow at the mention of the press.

"Is that so?" she asked.

Martha's sapping confidence was almost empty. This *had* been a bad idea. She shouldn't have talked herself into any of it. She should have stayed at home, she shouldn't have listened to Helen. She should have locked the door, drawn the curtains and sat in the dark, as close to putting her head in the sand as was possible.

Then something caught the corner of her eye. She hadn't seen it when she came in. But beside the wide archway that led from the main bar, hanging on the wall, was a portrait of the pub itself. Grainy and hazy, there was a huge crowd gathered outside, a banner above the door celebrating New Year's Eve 1978.

Martha had no idea if her parents had been there that night, or if they'd still bothered coming by that point in their relationship. But that didn't matter. It was a window into the past, her past, her family's past. Her mother's past, the same mother who was now gone, spiritually and, unfortunately physically. And that was why Martha was there, right now, cowering in front of Pope.

She felt a sudden surge. "It is," she said, although the voice didn't feel like her own. "It is so.

Pope remained stoic.

"We've been doing a bit of our own investigating," she continued. "I know you said not to, but what do you expect us to do? Sit on our backsides while nothing gets done. You're busy DI Pope, we understand that. We offered to help you but you rebuffed us. Now, after some digging, information has come to light that we think might be able to help in getting our mother's body back."

"And other people too," said Helen. "There are victims' families all over the city, could be all over the country for all we know. This is a serious problem, a scandal even. And we're just the tip of the iceberg."

"People need to know," said Martha. "They deserve to know. And the victims deserve to have their voices heard. Way beyond the confines of some awful forum online. It's not fair Detective Inspector. It's not right and you know it."

Pope sucked in a giant breath of air through her flaring nostrils.

"And you're telling me this because?" she asked.

"Because we thought we would give you the benefit of the doubt," said Helen. "We thought we would give you the chance to give us something concrete, a lead, something positive in the investigation. And not just palm us off."

"It's a peace deal," said Martha. "Give a little, get a little."

That drew a small laugh from Pope. Or as close to a laugh as she was capable.

"I see," she said, sucking her tongue. "So what you're effectively doing is bribing me. Is that it? You're telling me that if I've not found your mum's body you're going to the newspapers. That's not really in the spirit of the law, you both know that, don't you?"

"We know what we're doing," said Martha strongly. "This has all gone too far, too quickly and it's far too personal to just let go."

Martha could feel her legs shaking. Her knees were wobbling against each other and she was trying with all of her might not to throw up. This was going to be it.

"That's what we brought you here to tell you," said Martha. "It's as simple as that."

"So, what have you got for us?" asked Helen bluntly.

Pope smiled. It wasn't a confident smile, far from it. She looked more shellshocked than Martha was feeling.

"What have I got for you?" she baulked. "Absolutely nothing. The police don't answer questions like that, not outside of our own offices and certainly not in pubs to a victim's family like you two."

"Well that's that then," said Helen with a sigh. "I thought you might have at least tried, Pope."

"DI Pope to you," she said spitefully. "How do you know all of this anyway? You're threatening to go to the press, but they'll ask the same question."

"Geri's boyfriend works at the morgue," said Helen casually. "Matt, he's a nice bloke. Ow!"

Martha pinched her sister's thigh. She'd said too much. There was nothing they could do now, just press on.

"It doesn't matter how we know Detective Inspector," she said, trying to salvage the situation quickly. "All that matters is that we're willing to blow this whole thing wide open, if it means we get our mum back sooner rather than later. And that's something I'm sure you won't begrudge us in the long run."

Pope nodded.

"Okay," she said. "I can tell you've made up your minds. And that's fine. I can only advise you both that doing what you're proposing would be a very, very big mistake. As I've told you before, this is an ongoing investigation that a top team of police officers is working on. The people behind this are professionals, they know what they're doing and if they're willing to do what we think they do, then they won't take kindly to being exposed to the press. Not only that, you might force them underground, making it even *harder* for us to catch them and, ultimately, return your mum's remains to you. Do I make myself clear?"

"We've lost our mum," said Martha. "Don't you see? That's the problem. What have we got to lose?"

"I'm not being drawn into this with you, Parker," said Pope. "As far as I'm concerned, you're making rods for your own backs if you go to the press. And I cannot, and will not, placate you when it's against the rules. For that, I'm sorry. But my answer remains the same."

With that, Martha knew what she had to do. She hadn't expected Pope to offer them anything, even in way of off the record guidance. This whole meeting had been a courtesy, a last ditch effort to change her mind. Helen had been right to force the issue of course. She was a diligent and smart woman who didn't rush into anything—everything Martha felt she wasn't at the moment. Having her sage advice was valued.

"I think our business is concluded here, don't you, ladies?" Helen asked, drumming her fingers on her knees. "We appear to have reached an impasse and none of us wants to give up our position. A fairly stark conclusion, I reckon."

Pope said nothing. Helen stood up, Martha joined her. She eased past Pope, who reached out and stopped her before she could go.

"Think about this, carefully, Parker," she said, her voice quiet and low. "Think about what you're about to do and if it's really going to help matters. That's all I'm saying."

"I know," said Martha, her eyes heavy, a sad smile on her face. "But what option do I have? She was my mother."

Pope let her go. The Parkers walked past the barmaid who was finishing sweeping up the broken glasses and spilled juice. Pope watched them go out the door. She gave them a few seconds to get down the street before she shouted an expletive at the very top of her voice.

It was so loud she erupted into a fit of coughing almost immediately afterwards. Scrabbling for her inhaler, she sucked on it hard and slowly caught her breath. Not that she had any time. She had to act fast. She grabbed her phone and stormed out of the pub, dashing across the street towards the police station.

"Get me information on a Matt or Matthew that works at the city morgue," she said, flipping a finger at oncoming traffic trying not to run her over. "And get me a locator on Geri Parker's phone, right now. Something's come up and we need to act fast."

Seventeen

GERI WAS IN a world of her own. Consumed by the million thoughts that were washing over and over her mind like a relentless ocean, she didn't notice when Matt took her hand. They walked down the busy street in the city's west end for a few paces before she stopped.

"What are you doing?" she asked, looking up at him.

"What?" he laughed. "What are you talking about?"

"This," she said, lifting their joined hands. "This is what I'm talking about."

"What about it?" he asked.

"What about it? It's happened, here, in the outdoors, with people all about. It's in public. It's affectionate. You might even say it's a display. Do you see what I'm getting at here?"

Matt smiled. The bruising around his cheeks and eyes was fading already. Geri liked his face, she liked his smile. She liked Matt. And she only half-wanted answers.

"I don't know," he shrugged. "I just thought that you might want to hold hands as we went for a walk. It's what people in our position do, Geri. It's what normal people do, you know that."

"I'm not normal," she said. "Whatever that generic, catch-all term is supposed to mean anyway. And you certainly aren't normal. I think hanging around with dead people all day and all night has fried your brain if you think *this* is going to cut it."

She waved their clenched hands in front of his face

"I notice you haven't let go yet," he said.

She hadn't. And in truth, she didn't want to. She just felt the need—for her own benefit, not his—to at least pretend to be outraged. Geri had always despised such gestures. Kissing in public was a definite no, especially in daylight hours. Arms around each other was equally bad. But holding hands, in the middle of the street, that was about as bad as it could get. Or at least, it used to be.

"I'll allow it," she said, dropping their hands down and starting walking again. "But only because you've had a rough couple of days."

"Your generosity knows no bounds, Geri Parker," he said.

They walked along in comfortable silence, nowhere really to go, and with no purpose. The day was a comfortable temperature, the air crisp and clean. The denizens of Byres Road were all out in force. The huge sandstone buildings on either side of the busy street rose to greet them, filthy student flat windows winking in the winter sunlight as they walked past. Geri felt quite sick that these sorts of days had grown to be so important. She was putting it down to her grief. The world seemed to be awakening from the darkness that had plagued her for the better part of a fortnight. She was starting to awaken too. Despite everything that was going on.

"Have you heard from Martha and Helen?" asked Matt, as if reading her mind.

"Nope," she said, clicking her tongue. "And I don't expect I will for a good while now. They've got what they wanted."

"What's that?"

"You were pumped for all the information they needed," she shrugged. "You might not have noticed it, Matt, but my sisters gave you the full Parker's interrogation the other night there."

"Interrogation? That wasn't an interrogation. They didn't put matchsticks under my fingernails or shine a big, bright light in my face."

"No," Geri smiled. "There are many ways to get answers from a punter. Believe me. And the dynamic duo are experts in that field. They milked you for all you were worth and happily went on their way."

"I feel kind of dirty," he said, rubbing his chest. "Like I've been used. They were so lovely too. I mean, as lovely as your sisters could be. I don't mean I fancy them or something, it's not like that."

"You should feel used," said Geri. "That's what they do. It's the business."

"Being a private investigator?" he asked.

"Yep," she said. "You have to be ruthless and not waste any time. Especially if you're up against it. You have to be lean, mean and keen. That's one of my sayings by the way, feel free to use it."

"How long have you used it for?"

"About ten seconds, when I made it up just there."

They both started to laugh. The old iron gates of the city's Botanic Gardens came up on them. They turned into the park and strolled down the neat path that led between the gently sloping grass. The impossibly beautiful glass structure of the Kibble Palace loomed out of the barren gloom ahead of them, glistening in the grey sunlight. Packs of students were dotted about the lawns enjoying a late lunch and missing the mania of very early Christmas shopping.

"Are you still fighting with Martha?" he asked.

"Who said I was fighting with Martha?" Geri asked, her mouth tight.

"I might not be a private dick, Geri, but you don't have to be to see that you two are at each other's throats all the time."

"Hmmm," she grumbled. "Not sure I agree with that logic."

"It's the correct answer though, isn't it?"

"No comment," she said.

"Told you," he laughed.

They enjoyed the sights and sounds of the park in the early afternoon. Geri hated it when other people were right. They often rubbed it in her face. Nobody was as right as often as she was. It was just a scientific fact. When she was on the other end of a moral beating, there had to be something deeply wrong.

"What's it all about anyway?" asked Matt. "You and Martha. I thought the three of you were really tight."

"We were," said Geri. "We are. Of course we are. When you've been through the stickiest of situations like we have, you can't *help* but be tight."

"So what's changed?"

What had changed? Geri had spent the better part of a fortnight asking herself that same question. The truth was, an awful lot. They had lost their mother, quite literally. And the fallout from all of that felt like it was driving a thick wedge between them both.

Then there was Matt. Geri had never felt this way about another person before. She trusted him, implicitly, which was madness, when she thought about it. She'd known him well under a year and yet here she was, strolling through parks on a weekday, holding hands no less.

"People change," she said. "I guess that's what's happening with Martha and I. We've known each other a long time, well, she's known me all of my life, I guess. That's a long time to be in each other's company, pretty much all day every day. The firm has made sure I rarely don't see both of them."

"And you think you need a bit of space?" asked Matt.

"I'm not sure, maybe," she said. "I'm not particularly happy about bickering with Martha. She pretty much raised me. Mum was still working, so was Dad. I actually saw very little of either of them, especially when I was turning into this blossoming woman you see before you now. Martha was always there, though, even when she had her own family to look after. She always made time for Helen and me. We were effectively two more kids."

"Not your fault though," said Matt. "You couldn't help being born so much younger than the others. Just a twist of fate and circumstance."

"Yeah, I know. But I owe Martha a lot. Not just for watching out for me. For the way I think, the way I look at the world. She's absolutely hopeless with technology, though. Seriously, she'd be able to short circuit a battery if you gave her long enough. I'm talking about analytics and problem solving. Thinking outside the box. You need a lot of that when you do what we do. She's been my inspiration for a while."

Geri felt suddenly quite emotional. She swallowed hard, making sure she didn't start blubbering there in the middle of the park. Holding hands was bad enough. She couldn't very well have a full on breakdown with everyone watching. That would be far too much.

She was close to it though. Talking about her family, about Martha, it just reminded her of how important she was to her. How they had been so close for so very long. And, more importantly, how that dynamic, that relationship, was changing. Not necessarily for the better.

"I don't know," she said. "It's just life, isn't it? Life's just one big string of arguments and fallings out, stacked up in a row and there to punch you in the face when you least suspect it. I guess it's what keeps us on our toes eh?"

"Yeah, I guess," said Matt, rather deflated. "You shouldn't fall out with her though. She is still your sister. And you guys have been through a lot. Not just in the past few weeks. I'm talking about all the other stuff you've told me about. Good relationships are worth fighting for."

"And what if I've outgrown that relationship?" Geri asked. "What then?"

"Blimey," he laughed. "I wasn't expecting there to be any questions. I just thought I'd say some really corny bull and that would be that. I probably should have planned ahead a bit more."

Geri laughed at that. She stopped them in the middle of the path. Pulling Matt's head closer to hers, she leaned in and kissed him on the lips.

"Wow," he said. "Isn't that a bit too much like public affection?"

"Yes, it is," she said. "But I don't care. Not anymore. I just wanted to do it. So I did. I'm getting a bit bored of worrying what other folk think. It's tiresome and takes far too much effort."

"I like the sound of that," he said. "Shall we celebrate? With wine?"

"In vino veritas, as Doc Holliday would say."

"Doc who?" asked Matt.

"Oh, come on," said Geri, slapping him on the shoulder. "You're joking right? You don't know Doc Holliday? As portrayed by Val Kilmer in the quite frankly *epic* Tombstone from the nineties?"

"Never heard of it," he said. "Is that the one where Bruce Willis has to blow up an asteroid?"

Geri let out a groan of frustration. It didn't matter though. She took a hold of his arm and they started walking again, the path leading around the park and back out onto the main road. They headed for the traffic lights, set on spending the rest of the afternoon in the pub, when she heard the distant moan of sirens.

They stopped at the lights. The unmistakable sound got louder. Geri didn't know why, but the sirens were making her feel very uncomfortable. It was ridiculous, she kept trying to tell herself. It was just an ambulance, or a fire engine. They whizzed around the city all day and all night.

But she couldn't shake the unease. There was something about them, something haunting, like they were calling out to her. A flash on the horizon made her jump. She saw the blue lights blinking on and off at the far end of Byres Road, directly ahead of them. The wail was growing as the squad car weaved in and out of the busy traffic, thundering down the wrong side of the street as it barrelled towards the junction by the park.

"Blimey," said Matt. "They're in a rush."

The squad car didn't stop when it hit the busy junction. All lights and sirens blazing, traffic skidded to a standstill to avoid what would have been a deadly collision. Geri was starting to think the police were going somewhere else, that she had just been paranoid, when the squad car slid to a stop right in front of them.

Everyone took a frightened step back from the edge of the curb. Everyone but Geri. The inevitable was sinking in. A uniformed officer climbed out of the driver's side, closely followed by Detective Inspector Pope—a furious look on her plaid face.

"Geri," she said, stomping towards her. "Get in the car now."

"Wow, what's going on here?"

"Matthew Taylor-Brown?" asked Pope.

"Yes," he gulped.

"Right, both of you, into the car, now."

"What's going on here?" he asked. "What have we done?"

"Do as she says, Matt," said Geri with a defeated sigh. "There's no use arguing."

"What? We haven't done anything wrong."

"I know," she said. "But I don't think that matters. I have a feeling that my sisters might have done something incredibly stupid. And we're about to face the consequences."

Pope didn't answer her. She looked sour-faced as Geri and Matt climbed into the back of the squad car. Then again, thought Geri, she always looked like that.

Eighteen

"ARE YOU ABSOLUTELY sure you want to go ahead with this?"

Helen was asking the question that had been running around inside Martha's head for what felt like a thousand years. Was she absolutely sure about this? Did she really want to bring everything crashing down around her ears? Once more into the breach and all of that.

She held on to the steering wheel with as tight a grip as her tired hands could muster. The knuckles on each hand were white. She stared down at them, noting how old they looked. Tired, haggard, wrinkled. Time waited for no woman it seemed.

Outside, a grinning, neon Santa lit up the forecourt of the huge newspaper office block at the top of the town. *The Scottish Sentinel* was the number one news brand in the country. It was everywhere, an institution. Everyone read the newspaper, everyone read their website, at least, that's what their corporate logos and adverts said. A tabloid of the highest order, Martha had decided it was probably the best place to start with what she had to say. Not that she held any great opinions towards the different styles of news reporting. She was no media snob. She just wanted to get this story out there, get it off her chest and be free of it all.

Only it would never be that simple. She knew that. Speaking to journalists would just be the beginning. She knew that once the lid was off this particular Pandora's Box, there would be no closing it again. This was a keg of dynamite and it was ready to go off.

Santa was still smiling down at her from the roof of the newspaper's main building. His reflection was all around her, puddles in the forecourt where the rain had dampened the afternoon. The sky was darkening already. Another day going and another one since her mother's accident. Time, she thought, was slipping away. Just look at her hands.

"Martha? You with me?" asked Helen.

Her sister's voice was enough to snap her out of her daze.

"What? Yes, of course," she said.

"Yes, of course you're with me. Or yes, of course you want to go ahead with this?" asked Helen.

"Both," she said, feeling no more confident. "I think."

"You think?" Helen wrinkled her nose. "You had better make up your mind pretty quickly. Before the combined forces of Police Scotland come charging up the road behind us and throw us in a dungeon never to be seen again."

"Have you got those pictures there?" she said.

Helen looked about the footwell. Nothing. She opened the glovebox. Nothing. Martha started to panic.

"Helen," she said. "What have you done with—"

"Here!"

She pulled the pile of photos Hamish had given them out from under her backside, waving them around in front of her victoriously.

"Bloody hell, Helen," said Martha, snatching them from her. "You almost gave me a heart attack there."

"Sorry," she said.

Martha took one last look at the tall building of the Sentinel lying in wait. There was still time, she thought, to turn and go. Nobody would know they had been there. Nobody would know about everything they had learned. Pope wouldn't be able to do anything to them as nothing would come out. Their conversation in the pub would have been nothing more than an inconsequential exchange of ideas. No harm done, not really. Although Martha wouldn't be able to call in any favours from the disgruntled DI any time soon. She could live with that.

Then she remembered her mother. She *always* remembered her mother. That's what this was all about. While she and Helen had been running around, her mother's body was out there, somewhere it didn't belong, with God knows what happening to her. They could make no funeral plans, had no opportunity to say a final goodbye and bring this whole rotten affair to an end. That's why she had to act. That's why she had to do what she had to do.

"What's that quote from that film?" she asked Helen.

"Nice and vague, go on," said her sister.

"You either die a hero or live long enough to see yourself become the villain."

"Oh yeah," said Helen, snapping her fingers. "It's from one of the Batmans. Batmen? Batman movies."

"That's the one," said Martha. "I kind of feel that way just now. Rock and a hard place."

"Yeah, I know what you mean," said her sister. "Look, Mart, I'm sorry about earlier on. Pope and all of that. I just thought we had to make sure we were doing the right thing. We had to give her a chance to at least pretend like the cops were doing something. And, well, I feel like a bit of an idiot now, having spoken to her."

Martha took Helen's hand and squeezed it.

"You're not an idiot," she said. "And you never will be. No matter what we're about to do, I want you to know that I love you. You *and* Geri for that matter."

"Geri, yeah," said Helen. "Do you think we should get her permission for all of this? I mean, it's her mum too and all of that."

"Geri has her own life," said Martha coldly. "We don't have time. Like you said, we don't know what Pope is planning, as we speak. We need to act. And if we're going to act, we've got to do it now."

"Agreed," said Helen.

"Okay."

"Alright."

"Right."

"Yes."

"Here we go then."

"Here we go."

Martha gave the steering wheel a final squeeze before opening the door. The damp air hit her like a wall and she did well to keep her balance. Helen followed her as they walked across the forecourt, Santa getting bigger and brighter with every step. He glowed above the main door like a Yuletide bouncer outside a nightclub. Martha would be happy never to be in one of those places ever again.

The revolving doors squeaked as they headed into the main reception. It was cool and draughty inside. Everything seemed too big, a colossal amount of wasted space for the reception area of a newspaper. A small desk was directly ahead of them, a bored looking security guard perched behind, his eyes glazed over. When he saw the Parkers approach he did nothing, uninterested by the visitors.

"Can I help you?" he asked in a broad Welsh accent.

"Hi, yes, hello," said Martha, the nerves getting to her a bit. "My name is Martha Parker, I'm a private investigator. This is my sister Helen."

"Yo," said Helen.

The guard looked her over with lazy, bloodshot eyes.

"We were wondering if we could speak to one of your reporters please. We have a story that might be of interest to the newspaper."

"And online," said Helen.

"Yes, thank you Helen. And online," said Martha, apologetically.

The guard sniffed. He leaned back, revealing a huge, heaving beer belly that was barely contained by his woolly jumper.

"Do you have an appointment?" he asked lethargically.

"No," said Martha.

"Do you know who it is you want to speak to?"

"No, sorry," said Martha. "Maybe one of your crime writers or someone on the city desk?"

"Or the editor maybe?" asked Helen. "This is proper dynamite stuff we've got, could be very good for the paper."

None of this seemed to interest the security guard. He sniffed again, clearing his throat. Putting his hands behind his head, he rocked in his chair, the hinges squeaking under the weight.

"So you're telling me you don't have an appointment," he said. "And you don't know who you want to talk to. But you've got a really good story for the paper. Is that correct?"

"Yes," said Martha. "Is there a problem?"

"Listen love," he smiled a missing toothed grin. "Do you know how many crackpots we get in through those doors behind you? I've been doing this job for seventeen years. I've had everyone from people who spotted Elvis in Inverness to the punter who *really* killed JFK come up to me. And I'll tell you what I told them. No thank you."

"But... but this is important," said Martha.

"Sorry, can't help you, I'm afraid," he held up his hands. "We here at the Scottish Sentinel can't just let any old waif and stray in off the street. What happens if you've got a grudge against one of our staff? Or you've got a bomb? And I let you into the newsroom upstairs. What do you think would happen then, eh?"

"But we don't have a grudge," said Martha.

"And we certainly don't have a bomb," said Helen.

"Says who? You? No thanks, I'd rather not take the risk," laughed the guard. "I suggest that you go home and think about all of this. And if you think it's still a good story you've got, just email it in or something. Two good looking ladies like you must be able to work a computer between you, am I right?"

Martha couldn't be sure when she finally snapped. The attitude of the guard was utterly abhorrent. Had it been his relaxed and arrogant attitude that had forced her over the edge? Or maybe the fact he wasn't willing to listen to them? The blatantly sexist comments had certainly taken their toll. And now her blood was boiling like molten lava.

"Look here," she slammed her fists down hard on the guard's desk.

He sat bolt upright, the colour draining from his face. Martha didn't give him time to get his bearings.

"My sister and I have had a very long day and it's not even... not even... what time is it?" she asked.

"Three," said Helen. "Three-ish, I don't know."

"It's not even three-ish," said Martha. "We lost our mum to some maniac driver last week and now her body has been stolen from the city morgue. And we've got a whole pile of evidence right here with us that proves there's a massive cover-up scandal involving other stolen bodies and the police are doing nothing about it. Now, if you don't let us upstairs to speak with one of your reporters, we'll go somewhere else. And instead of being the hero who saved the Scottish Sentinel, you'll be the one who wouldn't even let the biggest story of the year in the door. How does that sound, *love*?"

The security guard took a dry, painful gulp. He shifted his wide-eyed gaze between Martha and Helen.

"Missing bodies," he said. "You mean like that crash at the mortuary the other night?"

"The very same," said Martha. "Only we've got evidence that it actually happened and there's something rotten going on. Now, as I say, we're happy to give this story to you guys or we can go somewhere else. That decision is on your shoulders now. I suggest you choose wisely."

"Yeah," he said. "Yeah okay, alright. Lifts are over there."

He pointed back over his shoulder as he lifted the phone beside his computer.

"Go up to the fifth floor, somebody will be waiting to meet you at the door," he said. "That okay?"

"Fifth floor, thank you," said Martha.

She strode purposely towards the row of elevators at the rear of the lofty reception area. Helen panted as she tried to keep up.

"Nicely done," she whispered. "Although evidence is pushing it a bit, don't you think?"

The lift doors opened and they climbed in. Martha pressed the button and they closed again behind them. The elevator began to climb, the numbers ascending as it did so.

"Sometimes you've got to go with what you know, Helen," she said morbidly. "Heroes and villains. Turns out there isn't much difference between them."

The doors pinged open and a short, middle-aged woman with thick glasses smiled at them.

"Hi," she said. "Welcome to the Scottish Sentinel. How can I help you?

Nineteen

ANOTHER POLICE STATION. Another interrogation. Geri wasn't quite sure what she had done in a previous life to warrant all of this. But she knew it must have been bad. Rotten even. This was torture, long, drawn out, protracted torture.

At least she wasn't alone this time. Matt was beside her. That made a refreshing change. Normally when she was about to be grilled by the police, she had to face them on her own. Having a bit of company felt like a novelty.

Matt, however, wasn't quite in the same jovial mood. He was pale and sweating, looking the hallway up and down nervously. Every noise, every opening and closing door, every cop that walked past had him on the edge of his seat. He drummed his hands together, impatient to find out what was going on while at the same time desperate to never know.

"You okay?" Geri rubbed his arm.

"What? Yeah, course, always," he lied.

"Is this your first time in a police station?"

"Yes, yes it is," he said. "I don't know what I was expecting. You see them on the telly don't you, see them all the time. They always look dull and dreary. This place isn't like that at all. It's just like an office."

He nodded at the pale walls and the frosted glass that separated the corridor from the main offices.

"It is an office Matt," she said. "A lot of policing is paperwork. I imagine it's a bloody nightmare. That's why I leave all of that boring stuff to Martha and Helen with the firm. I'm a woman of action you see."

She hoped her manner would calm him down. He didn't seem to pick up on the joke, still nervously watching the hallway.

"We're going to be fine, you know?" she said. "We haven't done anything wrong and we're not under arrest. Pope is a bit of a hard arse. But she's fair. She wouldn't try and fit us up with anything we hadn't done. She's a good cop, honest."

"So why are we here then?" he asked. "Why were we pretty much kidnapped from the street corner and sped across the city to be sitting here, right now."

"I don't know," Geri shrugged. "It'll be Martha and Helen. They'll have been up to their usual tricks and caused all kinds of hell. They have a tendency to do that sort of thing when I'm not there to keep them in check."

"I find that hard to believe," said Matt.

"Is that so?"

"Oh come on, Geri," he said. "You're not exactly a wallflower yourself, are you?"

"And what's that supposed to mean?" she grinned.

"It means that if there's any sort of bother, any sort of scandal or trouble, you're normally at the heart of it. It's like you love being in the eye of the storm, up to your neck in things."

Geri couldn't really argue with his assessment. Although things had changed recently, thanks to him. She was about to tell him so, when Pope appeared at the far end of the corridor.

"Heads up," she said, nudging Matt. "Here comes the ringmaster."

Pope charged up the corridor. Her shoes slapped hard on the linoleum floor, clicking and clacking like a freight train running out of control down the side of a mountain. Her whole appearance had an avalanche feel to it though. She was as dishevelled and tired as Geri had ever seen her. Thick bags drooped under her sharp eyes, her skin was covered in a greasy sheen. She shook up an inhaler and sucked on a shot as she neared them.

"Right you two, in here," she shouldered open a door beside them and ushered them in.

Inside was an interview room. The lights flickered into life, giving very little comfort to the stark and bleakly practical room.

"Sit down," said Pope, taking her own seat out from beneath the small table. "Now before you say anything, I'm sorry."

"You are?" asked Geri. "For what?"

"It's not exactly my style to go about lifting people off the streets," said the DI, raising her hands. "But this is a bit of a minor emergency."

"It's *always* a minor emergency when we're involved, Aileen," she said.

Pope didn't like that. Geri had thought about addressing the cop formally. But she wasn't under arrest and she'd just been given an apology. Still, she filed it away in the back of her mind not to call the DI by her first name again any time soon.

"I can't argue with that," said the senior cop. "This time though, it's a bit bigger than your usual carry on with cheating husbands and wives."

"Eh, hold on," said Geri, feeling put out. "We deal with a *lot* more than cheating husbands and wives. As you know only too well."

"I'm not in here to argue with your resumé, Geri," said Pope sternly. "I'm here to give you both a bit of a warning and a plea to talk some sense into those two mad wenches you call sisters."

Geri nudged Matt in the ribs. He winced in pain.

"Told you," she said.

"Told him what?" asked Pope.

"As soon as you picked us up, I knew it was Martha and Helen. It's *always* Martha and Helen. You might as well come out with it now, Detective Inspector. I highly doubt there's anything you can tell me that would shock me. Not with those two, they're quite capable of doing anything and everything. Especially when I'm not there."

Pope didn't bite. Geri thought that was odd. She was being complicit, she was helping, she wasn't resisting. She had accepted the apology and was happy to move on. So what was the problem?

"Matthew," said the cop, turning to him. "I'm going to ask you a very simple question and I'd like you to think about it before you answer. Do you understand?"

"Yes," said Matt, nodding. "Wait, hold on. Was that the question? Do I understand? Was that the one I was supposed to think about."

"No," sighed Pope. "That wasn't the question. I'd like you to tell me just how you and Geri have spoken to Martha and Helen Parker about the whole business at the morgue. The morgue you work at."

Geri didn't like where this was going. She had been cursing her sisters for getting Matt so involved. He had worked hard to get his internship. And while he'd been happy to reveal everything that had been going on, she didn't like him being implicated in anything they were doing.

"We're not under arrest," said Geri. "He doesn't need to answer that if he doesn't want to, yeah?"

"Yes," said Pope. "Technically."

"You don't have to say anything, Matt," she said to him.

"It's not like that Geri," said Pope. "I'm not interrogating you. You're not wanted for anything. I'm just trying to get a picture of what people know, that's all."

"Why?"

Pope clenched her hands into tight balls. She cleared her throat, wrestling with something Geri was unsure of.

"Martha and Helen have done something, or they're about to do something that's incredibly stupid," she said. "And I need to know what they know so I can try and stop them."

Geri felt suddenly quite cold. She shivered and rubbed her arms through her sweater. Despite everything that was going on between them, Martha and Helen were still her sisters. And if the police were trying to twist her arm to find out what she knew, then it had to be serious.

"What are they trying to do?" she asked.

"I had a meeting with them, about twenty minutes before I picked you both up," said Pope. "It was amicable enough, in the pub, no less. Martha dropped a two glasses and looked thoroughly embarrassed."

"She does that sometimes," said Geri.

"To cut a very long and boring story short, they told me that they were going to the papers with what they know about the bodies going missing. And that they hoped it would speed things along to try and find your mum's remains."

"What?" Geri shot up from her seat. "That's… that's absolute madness. What are they thinking?"

She began to pace around the room, everything whirling around inside her head. She tried to focus on what Pope had said, one word at a time. But it was too difficult.

"They're going to the press?" she asked. "But that's… that doesn't make any bloody sense. That's not going to catch Mum's kidnappers any quicker. If anything, it'll make them *harder* to catch."

"That's what I told them," said Pope, steepling her fingers. "I said that, by taking this whole issue public, they run the risk of jeopardising the whole case. And exactly as you say, forcing the dirtbags behind all of this mess further underground so we never catch them, let alone find your mum."

"This is insane," Geri kept saying.

"Sit down Geri," said Matt, trying to calm her down. "You're getting frustrated. You can't think straight when you're like that."

Geri reluctantly did as her boyfriend asked her. She sat down with a thump across from Pope, still rubbing her forehead.

"Did they say which paper they were going to?" she asked.

"No," said Pope. "And I didn't ask. It hardly matters, Geri. This is the biggest story of the year, it already is after that break-in at Matt's place of work. As soon as they get a witness testimony and whatever else it is your sisters have dug up then the whole of the country's media will be onto it."

"Wait, hold on," said Geri. "Matt's place of work. How did you know he worked at the mortuary?"

"Martha and Helen told me," she said flatly.

"They *what*?"

Geri leant on the table, arms stretched out in front of her.

"They told me," said Pope. "They said that they had an insider at the mortuary, your boyfriend. That's how they knew about all the other missing bodies we have on file. And that they were going to expose the whole thing to the press."

Geri felt sick. She had never been betrayed before, not like this anyway. She may have been fighting with her sisters more than usual lately. But she never expected them to cross that line, that unspoken rule of sibling confidentiality. Then she cursed herself. This was *exactly* why she didn't want Matt involved. It had been an unhappy coincidence, everything that had happened. Why couldn't the thieves have targeted another morgue in another city. Why had their mother been killed by a hit-and-run incident? Little moments in time, little strands of fate's great tapestry, all spinning on and on. In that moment she could have cried, just sat there and sobbed. Not because she was sad, but through sheer, unadulterated rage and anger at Martha and Helen.

"Where are they now?" she asked. "We need to stop them."

"I have no idea," said Pope. "And yes, stopping them would be very helpful. This is a huge case, Geri, a massive one. And it's above all protocols when it comes to sensitivity given what's been stolen."

"Who," said Matt.

"What?" asked the DI.

"Who has been stolen, not what," he said. "They're still people, even if they're dead."

For a brief moment Pope looked embarrassed. She quickly moved on before anyone could properly notice.

"You need to try and talk some sense into them, Geri. They'll hopefully listen to you," she said.

"Yeah, of course," she said, trying to shake off the anger. "I'll call them now."

"You need to try and make them see that we're doing all that we can," Pope went on. "Some of our best people are working on this case. We *are* trying. We've got officers from the major crime unit from down south also taking a look at what's going on. It's our top priority. That's why we need it to remain confidential for the moment, until we can establish if there's anything the public can do to help us. Then we'll gladly go to the press. But not before."

"I get it, yeah," said Geri, getting up again. "I understand. Are we free to go?"

Pope hesitated. She sat back in her chair, fingers drumming on the tabletop. She eyed Geri and then Matt up and down before making her decision.

"Yes," she said. "You need to call Martha and Helen right away though. I don't think they'll dally on this sort of thing."

"No," said Geri, rounding the table and heading for the door. "I don't imagine they will."

She pushed her way through the door and stomped out into the corridor. Matt lagged behind her. She could hear him calling after her, but it was dull, faded in her head. She clenched her fists open and closed as she made her way out of the police station and into the crisp, cool air. Fetching her phone, she tried Martha first. There was no answer. It was the same for Helen. She tried Martha again, this time getting the answerphone.

"Martha, this is Geri, you need to pick up your phone as soon as you get this message," she shouted down the line. "I've just been told by DI Pope that you and Helen are planning on telling journalists about what happened to Mum at the mortuary. You *cannot* do this, it's madness. Do you have any idea how much bother that would create, how many problems it will cause the police, Pope and Matt? Which reminds me—you got to speak to Matt the other night there in total confidence. I knew I shouldn't have let you, I bloody knew it. He told you all of that stuff in good faith that you wouldn't tell another soul. Now you've gone and dumped him in the deep end with the police. Do you know he could lose his job, his *career* over what he told you? And this is how you repay his trust, *my* trust! You need to answer me Martha, you need to call me back straight away, before you do something that we'll *all* regret!"

Geri hung up, her thumb pressing the screen on her phone so hard that it almost broke. She could hear her heart thumping in her ears, her breaths short as they smoked out in front of her.

The first pangs of pain from a headache made their way back and forth above her eyebrows. She clapped a clammy hand onto her forehead and turned around.

Matt was waiting for her. He startled her, just standing there, staring at her.

"This is madness," she said again. "I can't believe what those two knuckleheads are planning on doing. I'm sorry, this isn't your fight, you have nothing to do with this Matt."

He didn't say anything. Instead he just looked at her, his face slack, eyes glassy

"What's wrong?" she asked him, sniffing.

"What you just said there, on the phone, about my career," he said, pointing at her. "That I could lose my job, my career would be in ruins. I never thought about it until now, Geri. But you're right. You're absolutely right. It won't take the coroner's office long to work out that it was me who gave them the information. And if Martha and Helen have gone to the media then they'll know. They'll know."

"I know, I'm sorry Matt."

She stepped forward and reached out for his hand. He pulled away, the slackness in his face turning to panic.

"Oh my God," he said. "This could be it, this could be my whole career down the drain. Just like that, in the blink of an eye, in one conversation. I mean… I never thought they'd go public with it. What was I thinking? What was I thinking Geri?"

"Matt, it's okay," she said, trying to calm him down. "It's okay. We can still stop them, there's still time."

"No, there isn't," said Pope, emerging from the police station.

Geri turned to face her. The DI moved like a ghost, gliding over the gritted pavement. She held up a sticky note in her hand and waved it at them.

"This was waiting for me back at my desk," she said solemnly. "It's from the media team. Seems that there has been a press comment and statement request in from the Scottish Sentinel about allegations of a mass cover up of missing bodies from the city morgue. More missing bodies than the two I know your sisters already knew about. It would appear that they know everything, everything I assume you told them."

She stared directly at Matt. He shook his head, stepping back away from them both.

"No," he said. "No, no, no, this can't be happening. This can't be happening to me. This is my life, my livelihood."

"Matt, calm down," said Geri, trying to reach him. "Just calm down. We have to think."

"No," he said. His voice was loud and cut through the air like an axe that had been thrown at her head.

"You stay away from me. Do you hear me? You just stay the hell away from me, Geri. You've ruined my life. I'm... I'm finished."

"Matt!"

He turned and started running down the street, vanishing around the corner before Geri could do anything. She felt like her feet were glued to the pavement, that she was buried up to her neck in cement and there was no chance she could ever move again. Then the tears started to roll down her cheeks.

"Matt," she whispered. "What have I done?"

Twenty

FOR THE FIRST time in days, Martha hadn't slept. She had spent the night sitting in the darkness, chewing on what was left of her fingernails, wondering if what she had done was the right thing or not.

Around four in the morning she had decided that a pros and cons list was the best way forward. While it was already too late to change anything, at least that way she could get everything out of her head and down onto paper. Not that it made very good or pleasant reading.

When that pointless exercise was exhausted, she had gone back upstairs to bed. She listened to Geri's message for the millionth time and lay awake until the first cracks of the winter dawn had crept beneath the curtain's edge. It was morning again, another day. Only this time she had a stake in what was going to be on the news agenda.

Helen hadn't called by six, which she thought was unusual. She had been expecting the phone to buzz as soon as Helen stirred from her scratcher and checked online. Martha had refrained from going near her phone now, especially not the internet. She didn't want to know how big or how small her decision had been interpreted. She almost wanted it to be over and done with, so she could say she had done everything she could to get her mother home. But she didn't want to deal with the consequences. Cake and eating it all at once.

Eventually, just after seven, there was a knock at the door. Martha knew who it was even before she opened it. She pulled the door open and was met with a newspaper floating in front of her nose.

"We made the front page," said Helen, emerging from behind.

She handed Martha the paper and pushed her way into the house, heading straight for the TV. Helen turned on the screen and started flicking through the channels, searching for the news. Martha, meanwhile, had to try her very hardest not to keel over at the door.

Helen was right, the story was on the front page of the Sentinel. A picture of the huge, ugly hole in the side of the morgue dominated everything. Beside it was the headline, one that made Martha turn white.

**THIEVES STOLE MY MUM'S BODY –
AND SHE'S NOT THE ONLY ONE**

Martha flipped through the next few pages. The rest of the story was emblazoned across the paper in front of her. The pictures Hamish had given her were there, the vaguest outlines of people and a van dotted and enhanced by the paper. She started to skim through the words, remembering her conversation with the crime reporter Annie Anderson. There was even room for a small photo of Annie beneath her byline, the same middle-aged friendly smile that had coached and coaxed all of the gory details from her in the newspaper office the afternoon before.

At the end of the article was a comment from the police. Martha read it then reread it, just to be sure of what it said. Then she read it a third time while she unpacked and unscrambled the comment.

"Have you read this?" she called after Helen.

"Of course I have," shouted Helen. "Cover to cover."

"The bit from the police."

"Yes."

"Where they say that they are aware of ongoing investigations into the alleged disappearances of cadavers from the Glasgow mortuary. And that they are monitoring the situation closely along with colleagues from other constabularies to establish the role of organised crime syndicates."

"Yes, I read it Mart," Helen shouted back.

Martha felt numb. She wandered into the living room and sat down on the sofa across from her sister. Helen was still furiously rattling through the various channels, trying to find some coverage of the story. Martha stared down at the newspaper in her lap. Annie Anderson had persuaded them that being named and pictured would give the story some weight, especially given their minor celebrity. A photo of the three Parkers Helen had dug out from her phone was in the bottom left corner of the spread. They all looked happy, bathed in summer sunshine. Martha wondered if she would ever be that happy again. Or if they would ever be able to pose for a picture together like that again. She touched the photo where Geri stood and felt suddenly very alone.

"Nothing," Helen tutted. "Absolutely nothing. No major news channel has picked it up. What a disgrace."

"Give it time," said Martha. "It's still early."

"I suppose," she said. "Have you heard from Geri?"

"Yes, I'm afraid so," said Martha solemnly. "She left a message on my phone. You?"

"Not since last night, when we came out of the newspaper and *that* message she left for both of us. I didn't call her back."

"No, neither did I," said Martha.

"She'll know we'll have heard it by now."

"I suspect so," said Martha. "She'll also know that we didn't get it until it was too late."

"I somehow don't imagine that'll fly very far as an excuse with Geri, Mart," said Helen. "You know what she's like."

"Yes, I do," she said. "I can't deal with that right now. We need to concentrate on this whole thing being exposed. It might actually get us somewhere close to finding Mum's body."

"Yeah, I was thinking about that last night," said Helen, tucking her feet under her legs and sitting on them. "Have you ever heard of a thing called a ghost wedding?"

Martha wasn't listening, not fully anyway. She was still looking down at the picture of the three sisters together. Beside it was a photo of their mother. The Sentinel had insisted on using an image of her, to 'tug at the heartstrings' as Annie had put it.

"No," she said eventually.

"Nor had I," said Helen. "But Hamish and his online pals—who I'm sure will be delighted with all of this coverage—brought it up on the forums the other night. It's a pretty mad thing but apparently it's big business."

Martha closed her eyes tightly. She had to try to listen, to think of something other than Geri and the message she'd left. As soon as Martha had seen the voicemail message on her phone, she knew her youngest sister was angry. She knew she'd want to protect Matt as much as possible. Martha also knew that in time she would probably forgive that breach of trust. The ends always justified the means in Geri's eyes. This was no different.

"What's big business sorry?" she asked.

"Ghost weddings," said Helen. "Essentially it sees people marrying dead bodies in order to bring them peace in the afterlife. It's been going for about three thousand years in the far east. Apparently, it used to be just between two cadavers. So somebody would have a marriage ceremony for two dead people who were unmarried when they were alive. Now, apparently, you're getting living people who are marrying corpses to keep the tradition going. Like I said, it's big business out there."

"That's dreadful," said Martha. "Why are you telling me this Helen, now, of all times. Don't you think we've got enough on our plate?"

"Yes, Mart, I know *exactly* how much we've got on our plate. I just thought I'd tell you about a bit of research I've been doing."

"Why would you research something like that?" she asked.

"The forums, the ones that Hamish is part of," said Helen. "I just told you this. A couple of them on there think that the reason dead people are vanishing is because of this ghost wedding malarkey. They reckon that their loved ones, including our mum, have been stolen to be sold to the far east market for this ghost wedding business."

"Bloody hell," said Martha, leaning forward and burying her face in her hands. "I don't think I can take much more of this. I think my head is going to explode."

"I'm telling you, Mart, people make hundreds of thousands in shipping these bodies about the place to get married," said Helen. "I mean, I don't think it's *actually* happening, not here anyway. You know what these internet crackpots are like. Just gets you thinking, doesn't it?"

"Oh yes, absolutely," said Martha. "I'm really loving thinking about our mum being married off to some rich singleton in Beijing or Shanghai. Really quite lovely stuff Helen, thank you."

Martha felt sick. Her stomach rumbled, her throat dry. She looked down at the paper and closed it over, leaving it on the back page rather than the front.

"You wouldn't be making a pot of tea would you?" asked Helen. "I'm rasping here."

"Yes, I think that's probably a good idea," she said. "About your only good idea for the past few weeks."

"Hey, that's not fair," she called after her sister. "I have plenty of good ideas. It was me who put us in touch with Hamish. If I hadn't been such a tech nerd, we never would have had enough evidence for the newspaper."

"I'm still not convinced we did," said Martha. "But I believe that's what Annie Anderson called 'taking a punt.' Or something like that anyway, I can't recall."

"Well it worked," said Helen, checking her phone. "Looks like other newspapers are running it online now too and crediting the Sentinel. We're starting to go viral."

"Not again," Martha shook her head.

She walked out of the living room and felt a cold breeze gust up about her ankles and dressing gown. She wrapped herself in the house coat and noticed the front door was lying wide open.

"Helen," she called back into the living room. "Didn't you close the front door when you came in?"

"You came in behind me," shouted her sister.

"Oh," said Martha. "I thought I closed it."

She wandered over to the front door, the breeze getting stronger. She was about to close the door when she spotted a large, black Range Rover parked at the end of the driveway. The engine was running, a man in dark clothes in the driver's seat. It was nothing new for this area, there were plenty of luxury cars and men who drove them about. Only something didn't seem right about this. Martha didn't recognise the car, or the driver.

She stepped out onto the porch when something hit her from behind.

She tumbled forward, hitting the ground hard. She let out a groan as the biting warmth of blood filled her mouth. Groggily she tried to roll over but she didn't have the energy. Her vision was blurred and she felt something looming over her. A shadowy figure appeared and she tried to blink away her haze.

"That her?" came a thick Glaswegian accent.

"Aye, that's her," said another.

Martha tried to work words around in her mouth but nothing would work. She felt a set of hands grab her ankles, another pair take her wrists. They lifted her up and she was carried down the driveway. She felt the warmth of the Range Rover tingle her skin. Then everything went dark.

Twenty-one

"SORRY ABOUT THE bump on the head. You can't take any chances in my line of work."

The world went from darkness to light in a split second. The adjustment sent a sharp, stinging pain through Martha's brain. She winced, still tasting blood. Her eyes started to adjust to the light and she was able to see again. Much to her surprise, the skyline of Edinburgh was waiting for her.

The huge, imposing castle was up to her left, perched atop the volcanic mountain in the middle of the city that wore the fortress like a crown. The spires of St Giles Cathedral and General Assembly Hall of the Church of Scotland stuck out above the other rooftops, dark fingers on the clear blue sky.

The room she was in was luxurious, if sparse. Minimalist furniture gave everything a cool and classy feel. Even in her scrambled mind Martha acknowledged this wasn't the type of place to fill with clutter. Not with one of the most stunning views of the Scottish capital just sitting there for all to see and enjoy.

It took Martha a moment to process what was going on. She went to rub the back of her head and found her hands were tightly bound to the legs of her chair. She struggled but it was useless. Every move was painful and she quickly gave up.

"The boys can be a bit rough when they put their minds to it," came the same voice that had woken her.

Martha looked about. She felt something brush past the back of her head. A tall, elegant woman came into view as she rounded past her. Rakishly thin, she wore a fashionably loose blouse and high waisted trousers. Her six inch heels clicked on the polished floor of the room. The soles of the stilettos were blood red, matching the cascading head of hair that seemed unnaturally shiny and well kept. Martha suspected it was a wig. The woman strutted over to the huge panoramic windows that offered the view of the city's skyline.

"I'm sorry," she said. "Do I know you?"

"I highly doubt it, Martha," said the red haired woman, her back still turned on Martha. "I'm sure you won't lose any sleep if I tell you that you're probably not big time enough to know who I am. And I don't say that with any airs or graces. If you *did* know me, you wouldn't be so calm."

Martha was struggling to concentrate. She had a thumping headache and the taste of blood wasn't a good sign. She tried to remember what had happened at the front door. Then she calculated she must have been unconscious for at least an hour if she was now in Edinburgh. That didn't account for traffic or parking. Or, indeed, getting her up the stairs to this wonderful suite.

It was all pointing to one thing. Professionals who did this sort of thing for a living. That made Martha clench everything tighter.

"Okay," she managed. "If that's the case then there's probably no need for me to be tied up is there? I mean, if I don't know who you are then how could I possibly be a threat."

The red haired woman's head twitched to the side. Martha wasn't sure where her logic had come from. But it sounded good at least.

"Very good Martha, very good indeed," said the stranger.

She slowly turned away from the windows. Facing Martha at last, she was much older than she had been expecting. Her face was heavily made up, but Martha could still see the wrinkles, the crow's feet of a woman well into her fifties. There was an air of superiority about her, a command, a confidence that Martha had seen in women of power before. Only this had a danger about it, a malice. There was something about the woman's eyes that couldn't be trusted. They were both alive with zest and intelligence but dead at the same time. She gave Martha the chills.

"My name is Nicola Wu. And I run this country," she said.

Martha was speechless. There was a lot to unpack there.

"Okay," was all she managed. "Although, if you don't mind me saying so, I think there are probably quite a few people just over the road in the Scottish Parliament that would probably disagree with you."

"The Scottish Parliament," that drew a smile from Wu. "If you think my methods are brutal, they're not a patch on that lot, believe me. I could tell you a few stories about the Scottish Parliament and the right honourable folk who call it home. They would turn your hair white and anything else you had. Trust me."

"You'll forgive me if I don't take you up on that offer, Ms Wu," said Martha. "But I tend to not trust people who bash me over the head and kidnap me to Edinburgh."

Wu nodded in agreement. She walked smartly over to a broad, stylish desk at the far end of the huge suite. Producing a packet of cigarettes and quite possibly the shiniest lighter Martha had ever seen, she lit one and blew the smoke out in front of her. She gave a slight nod and two men appeared behind Martha. They quickly untied her and then retreated again.

"Like I said before," said Wu. "Sorry about that."

Martha rubbed at the marks on her wrists. She looked about to see the two heavies standing guard at a wide entranceway. She didn't imagine she was going to just walk out of there. Clearly she had been brought to the capital for a reason.

In days gone by she might have tried to work out why ahead of time. Staying ahead of whoever it was that meant you harm had been a handy asset to have up the sleeve of her cardigan. The way she felt now though, with everything that was going on, she just didn't have the energy.

"Ms Wu," she started. "I'm sure you've got your reasons for bringing me here. Some of them I might even agree with. But I would really appreciate it if you didn't mess me around. I've had a very stressful few weeks and I'd like to get back to some semblance of normality."

"Ah yes, normality, of course," said Wu, sucking on her cigarette. "Parkers Investigations, that's the name of your company isn't it? You and your sisters, Helen and Geri, the youngest yes? You guys are the absolute epitome of normal aren't you? I mean, catching the killer of a high flying banker, that seems fairly hum drum. Or at least it does compared to your exploits with the Steiners."

Martha was starting to panic. Who was this woman? And why did she know everything about her?

"It would seem that normal isn't in your vocabulary, Martha. Far from it in fact."

"Okay," she said. "I get it. You're trying to intimidate me for some reason."

Wu laughed loudly. She walked across to the huge windows and pressed a button beside one of the panels. It opened, letting the hustle and bustle of Edinburgh's traffic disturb the tranquillity of the suite.

"Come on," she said, beckoning Martha like a dog.

Martha didn't really have a choice. She looked at the goons who were standing guard behind her. They both took a step forward in tandem, signalling that she shouldn't keep their boss waiting. Martha got up and walked gingerly over to the open door.

The wind kicked up and cleared away some of her cobwebs. A thin strip of balcony ran along the outside edge of the building, disappearing around the corner. The views were even more stunning from outside, all the colours and life of Edinburgh painted out in front of her like a masterpiece. Foolishly, Martha dared a quick peek over the edge. It was a long way down and there was a lot of traffic. If she was going to be thrown over it would be *very* public. Not that it would matter to her.

"I'm sorry about what's happened to your mother's remains," said Wu, totally unaffected by the view, the height, or the billowing wind. "Death is a sacred thing. It shouldn't be interfered with. My father always told me that."

"Did your father tell you that smoking is bad for your chest too?" asked Martha, unsure of where that had come from.

Wu finished her cigarette. She flicked the end away, black painted nails catching the bright sunlight.

"I read your piece in the news today," said Wu. "It concerned me a great deal to see that the police are considering everything that's happening to be the work of organised crime gangs. I don't like the police Martha. I don't like them for a whole number of reasons I won't bore you with. But I especially don't like them snooping around my business interests."

"Business interests?" Martha asked. "And what business interests would these be?"

Wu smiled. She leaned on the balcony barrier and stared longingly out at the skyline.

"This place used to be a swamp," she said. "That's why it's called Auld Reekie. No amount of UNESCO heritage awards and tourist tripe can ever fully clean away the past. If something stinks then it'll always stink. A swamp is a swamp and you can't polish a turd. Everywhere you look there's something crooked, Martha. Everywhere, there's something rotten, something wicked. Everyone has their price and it's usually not a lot. Desperation, fear, anxiety, whatever. It all means people can be bought. And when that happens, they start to fear you, respect you. As long as you can give them what they want, they'll be yours forever."

The wind whistled in Martha's ears. The taste of blood was still in her mouth. She decided to hold on to the balcony barrier just to be sure.

"So what are you telling me?" she asked. "That you're some sort of Godmother?"

"I'm not telling you anything, Martha," said Wu, unflinching. "It's merely two businesswomen having a casual conversation about life and its troubles. Simple really, nothing sinister in that."

"No, but you did have me brought here in the back of a car," she said. "You did have one of your goons hit me on the back of the head. I reckon that's assault, if I go to the police."

Wu nodded.

"Yes, I think you're about right," she said with a smile. "But you wouldn't do that, not if you knew what was good for you, for Helen and for Geri. Who, I understand, you're not really seeing eye-to-eye with at the moment."

The wind had been cold. But Wu's words were positively frozen. Martha pushed the hair from her face.

"What do you know about that?" she asked. "How do you—"

"It doesn't matter what I know and how I know it Martha," said Wu. "I know it, that's what matters. And you'd be wise to follow my counsel when I offer you an olive branch. I'm not the type of person you want to see get angry. Plenty of people have and they don't see much of anything after that."

The wind died down. Martha could feel her heart beating hard in her chest. It couldn't be good for her, too much stress, too much action. She had to calm down, and quickly. Otherwise it wouldn't be Wu who would bump her off. It would be herself.

"Okay," she said. "You've got my attention. I get it, you run this town. What does that have to do with me and my sisters?"

"Nothing, not really," said Wu casually. "Absolutely nothing at all. From what I gather you three have just been in the wrong place at the wrong time. It's unfortunate, you weren't to know. But it's happened and you've blabbed to the press. No doubt against the wishes of the police. How is DI Pope these days, anyway? I haven't heard from her since she got promoted. Good detective, if on the pale side. She and her wife could be doing with a holiday."

Martha felt sick. Was there anything Wu didn't know?

"I'll be sure to pass on your concerns the next time I see her," she said. "Although I don't think that'll be anytime soon. Not after the news broke this morning."

"I thought so," said Wu. "A shame, when something like this drives a wedge between people. I've seen it happen all too many times. But business is business as they say."

"And your business is?"

"Lots of things," said Wu. "In fact, I just signed a multi-million pound deal to have this whole building completely renovated and turned into luxury apartments. The one in there, that's just a demo for the investors. I reckon in about a decade

I'll have tripled my investment. A shrewd move, if I do say so myself."

"And you do," said Martha.

"You see, this is the problem Martha, this is the problem I have with your editorial in todays' papers. It's brought a very private, unfortunate and very much unwanted attention onto parts of society that should just be left alone."

"You mean crooks," she said.

"That's one word for it. I like to think of it as unauthorised business opportunities."

"And the trading of dead people is a business opportunity to you?"

Martha could feel herself getting hotter. The ice in her veins was melting. Wu shook her head. She pulled back the sleeve of her blouse to reveal a gaudy, glittering watch. She unfastened it and held it up to Martha.

"You see this? It's worth a hundred grand," she said. "Diamond encrusted, brushed gold, blah blah blah. All of the bells and whistles."

She then did something Martha wasn't expecting. In a fluid motion she hurled the watch off the balcony. They both watched it as it sailed through the air before plummeting down towards the road below. It smashed on impact, scattering the diamonds about the street. A bus ran over it in a final mark of indignation.

"Hundred grand, so what?" asked Wu. "Plenty more like it out there and it's easily replaced."

"Bloody hell, what a waste," said Martha. "What could a charity have done with that money?"

"You're missing my point," said Wu.

"There was a point to this?"

"The watch is material, Martha. It's a thing, an object—an expensive one, but a thing nonetheless. People, they aren't objects and they're certainly not things. They can't be replaced. Everyone is individual, good, bad or indifferent. It's what makes the world tick, if you pardon the awful pun."

Martha winced.

"What I'm trying to tell you, Martha, nobody in my organisation, or *any* organisation, if you want to call it that, has been stealing bodies. If they were, I'd know about it. I know about everything else."

It took a moment for Martha to realise what she was being told. She was still shocked by the watch.

"So you're saying the police have got it wrong?" she asked.

"It wouldn't be the first time," sniffed Wu. "They're not the brightest sparks. DI Pope is though. But she works with idiots. How do you think I can afford to throw away a hundred thousand pounds worth of diamonds to prove a point to a complete stranger?"

"Fair enough," said Martha. "So if the underworld isn't stealing the bodies. Then… who is?"

Wu laughed at that. She shrugged.

"Beats me," she said. "And believe me, I don't say that very often. It would seem there is somebody out there in the big bad world who fancies themselves as a Burke and Hare tribute act. Although why they would want to mess with the dead I'll never understand."

Martha needed a moment. This was all getting too much. The police were convinced gangsters were behind the thefts. Now the top kingpin, or was it queenpin, by her own admission, was letting her know that it wasn't the case.

"Why are you telling me all of this?" she asked. "What does it matter to you if my mum's body is missing. Or indeed anyone's body is missing? What do you care?"

"I don't care," said Wu. "Not really. I'm sorry for your loss. Like I said, death is sacred and all of that. What I *do* care about is having extra police patrols around my businesses. Extra attention and extra care being given to the people that work for and with me. Do you have any idea what it's like to be harassed by the biggest, best organised and equipped gang in the land? That's what it's like for me when the police get a bee in their bonnets."

The taste of blood made it hard for Martha to have any sympathy.

"You can do me one small favour, though," said Wu, walking past her.

They stepped back inside and Martha was relieved to be away from the dangerous edge. Wu walked back over to the huge desk and opened a drawer near the bottom. She produced a long, white envelope, DI Pope's name handwritten on the front.

"Give this to your cop pal," said Wu. "It's a love letter from me to her that should set things straight. I don't know if she'll pay it much attention, you know what she's like at times. But if it stops them wasting time on a fruitless investigation and gives my people breathing space then it would be greatly appreciated."

Martha took the letter. She turned it over in her hands.

"You don't trust me, do you?" Wu smiled.

"Can you blame me?" asked Martha. "You kidnapped me from my front door. I'm still in my dressing gown for goodness sake."

"Sometimes it's all about the pizazz, the glamour," said the businesswoman. "One of my drivers will deliver you safely back to your gaff Martha, untouched. I'd get that lump on the back of your head looked at though, concussion protocol and all of that."

Wu rounded the desk. She took a hold of Martha's arm, her grip light but strong. Guiding her towards the double doors, the goons pulled them open as they approached. A small gaggle of similarly smart and brutish heavies were waiting on the other side. They all stood stiffer as Wu walked down their ranks.

"Deliver that letter to Pope personally," she said. "I'll know if it doesn't reach her."

"I will," said Martha.

"I am truly sorry for your loss, Martha. Losing your parents isn't easy, no matter what time of life it happens. Sometimes, in fact, it's even harder if you've had them for a very long time. I wish you well on your journey to finding whoever did this to your mother. But I can assure you, whether you want to believe me or not, organised crime isn't where your answers lie."

She gave a weak smile and clapped Martha on the shoulder. Then she turned and strutted off back towards the suite. She snapped her fingers and the doors of a lift opened behind Martha by command.

She stepped inside, joined by half a dozen heavies who surrounded her like bodyguards. It was going to be another one of those days.

Twenty-two

GERI BANGED ON the door. She banged on it so hard that her hands hurt. It didn't stop her though. She was determined to get inside. She was owed some answers from her family.

"Martha! I know you're in there. I can see that your phone is active and inside," she shouted, her voice waking up the whole street. "Let me in or I'm going to break something. In fact, let me in so I *can* break something."

There was no answer. Geri took a step back. She was sweating, her jumper and jacket feeling like they weighed tonnes. She looked up at the dark windows of the second floor of Martha's house. The curtains were open but there was no sign of life. Geri was getting angrier with each passing moment. She checked her phone again. The tracking service showed that Martha's mobile was inside. So why was she ignoring her?

"Let me in Martha," she shouted. "I'm not going anywhere. Let me in or I'm breaking in."

Her voice echoed down the quiet suburban street. A few lazy birds, not yet south for the winter, flapped out of bare branches at the sudden disturbance. Geri watched the front door, expecting it to open and her sister to be there, perhaps apologetic. But there was nothing. Just the silence and stillness of a residential street a few weeks out from Christmas.

Something wasn't adding up here. In all of her anger, Geri hadn't considered that there might be something suspicious going on. She checked her phone again. It definitely showed

Martha's mobile at the address. And she wasn't aware of any bugs or faults.

"Martha?" she shouted again, this time more cautious.

Silence. Geri walked back towards the door, her boots crunching on the damp gravel of the driveway. She looked down and saw other footprints there. They looked odd, dragged out, like somebody had been shuffling along.

Geri quickly called her sister. It rang out and went to the answerphone. She hung up and hurried over to the bay windows of the living room. It was dark inside. She tried calling again and saw the screen of Martha's phone light up on the far off sofa.

"Right, now that is odd," she said.

A clank from around the back of the house disturbed her. Geri backed away from the window. She stared down at the corner of the house where the path led to the back garden. She looked about to see if there was anyone around. Of course there wasn't, this was the suburbs. There was never *anyone* around when they were needed. They were too busy on the golf courses or in country clubs, sipping Pimms and talking about each other.

Geri slowly made her away along the path, trying not to make a sound. She hugged the wall, hoping that whatever was around there, if anything, wouldn't see her coming. She scanned the path and garden for a weapon, but there was nothing. Again, she reminded herself, this was the suburbs. There was no litter, no abandoned iron poles or crowbars dotted about the place.

Another clank made her jump. She gave one more look about for some last minute support. There was, of course, none. She was on her own. She paused at the edge of the house and took a deep breath. Whatever was making that noise was just around the corner. Thinking the worst, Geri hurried around, her arms outstretched and fists clenched for action.

Toby the tomcat was waiting for her. He stopped his pawing at a half-opened bin bag, cans clanking as they toppled out onto the path. Geri stopped, halted herself before she stood on him. Not that he seemed bothered. He gave her one cursory glance, emerald green eyes unblinking, before he returned to his foraging.

"Bloody hell fire," said Geri. "And there was me going to punch you up the bracket, Toby."

"You're fighting with the cat now?"

Helen's voice from behind her made Geri jump. She felt like her skeleton had been electrocuted, rattling from head to toe. When she landed, she turned to face her sister who looked totally perplexed.

"What? No. I heard a sound, something banging or something. I thought, I thought somebody was breaking in."

"Into Martha's house? Are you mad? She's got nothing to steal."

"I don't know what I was thinking, okay? I'm not thinking straight. Hell, I'm not thinking at all. Cut me some slack Helen."

She pushed past her sister and rounded the corner, past the front of the house. Then she remembered who she was talking to and stopped.

"And another thing, I'm not talking to you," she shouted.

"What? Why?" asked Helen, following her.

"Why? I think it's pretty bloody obvious why."

"If it was so obvious, then I'd know."

"Oh, you know alright. You and Martha, a neat little coven you're forming. And as soon as my back is turned, you're off blabbing to the press, talking to journalists with information that was told to you in confidence."

"Oh," said Helen. "That thing."

"Where is she?" asked Geri, heading to the front door again. "Where is Martha? I want to talk to her. Right now. I'll break down this door if I have to."

"Geri, calm down. You're clearly tired and emotional."

Geri knew her sister Helen wasn't the most eloquent when it came to confrontation. In fact, she was as subtle as a bull in a china shop. A bull with a sore head and a penchant for smashing things into oblivion would be the most accurate way to describe her. She should have known better than to let it bother her. But the morning, the previous evening, the two weeks, the month and life Geri Parker was having, she was in need of venting.

"Calm down?" she said, stomping back towards Helen. "Calm down? You're telling *me* to calm down? Are you off your head, Helen? What could I possibly have that could calm me down, eh? No, please, go ahead and tell me. I'm all ears."

"You're acting like a complete arse," said Helen.

"*I'm* the complete arse? Are you serious? I don't believe I'm hearing this."

"Well you should take the wax out of your ears then. Or not listen to all that bloody brain rotting music so loud."

"Don't," Geri said, holding up a stiff finger. "Just don't. I'm not in the mood this morning Helen. I'm really, *really* not in the mood to start this with you."

"Start what?"

"This," she spun her hands around like she was mixing dough. "This whole why are we a family at war thing. The cold shoulder thing. The fact that you guys not only went behind my back over something that affects *all* of us. But that you used information that *my* boyfriend, the man I'm very, very close to, told you, believing it wouldn't leave the four walls of my flat. And instead here we are, shouting and screaming at each other like a couple of petty schoolgirls and Matt is off somewhere, probably deleting me from his life and I'll never see him again. That hurt, Helen, that really, *really* hurt. As if it wasn't bad enough with Mum dying and then going missing, I'm now wandering about in a bloomin' trance like some stupid lovesick idiot who doesn't know what to do with herself. Me, Helen. Me!"

She shook her head, eyes glassy with tears.

"There, satisfied?" she said. "Is that what you wanted to hear? Is that what you needed me to confess to you out here on Martha's lawn to unlock the gates and let me at her?"

"She's missing," said Helen.

Geri took a moment. She was sure she heard what her sister had said, but it didn't make any sense. She was angry and she'd accepted that was all the emotion she was going to pour out. In the cab over, she had practised everything she was going to say to Martha, the lack of trust, the betrayal, the fact that she loved Matt. All of it. Now the carefully rehearsed production was in tatters.

"What?" was all she managed in the end.

"She's gone. Missing," said Helen. "I was around here first thing, I brought the paper. She went to make us a cup of tea and then the next thing I hear is a car taking off down the road. I went out and checked and the front door was wide open. She's gone."

"What do you mean she's gone. This is Martha we're talking about," said Geri. "She's never just gotten up and gone anywhere without a reason. She gets a nosebleed when she has to go anywhere she doesn't know."

"Geri, I'm telling you what happened," said Helen. "I can't add anything else to it, as I don't know."

"Did you see the car?"

"No."

"Well, do you know what direction it went in?"

"Nope."

Geri clenched her teeth. She really didn't need this, not this morning.

"Are you of any help at all?" she asked.

"I told you she's missing," said Helen. "And you won't need to kick the door down, it's not locked."

"Didn't you hear me banging?" asked Geri.

"I was in the office in the garage," said Helen. "I'm doing a bit of research. Have you heard of this thing called ghost weddings or ghost marriages?"

"Not now," said Geri, heading straight for the front door.

She opened it with ease and darted for the living room. She picked up Martha's phone from the couch and scrolled through the missed calls and messages. There was nothing out of the ordinary.

"Have you called Pope or the cops?" she called to Helen, sauntering in behind her.

"No," she said. "I didn't think it was that serious."

"Are you kidding me?" asked Geri. "Helen, Martha has gone missing. You don't know where she is. She's a private investigator, who's mum has just died and vanished and had her face plastered over a national newspaper. You don't think any of that is worthy enough of flagging to the police?"

"Well…" said Helen, trailing off. "When you put it like that I suppose there's a chance that…"

A loud thump interrupted her. The sound of crunching feet on the gravel of the pathway made Geri nervous. The roar of an engine followed, screeching tires screaming up the road that ran along the front of the house.

She bolted for the front door, pushing past Helen. But she stopped before she could get outside. Martha came stumbling towards her, cheeks flushed, tears running down her face as she hobbled towards her home, dressing gown wrapped tightly about her.

"Martha!" Geri shouted.

She collapsed into her youngest sister's arms.

"Helen. Quick," shouted Geri. "It's Martha. She's back!"

Twenty-three

MARTHA SAT PERFECTLY still, her hands wrapped about her mug. She had her trusty blanket slung over her shoulders. Her face was still cold, nose with a permanent drip at the end. She sniffed for the hundredth time to make it go away. But it remained a constant in an ever changing world.

She had experienced many strange mornings in her life. Martha Parker was no stranger to the out of body experience. It came with being a private investigator. She'd been dragged kicking and screaming to almost every corner of the country at some point. The good people of Glasgow and beyond believed that she, along with Helen and Geri, were the best in the business. They had been on the frontline, stared death in the face and all of that. She still couldn't quite believe it. This had been a side project, a hobby even, something to fill up her days while her husband worked and her daughter grew up faster than time itself.

Never, as long as she lived, did expect things to turn out the way they had. From dead bankers to murdered celebrities. And now her own mother's body, missing without a trace. In the past few years she had shared conversations with some of the most powerful people in the world. She'd seen the sights and the stars, the world beyond the real world, the bubble of celebrity and power and wealth. She'd been chased through parks by the police, fallen through rooftops and been harangued by bouncers, security guards and all kinds of official people. She'd even been in a plane crash, kidnapped, shot at and threatened more times than she could count.

Life, it seemed, had been one long thrill ride. At least that's what everyone else thought when they looked at Martha Parker and her sisters. The reality, as she was finding out, was very, very different. The reality was here and now. Sat cradling a cup of tea that had gone cold an hour ago, wondering just what the hell was going on.

"Still nothing on the main news channels," said Helen.

She was fidgeting with the buttons on the TV. Geri ignored her, one leg dangling over the couch arm, locked on her phone. Martha watched her two sisters. There was something deeply comforting about them all being in the same room again. Sure, they had been together only a matter of days ago. But not like this. She reckoned that this was the first time the three had been alone, in each other's company, since their mum's passing. Since that fateful night in the hospital there had been a constant stream of other people, outsiders. They may have meant well and all of that. But they weren't Parkers. They weren't family. They were them.

She watched Helen and Geri silently, and wished things had been different. She wished once again that she hadn't put them in as much danger as she had. All those threats, bullets, plane crashes and more had involved them too. They had been right by her side, through thick and thin. She had a duty to protect them, she always had, being so much older. That was double now, infinitely more pressing. She had always been another mother to both of them, especially Geri. Now she would have to be her sole mum. And that started now, with an apology.

"Geri," she said, shifting for the first time in forty minutes. "I'm sorry."

Geri looked up from her phone. Her face was as hard as granite, unflinching. She was blasé, bordering on uncaring.

"Whatever Martha," she said. "I'm so tired of it all, I actually don't care anymore."

"Tired of what?" asked Helen. "You're not the one who was kidnapped by gangsters and whisked off to Edinburgh. Lovely city, right enough, did you see the castle, Mart?"

Martha ignored her.

"I'm sorry Geri, about everything that's happened," she said. "I know you're probably not in the right frame of mind to forgive me."

"What an understatement," said Geri. "Which in itself is an understatement for this family."

"But I need you to know, when you come around, *if* you come around, that my thinking and my intentions were only good."

"Like I said, Martha," Geri shook her head. "Whatever. I'm over it. Is that what you want me to say?"

"Don't be like that, Geri," said Martha.

"Then what should I be like?"

Geri sat upright on the couch and stared both Martha and Helen down.

"What the hell kind of reaction were you two expecting from me? You've completely betrayed my trust. I can't trust you, either of you. Do you have any idea how that feels? You're my sisters, my blood. My *only* blood as it happens, now that mum has gone. I get pulled into a police car by Pope, put through the ringer by her, only for her to twist Matt's arm. And what do you think he does? He runs. Can I blame him? Absolutely not. I wish I could run too. I wish I could run out of that door and never come back. And it feels absolutely bloody horrible!"

She panted, gulping for breath. She got up and walked over to the window. Martha thought, just for a moment, that she might actually go and they'd never see her again. Instinctively she shot to her feet, ready to give chase. Instead Geri leaned on the sill, staring out at the front lawn.

"I know you're hurt Geri, and I don't blame you," she said. "I knew this would happen, I didn't want it to be this way. But it was the only option."

"There's always another option Martha," she said bitterly. "How the hell could grassing on Matt and telling the press everything he knows be the only option? He's probably going to lose his job now. His bosses will know it was him, it's all logged on the various systems. He's a sitting duck. And for what? So you could pressure the police into doing their jobs? Well, I hope it was worth it. I really do."

Martha stood, her head bowed. She stared down at her feet, pale, ghostly against the dark rug. She looked like a corpse, a dead woman. All she needed was the toe tag and she could have passed for a cadaver.

It gave her chills as she thought about her mother, their mother. She had been like that only a few days ago. Maybe she still was, somewhere, out there. The thought made her angry, it made her sad. She was being torn apart from the inside out. She had to do something.

"She was our mum," she said.

Helen looked up at her, stopping her pretend channel surfing. Geri didn't move, still staring out the window.

"She was our mother. She gave birth to us. She raised us, she looked after us and she taught us everything we know. She made us birthday cakes and she bought us Christmas presents. She worked hard to send us to good schools and she was there when we all graduated. She thought the sun shone out of our backsides and she would never hear a bad word said about any of us, ever. She broke her back to make us happy. She taught us to be generous, to be kind, to be forgiving, not just to the outside world but to each other too. And most of all, above everything else, she loved us unconditionally for who we are, who we became, who she saw us all, all three of us, grow up to be. She was our mum but she was so much more than that. So, so much more than that one simple word could ever describe. She was my world, your world, our world. And she was taken away from us far too early. Not only that, she was stolen, robbed. That means none of us has been given a chance to say our goodbyes, to celebrate her life and all the wonderful moments that will live forever in our memories and beyond.

"That's why I did what I did Geri. That's why I risked your happiness, your trust in me and your sister. I didn't want to. But I had no choice. Our mother's remains are missing, taken by God knows who and the police and even the criminal underworld don't know where she is. We've lost the only person in all of our lives who stayed forever true, forever faithful. All I want to do is have her back, to hug her, to tell her one more time that I love her and that I'll look after you two now that she's gone. That's why I did what I did. And do you know something else? I'd do it again."

She was shaking. Her legs went weak, the world spun. She fought on, she had to. She'd put a lot on the line for her family, for Helen and for Geri. She needed them to understand her motivations and what the last few days had been like for her. If they couldn't forgive her now, then Martha believed, truly believed, that they never would.

"That's it," she said. "That's all I've got. I'm tired. I'm drained. I've got a lump on the back of my head the size of a golf ball. I've got a letter from Scotland's premier gangster addressed to a police officer who thinks my name is mud. And, most of all, I've got my youngest sister who hates my guts, while the other one thinks I'm an idiot. Not a bad week's work, even by my standards."

She laughed and wiped the dribble from the end of her nose onto the sleeve of her dressing gown. It was filthy and Martha was sure she spotted some blood on there. Looking about the room, Geri hadn't moved. Helen, however, stood up.

"Blimey Martha," she said. "That was quite a speech. And for the record, I don't think you're an idiot. I think you're absolutely bonkers, but not an idiot. Never that."

"Thank you Helen," she smiled weakly.

"But I guess it's not what I think that matters. Is it Geri?"

They both looked over at their sister. She stared out the window, head held high. She was silent, unmoving. Even though Martha knew she was a fully grown woman, fiercely independent and everything else, in that brief moment she was the little girl in pigtails she used to collect from primary school. Decades rolled backwards and they were all younger, more innocent, when the world was less complicated, when they were free. Martha had never been big on prayer, it had never really formed part of her life. But she prayed now as she stared at the back of Geri's head. She prayed that her youngest sister would understand.

Geri took a deep sigh, her shoulders bobbing up and down. Then she turned around to reveal her bright red face covered in tears and snot. She threw her arms open and lunged towards the others. Martha and Helen grabbed her tightly and the three Parkers embraced, as they had done so many times for so many years.

"I love you," Martha whispered "And I always will."

Twenty-four

THE NIGHT HAD fallen and everything was colder. The frost was already making the pavements sparkle. Breaths bloomed from beneath woolly hats and above tightly wrapped scarves. The late night Christmas shoppers were feeling the fatigue. They weren't the only ones.

Martha buried her hands in her pockets. It was nice to be wearing some proper clothes again. Her jaunt through to Edinburgh in just her dressing gown hadn't been ideal. A warm shower and quick bite to eat and she was feeling herself again. Sort of. There was only so much you could feel yourself given everything she had been put through.

She had Geri and Helen back onside though, which made her feel better. The three sisters walked up Buchanan Street, bathed in the glow of the shop window displays and the Christmas decorations hanging from the streetlights. In another time, in another life, this might have been enjoyable, even fun. But the three Parker sisters had business to attend to tonight. And it wasn't going to be pleasant.

"Have you opened the letter?" asked Geri.

Martha felt the envelope in her pocket. She ran her fingers along the edge.

"No," she said. "Nicola Wu was pretty adamant that I should deliver it to Pope in person. And she doesn't strike me as the type of woman who approves of her mail being tampered with."

"We're PIs, Mart, not the Royal Mail," said Helen. "I would have told her where to stick it."

"Yes, of course you would, Helen," said Geri. "You have a notoriety around these parts for sticking up to criminal kingpins don't you. In fact, what is it the press dubbed you in today's paper? The last of the tough guys?"

"Shut up."

"Oh, okay. Better do what you say, or you'll have me wearing a concrete overcoat before the night is out."

Martha smiled. She had missed this, missed it more than she ever thought possible. Walking with her sisters on either side of her, she felt safe for the first time in a very long while. She had spent her life putting a brave face on things, being the leader. Now, it seemed, she was human after all.

"No, I haven't read the letter is the answer to your question, Geri," she said.

"Do we have any idea what it says?" asked Helen.

"No, I'm afraid not," she said. "Wu was adamant that all of this had nothing to do with organised crime gangs, namely hers."

"Do you trust her?"

"No, of course not," said Martha. "Mind, I don't imagine she has anything to gain by saying it's not somebody she knows, or her own business dealings as she liked to call it. I mean, she went to all the trouble of having me kidnapped from my front door and taken through to Edinburgh. She quite easily could have remained in the shadows and we would have been none the wiser."

"That's true," agreed Helen. "Although it kind of feels excessive don't you think? She effectively broke the law in a serious way to tell you she wasn't breaking the law. Could be a case of the lady doth protest too much."

"I don't think so," said Geri. "From what Martha has said, this is a woman who is cold and calculating. She knew everything about us, that means she did her research before Martha was nabbed. If she was trying to do a double bluff, it's too risky. Whatever she says in the letter will clear it up I suppose. But I'm of a mind to believe her, as crazy as that sounds."

Martha agreed. She'd spent the drive back from Edinburgh wondering the exact same thing.

"It doesn't really help us though," she said, as they continued up the glowing street. "If anything, it puts us right back to square one. If the gangsters aren't stealing the bodies then just who is?"

"Maybe Pope has had a breakthrough," Helen snorted. "And maybe I'm going to win Mr Universe."

They all laughed at that. They reached the top of the street and the police station came into view. Martha was getting very sick of seeing the boring, drab grey building. Not just because it was Christmas, but she'd spent far too much time in the past few weeks in and around this place.

"Does she know we're coming?" asked Geri.

"No," said Martha.

"You thought we'd surprise her, good plan," said Helen. "If there's one thing we've learned about DI Aileen Pope, it's that she loves an unwelcome surprise."

"Maybe we should phone her," said Geri.

"And say what?" asked Martha. "That I've got a handwritten letter here from one of Scotland's most notorious underworld figures, the one who gave it to me when she kidnapped me from my doorstep this morning? I can't see that flying can you?"

"Then what are we going to do?" asked Helen.

"We wait," said Martha.

"Wait? It's freezing out here, Martha."

"We wait until she comes out and then we corner her. She won't have any choice but to listen to us."

Geri and Helen looked at each other. Martha expected a rebuke but there was none forthcoming.

"What?" she asked. "No arguments? No shouting and arguing?"

"Nope," said Helen.

"Not from me," said Geri.

"It's not the worst plan. So I suppose we should hunker down for the long game."

Martha felt a sudden lump in her throat. Once again, she was so delighted to have her sisters back onside.

A bus stop stood dilapidated and graffitied across from the police station. The sisters all hurried inside and took a seat on the uncomfortable bench inside. They settled down and waited. Martha touched the letter in her pocket. It felt heavy, unnaturally heavy, like it was packed full of secrets. As the time passed, she felt more and more compelled to open it up and read it. She wanted to know what Wu had written to Pope. She wanted to know all the gory details, the gossip, anything and everything that might give them a clue to solving this terrible mystery.

Then she started to think about her mother and what she would have thought of all of this.

"I wonder if Mum is watching us," she said to the others.

"Eh?" asked Helen, snorting herself awake.

"Right now. I wonder if Mum is watching us all. The three of us, sat here in the freezing cold waiting for Pope to come out of the police station. I wonder what she would think if she could see us right now."

"She'd probably think Geri wasn't wearing enough clothes," said Helen, nodding down at her sister's bare legs.

"And she'd probably think you were dressed like an explosion at a knitting factory," Geri fired back. "Seriously, how old is that jumper?"

"This?" she flattened her sweater. "I don't know. Ten years, maybe twelve."

"Blimey," said Geri. "You're the epitome of net zero aren't you?"

"Hey, there's nothing wrong with a sustainable wardrobe, save the planet and all of that."

Martha smiled. For once she was happy to let them argue among themselves. It was just nice to hear them talking. Although she knew it couldn't last forever. There was still work to do.

"Have you heard from Matt?" she asked, nervously.

"No," said Geri with a sigh. "And I don't expect I will either. He's very angry, very upset and very scared. The last thing he'll want to do is talk to me, or us for that matter. Can't say I blame him, we've single-handedly ruined his life."

"It can't be that bad, Geri," said Helen.

"Oh, it is," she said. "It is Helen. He'll get fired from the gig at the mortuary, if he's lucky. I don't know what their HR system is like, but I don't imagine they'll look too kindly on leaks to the media."

"He'll get another job," said Martha. "He's a clever boy."

"He is," sighed Geri. "But he has terrible anxiety. He gets really nervous in job interviews, or anything that involves people really. That's why he works with dead bodies. Worked with dead bodies. He always said they didn't talk back so he could say what he wanted to them."

She laughed at that. Martha was feeling awful.

"I guess he will get a new job in time," said Geri. "Which isn't such a bad thing. He might find something else. It's not like he's skint or anything."

"No?" asked Helen, her ears pricking up. "Do tell."

"It's nothing," said Geri. "His dad used to be some consulate out in Hong Kong or somewhere like that. He lived in like ten different countries before he was a teenager. Travelled and saw the world with his dad's job. Then his parents were killed in a plane crash when he was at boarding school and he kind of went off the rails. Dropped out of school and bummed around for a decade before winding up here."

"And the money?" asked Helen. "What about the money?"

"He would have had an inheritance, surely," said Geri. "Jetting about the world, that sort of job affords a high salary. I don't know though, we never talked about money or his background very much. Suppose you can understand why, orphaned at twelve years old, that's a tough gig."

"We're orphans now," said Helen sadly.

"Yes, we are Helen, thanks for that," said Geri. "Matt is slightly different though. We're fully grown women. He was a schoolboy when it happened. You can't really blame him for being anxious, I suppose. He passed through a lot of hands before he was grown up."

"It must have been tough," said Martha. "You're making me feel worse than I already do, Geri."

"Yeah, well, these things happen I suppose," she said. "I'm still not very happy with you, with *either* of you. But your hearts were in the right place, at least. And hey, maybe it wasn't meant to work out between Matt and I after all. The universe has a way of telling you these things, doesn't it? Or maybe it's Mum. Who knows? Who cares?"

Martha nodded. Helen did the same.

"Hey, is that Pope?" Helen pointed across the street.

A tall, hunched-over woman in a thick coat strode down the street away from the police station. Even at this distance Martha knew it was the DI.

"Come on," she said, bolting out of the bus stop.

She ran across the road as the rain started. It fell in chilly rods and Martha was soaked to the bone before she reached the other side of the street.

"DI Pope," she called out.

The woman didn't stop. Martha panicked. Did she have the right person after all?

"Oi! Aileen!" Geri shouted.

That was enough to get her attention. Martha had been right. Pope stopped suddenly and turned around.

"Oh, you've got to be kidding me," said the detective inspector. "Seriously? All three of you? At once? Is this some sort of bad dream?"

"No," said Martha. "I'm afraid it's not. And I think it's probably going to get worse before it gets better."

"Not for me Parker, I'm done with you, with the lot of you."

Pope turned on her heels and headed down the street.

"We have to talk," shouted Martha, the rain getting heavier.

"Not with me you don't," Pope called back over her shoulder. "Find yourselves some other moron who had the misfortune of trusting you. I'm finished with you all."

"But it's important," Helen cried.

"We have a letter for you," shouted Geri.

"It's from Nicola Wu."

Pope stopped dead. Her hunched back uncurled as she stood to her full height. She turned sharply, rain plastering her short hair to her forehead and running off her sharp nose.

"Nicola Wu?" she asked. "How the hell do you know her?"

Martha pulled the letter from her pocket and waved it at the DI.

"She gave it to me this morning," she said. "With the explicit instructions that I had to deliver it in person. It's about the missing bodies. She says she has nothing to do with it."

Pope stared through the rain at the letter. She went to speak, but stopped herself several times. Then she looked up at the heavens and let out as frustrated and angry a roar as the Parkers had ever heard.

"You bloody three," she shouted at them. "What did I do so wrong in a previous life to deserve being stuck with you? Honestly, it's like I'm being punished at a divine level."

"The letter, that's all we're here for," said Martha.

"You're not getting out of it that easily Parker," said Pope, stalking towards them and taking the envelope. "You owe me a very, very large brandy."

Twenty-five

MARTHA WASN'T REALLY sure why she'd ordered them all brandy. It seemed like a good idea at the time. Now the rich, brown liquor was staring back at her from the beautiful glass and she was considerably worse off financially.

The old man's pub had been replaced by a swish, up-market bar close to the police station. Christmas was tasteful here. There were no gaudy baubles or multicoloured lights like the ones she had at home. Instead it was minimalist chic—reindeers that glittered and just the outlines of Christmas trees—not the full bushy numbers.

The clientele was equally designer. Martha was pretty sure some of the coats, jackets, probably even the scarves, were worth more than the Parkers' outfits all put together. The air was refined and clean, no chance of catching a whiff of fifty year old smoke or yesterday's lunch special in this place.

Pope had insisted this was to be the venue of their showdown. She had marched them through the rain with no more of an explanation or even a word. Martha knew better than to argue with the Detective Inspector. She wasn't a woman to trifle with when she was in a good mood. And the luck that she had pushed so far might be enough to tip Pope over the edge of her hospitality.

The cop sat across from them, a high table and stools giving them all the look of vultures perched on a tree branch high above the Serengeti. She sipped from her brandy glass and savoured the taste, the smell. She sloshed it around and examined the colour against the comfortably dull light of the bar. The Parkers could only watch on, half in awe, half in curious fascination.

"You know," said Pope, draining her glass. "I don't have a clue about brandy. I couldn't tell you the first thing about this stuff, other than it costs a small fortune. Thank you, by the way Martha. That was very generous of you."

"A pleasure," said Martha.

"I don't know what all the fuss is about," said Helen, sniffing at her own glass. "It's just booze, what's the big deal?"

"You can get a bottle of Napoleon brandy, whatever that is, for like six quid in the supermarket," said Geri. "How much was this round Mart?"

"It doesn't matter," she said, lying. "What matters is that we have company, and we should act accordingly."

It was the most motherly thing Martha had said, probably since their own mum had died.

"Right, to business," said Pope.

Martha, Helen and Geri all sat up straighter.

"You have about ten minutes by my reckoning," said Pope, checking her watch. "Before my wife walks in through those doors over there and we begin our anniversary celebrations. Contrary to popular belief, you three are *not* invited, as I would like to spend the evening in the company of someone that I actually care for. So, if we have no further distractions, Parkers, do you want to tell me what the hell is going on here?"

Martha pushed her brandy to one side. She held up her hands.

"Firstly, I want to say thank you, from all of us," she said. "I really do appreciate you meeting us like this."

"Parker, please," said Pope. "I don't need your feigned apologies. You've done what you've done. It's out there now, we're at a dead end. Where's the chase and how do we cut to it? I've got a letter here that you claim is from Nicola Wu—who, I should add, is not a very nice person and you'd be wise not to become best pals with her."

"I can assure you Detective Inspector, that *won't* be happening," said Martha.

Pope reached over the table and took Martha's brandy. She sank it in one gulp and then turned her attention to the letter.

"Have you opened this already?" she asked.

"No," they all said at once.

"Alright, alright," she said. "I wasn't accusing you."

She cleared her throat as she unfurled the letter from the envelope. Martha, Helen and Geri all sat staring at her. The tension was almost too much to take. Pope raised one eyebrow and folded the letter over again and tucked it back into the envelope.

"Well?" asked Helen.

"We're on tenterhooks here Pope," said Geri.

"We really would like to know what it says Detective Inspector," said Martha.

Pope said nothing. She leaned across the table and took Helen's brandy from under her nose. Again, in one well-practised swoop, she sank the drink in one swallow. She politely wiped her lips clean and replaced the glass on the table.

"It would appear that Ms Wu, who is a person of great interest to Police Scotland, has nothing to do with the disappearing cadavers, including your mother. And that she would appreciate no further harassment or investigation on our part."

Martha, Helen and Geri all let out the same frustrated groan. Their shoulders sank and their heads all bowed. Pope blinked, unsure of what she was seeing.

"I'm sorry, was that not what you wanted to hear?" she asked.

"We knew that already," said Helen. "It's what Wu told Martha when she kidnapped her earlier."

"You were what?" the cop squeaked. "Kidnapped?"

"It doesn't matter," said Martha.

"Doesn't matter? It's against the law."

"What does the letter say, exactly," said Martha. "What does Wu write? Is there any clue in there as to who *is* behind the thefts?"

"No," said Pope. "There's nothing. It's two lines, two sentences where she respectfully asks for her business interests to be left well alone or she'll pursue legal action."

"And you believe her?" asked Geri.

"It's Nicola Wu," said Pope, leaning in closer. "If you think she doesn't already know that we're all in here, drinking together, then your head buttons up the back. She's the most connected, well-informed person in the country. And she's as dangerous as they come. Ruthless, utterly ruthless. She is, in a strange turn of events, quite honest too. If she has gone to the bother of writing to a police officer, an investigating officer at that, then I have no reason to disbelieve her. She wouldn't do something like that unless she was absolutely watertight that it put a good distance between her and the action. Which is ultimately the kick in the crotch that I didn't need right now."

"Why?" asked Helen.

Both Martha and Geri tutted in frustration.

"Why?" asked Pope. "Because Helen, you're Helen aren't you? Because Helen, I now have at least a dozen missing bodies and more reports coming in by the minute, thanks to you blabbing to the newspapers. And we have absolutely no clue where they're going or who's taking them."

"Wait, you said *more* calls?" asked Martha. "You mean more than what we reported?"

"Yes," said Pope, tucking the letter into her pocket. "This is why we don't go public until it's the right time, Parker. My team have spent the day fielding messages from all over the country. Bodies vanishing, being sent to morgues and mortuaries and never being released to families and next of kin. Whoever is out there doing this is doing it deliberately and for some reason that's beyond even my warped imagination."

"Have you ever heard of a ghost wedding, Detective Inspector?" asked Helen.

"Helen," said Martha, rubbing her forehead. "Not now."

"What? I'm only asking."

"No, Helen, I've not," said Pope sternly. "And quite frankly, I don't care either. I have enough problems and enough on my 'to be read' pile without taking recommendations from you, if it's all the same."

"Suit yourself," said Helen, huffing.

"This is a mess," said Martha.

"You're telling me," said Pope. "It was a mess *before* you took it to the media. Now it's escalated a hundred fold. Instead of being out there catching the criminals, my team are having to wade through more and more reports to find out if they're genuine or just bogus. There are people out there who like to wind up us bobbies for a laugh. Especially if they, oh I don't know, have read about a terrible story in the newspapers and online."

If Martha hadn't been feeling low already, she certainly was now. Pope clapped her hands on the table.

"Right, I've had enough of all three of you," she said, standing up. "You've caused me no end of misery and it seems your knack for disappointing me knows no bounds."

"Oh come on, that's not fair," said Geri.

"Yeah," echoed Helen. "If it wasn't for us you'd still be thinking this was gangsters."

"Forgive me if I don't celebrate wildly and start singing karaoke," said Pope.

As she rounded the table she took Geri's brandy and swirled it around.

"By the way, some good news, if you want to call it that," said Pope as she left. "We found the vehicle that hit your mum."

"What?" asked Martha, turning to face her.

In all of the madness she had forgotten all about the hit-and-run. It was an open investigation, a dangerous driver still out on the roads.

"Yeah. It was a van," said Pope. "It was discovered burned out about ten miles from your mum's house. The forensics team are going through it now. They should have something for me by the end of the week."

"That's good news," said Geri. "Progress on one front."

"You'll forgive us Detective Inspector," said Helen. "But we won't be celebrating wildly and singing karaoke."

Pope smirked and wagged a finger at Helen as she walked off towards the door. Her wife Laura was speaking to the Maître d'. She looked wonderful, a sparkly dress emerging from beneath her winter coat like an eruption of stars. The Parkers watched as Pope went over and kissed her warmly on the lips. They were then whisked away by the staff to somewhere away from them. Pope didn't bother to look back.

"Well, that's that then," said Helen. "A dead end. Nothing from Wu. Nothing from Pope, and nothing to point us in the direction of mum's body."

"Totally goosed," said Geri, trying to catch the eye of a waiter.

"What are you doing?" asked Martha.

"I don't know about you two, but I am absolutely famished. And I've had a few weeks that have seen me lose my mother, lose my boyfriend and pretty much lose my marbles. So I'm planning on drinking until I can't feel my face anymore. Anyone who is interested in that sort of debauchery is more than welcome to join me."

"Oh yes, that sounds like just my sort of party," said Helen. "I'll have what you're having."

"Good," said Geri as the waiter arrived. "Martha?"

She thought about saying no. She thought about being sensible and going home to do more research, to comb over everything they had learned, everything they had seen and done to try and find something they had missed. Then she thought better of it. Times had been tough these past few days and weeks. Geri was right. They deserved to have a break, even for an hour or two.

"A glass of Chilean red," she said to the waiter. "And make it a large one."

Twenty-six

GERI DIDN'T WANT to open her eyes. The thought alone was far too painful, even before she actually put any muscles to use. The taste in her mouth was too foul to think about, too. Everything hurt and she wished dearly that she had been much more sensible.

It was always the same after a night of heavy drinking and staying out late. She never would learn. It was also much harder than it used to be. When she was a teenager, she could get up after only a few hours. Now she'd be lucky if she felt even close to normal by the end of the day. And no amount of scrubbing and scouring of her teeth and tongue was going to make the blindest bit of difference.

In all of the pain, her thoughts fell to Matt. Just what she needed. It had been two whole days since she'd seen him now, and no word at all, nothing. Not even a text message. She had given up on trying to message him. Exactly as she had told Martha and Helen, she couldn't blame him for vanishing into thin air. They had put a spanner in his works so big that he might never recover. And that was putting it mildly.

Geri's head hurt at the thought of that, the implications. They had all played high stakes gambles before. It seemed it wouldn't be a Parkers investigation without something huge being on the line. But this was different. This was the man that she loved.

She opened her eyes. The brightness did nothing to help her hangover. She pushed back the duvet and kicked her legs over the side of the bed.

"Oh God," she said out loud. "I didn't just think that, did I?"

Geri stared at her feet. She wriggled her toes, trying to get some feeling back into them. This wasn't good. This wasn't good at all. But it was inevitable, this was always going to happen. She had been denying herself it for so long that it had almost become a joke. She loved Matt. She loved him with all of her heart. Even thinking about it now made her feel a bit sick.

She stood up, pausing for a moment to make sure all the blood was circulating properly. Taking some tentative steps to test her balance, she scurried for the door and out into the hallway of her flat. She stopped almost immediately, her sister Helen sprawled out on the carpet right outside her room.

"Helen," she shouted.

Helen sat up immediately. Her eyes went wide and then the lids dropped.

"Yes," she said. "I'm up, I'm awake. What's happening, where am I? What day is it? Is it noon already?"

Geri kneeled down beside her sister. She took her by the shoulders.

"I love him," she said to her, quietly.

"What? Who? When?" asked Helen, licking her dry lips and pulling several long strands of frizzy hair out of her mouth. "You what Geri?"

"I love him," she said again, laughing. "Matt. I love him Helen. I didn't want to admit it to myself. But it's true. I love him. I have to get him back."

Before Helen could react, Geri was off. She searched the flat for Martha, even calling out for her oldest sister. Eventually she found her in the bathroom, slumped in the bath, sound asleep with her coat over her.

"Martha," Geri said.

Her voice echoed off the tiles, making it louder than she had intended. Martha didn't stir, a peaceful tranquility on her face as she lay snoring. Geri reached for the shower head and turned on the tap. A jet of cold water doused Martha's face and she leapt to her feet before she knew what was going on.

"Bloody hell," she gasped. "Bloody hell, Geri. Why did you do that? You could have given me a heart attack."

"I love him," said Geri, smiling like a buffoon.

"You what?" asked Martha.

"Matt. I love him. I just told Helen. I love him, Martha. And I need to get him back."

Martha let out something that closely resembled a groan, although it wouldn't have been out of place at a zoo or safari park. She stepped out of the bath and squelched her way over to get a towel. Drying her face off, she took long blinks to try and waken herself up more.

"Are you still drunk?" she asked her sister.

"That's rude," said Geri. "But in fairness, I did ask myself that. I'm not, as it happens, as the dehydrated hangover that's burrowing its way through my skull will tell you."

"Sorry, I just had to ask," said Martha. "You're not exactly known for your long-term relationships, Geri. In fact, this is about the longest I think I've ever known you to be with the one person."

"Again, rude, but you're right," said her sister. "But none of that matters, not anymore. Not now that I'm being honest with myself. What is it you always say? You should *always* be honest with yourself. Well here I am."

"She's told you then, I take it," said Helen, appearing at the bathroom door.

"She has," said Martha. "And we've established that she's not drunk."

"I'm glad one of us isn't," said Helen. "I think there's more alcohol coursing about my veins than blood at the moment. Why the hell did we agree to keep drinking? It doesn't feel like something we would do. We're better than that surely."

"Nobody's better than an all-night session," said Geri. "The first big mistake you make is thinking that you are. It gets you every time."

"Can we please stop talking about drink and veins and blood please," said Martha, rubbing her tummy. "I don't think I can stomach much more of it."

"Agreed," said Geri.

She led them out of the bathroom and into the kitchen where she put the kettle on. Helen began raiding the cupboards and settled on a box of opened cereal. She didn't bother with a bowl or spoon or even milk. She sat down on the floor cross-legged and started eating straight from the box.

"So," said Martha. "You love Matt then."

"Yes," smiled Geri, pouring the tea. "I do. And I need to get him back."

"Do you think that's wise?" asked Helen.

"I think, if I love him, I should do anything and everything I can to try and get him back. Don't you?"

"I suppose," shrugged Helen. "It's just, well, you don't exactly have the strongest starting point do you? I mean, we practically ruined the guy."

"Not practically Helen, *did*. You *did* ruin him," said Geri. "And less of the we too, it was you pair, not me."

She handed each of them a mug of tea. Martha was grateful to taste something that wasn't laced with booze. It felt like it had been a very long time since that first glass of wine.

"Are you sure about this, Geri?" she asked her youngest sister. "It seems like a very quick turnaround from last night. I mean, you seemed pretty resigned to having lost him when we met with Pope. And now you're saying you want to try and get him back. What's happened between now and then?"

Geri thought it was a fair question. And in truth, she wasn't entirely sure she knew the answer. There was a yearning in her heart to be with him again. She missed him, she wanted to see him, and the idea she might have hurt him made her feel sick.

"When you know, you know," she said. "I know it sounds like something straight from a Valentine's card. But it's true, Mart. And I know, now, finally."

Helen rolled her eyes. Martha, however, was much more sympathetic.

"Okay," said Martha. "What's the plan?"

"I don't know," said Geri. "He won't return my calls, won't answer my messages. I've got no way of getting in touch with him."

"What about his house?" asked Helen. "We could go around there and just knock on the door."

"I don't know where he lives," said Geri.

"What?" said Martha and Helen.

"I know, I know," said Geri, throwing her hands up in the air. "I know it's weird right, I get that. He's always just come around here before and after work. I never thought to ask..."

"Oh Geri," said Martha.

"You've got it bad for this brochacho, haven't you?" asked Helen.

"Please, please, please don't *ever* try to speak like that again, not when I'm around you, Helen," said Geri. "For the record, I've been dealing with a lot recently. And yes, we've been seeing each other for months now, but it just never came up in conversation. I figured if he *did* want to talk about it or invite me round then he would in his own time. He's anxious, isn't he? Maybe it's a bedsit or a dump or something and he's embarrassed. I don't know."

Martha nodded.

"Fine," she said. "It's not the end of the world. We're specialists in this field, remember. All we have to do is think of another way of finding out where he stays. I mean, it can't be that hard, can it?"

The three Parker sisters prided themselves on their abilities to think outside the box. Sometimes, however, it was the simplest explanation that were the best ones. They all seemed to come to the same conclusion at the exact same time—a familial epiphany.

"The morgue," they said in unison.

Geri put her mug down. Martha did the same. Even Helen was able to drag herself away from the box of cereal.

"He's meant to be back at work," said Geri. "What time is it?"

"Just after nine," said Helen, pointing to the clock on the oven. "Is the morgue even open? I mean, it's always open, it's not a pub or a garden centre. But is the building open after, you know, the incident?"

"Only one way to find out," said Martha. "If it's open, he'll be down there. And if not, well, we'll just have to think of something else. But you have to be sure this is what you want, Geri. He's been ignoring you for a reason. Helen and I can only apologise so many times. It's you who has to tell him how you feel."

"I know," said Geri. "And I'm ready to do that now."

"Right," said Helen. "Let's be having it then. No time like the present, don't put off until tomorrow what you can do today, and all of that."

"Thanks Helen," said Geri sarcastically. "Just the motivation we all needed."

Twenty-seven

THE MORTUARY WAS still in a bit of a state. The whole outer wall that had been demolished only a few nights before was covered by scaffolding and a giant tarpaulin that flapped and clapped in the wind. The police road block had been removed though and there was no sign of any officers still standing guard.

Martha took that as a good sign as they approached. The taxi dropped them off around the corner and they walked the short distance past the High Court building. It was busy already, a steady stream of people going in and out. Martha had always found courts to be the best place for people watching. You could tell the accused, guilty or innocent, just by the expressions on their faces. Worried, relieved, apathetic, it was all on show in that corner of the city in the shadow of the giant Crown Office logo.

A few journalists and a camera crew were kicking around outside the building too. Martha saw their notepads and shuddered, memories of her interview flooding back. She wanted to put all of this behind her and move on. One way she could do that was by making peace with Matt and apologising. Her gamble hadn't paid off. Even if it had and they were closer to finding their mother's body, the risk had been too great. He didn't deserve to suffer because of her choices. And she hoped to speak with his superiors to explain everything that had gone on.

"This place gives me the creeps," said Helen.

"It's not exactly designed to be a fun factory," said Geri. "It's a place where the dead come to stay. Or should do."

"I know that," she fired back. "I might be hungover, Geri, but I'm not a bozo. I mean the building, the actual building itself. There's something unnerving about it. And that great big hole in its side makes it look even more monstrous."

"It's just a building Helen, it's not going to eat you."

"That's where we differ, Geri, I'm a romantic, an artist, I can see things that aren't there. You're just a blunt-force logic machine. Everything is zeros and ones with you."

"Okay, calm down you two," said Martha, acting as the referee once again. "Can we remember why we're here and show Geri some support please Helen. And Geri, lay off Helen's irrational fears of buildings. You know she's very sensitive about all of that."

The sisters begrudgingly called a truce. They rounded the corner and headed up the steps towards the entranceway of the morgue. The doors were closed, the windows dark.

"Is it even open?" asked Helen.

"It has to be," said Geri. "Matt told me he was going back to work today at the mortuary. He said that they'd been sent emails about when it was safe to return."

"It looks closed to me."

"Hold on," said Martha.

She pressed a button on a small intercom beside the door. It looked ancient, the button barely clicking. There was no sound or any sign that the device was still working. They stood around in silence, huddled around the mortuary door.

"Wait a minute," said Geri.

She stepped forward and pulled the door handle. It opened with a squeak, its hinges needing oil. Martha and Helen felt suddenly foolish.

"Don't miss the obvious ladies," she said. "I did it once before. Never again."

They headed inside. The door closed with a thump behind them. It echoed down a long, single corridor that Martha vaguely recognised. Inside was warm. She brushed her hand against a nearby radiator as they made their way down the hall.

"Somebody is in at least," she said. "The central heating is on."

At the end of the hall was a very small and dusty reception area. It looked abandoned, faded posters peeling off the walls and frosted glass above the desk. There was a bell so Martha pressed it.

"Makes sense," she said, looking to the others for approval. "If you want service you just ring the bell."

Again they waited. The faint smell of formaldehyde was still lingering in the air. It took Martha back to that fateful morning when they'd found out about their mother. She didn't need reminding. The smell was still potent enough to make her gag. Mixed with her hangover, it was almost unbearable.

She was distracted by a figure that appeared by the frosted glass window. When the screen was pulled back, Professor Vass, the woman who had been talking to Pope on that fateful morning, was on the other side.

The head of the coroner's office looked wide-eyed at the three Parkers on the other side of the reception desk. When she recognised them, she tried to close the screen.

"No," Helen shouted.

She leapt forward and jammed her arm into the gap. The screen hit her hard and bounced out of its rickety brackets, shattering on the ground. Vass stared at them like a rabbit caught in the headlights of an eighteen-wheel lorry. Then she made a break for it.

"Oh lord," said Martha. "This is the last thing we need."

"Get after her," shouted Helen, already clambering over the desk.

"Why, who is she?" asked Geri, giving chase too.

"She's Matt's boss," Martha explained.

They scrambled over the reception desk and into the inner workings of the morgue. Vass was up ahead, her white coat flapping behind her. She wasn't very fast and even in their decrepit, hungover states, the Parkers were more than capable of catching up with her. They stopped her just shy of her office, Helen barring the way inside.

"Alright Vass, cough up. Why are you running? Got something to hide?" she said, grabbing the pathologist by the lapels. "Talk, or we'll have something to say about it."

"Helen," Martha shouted. "Let her go."

"Eh?"

"Let her go," said Geri. "We're not here to interrogate her."

Vass looked terrified. She was mouthing something, but couldn't get the words out. Helen released her and took a step back.

"I'm sorry Professor," she said. "My sister gets over-excited at times."

"Over- excited?" Helen sneered.

"Yes, over-excited," Martha said. "We were just in the neighbourhood and wondered if we could talk to you for a moment about your intern Matthew Taylor-Brown."

"I know you," said Vass. "You're the ones who broke in when the wall was damaged. DI Pope told me I had to be careful of you, careful of everyone who came snooping around here. Who are you? Journalists? Police?"

"We're neither professor," said Geri. "I'm Matt's girlfriend. Or at least, I used to be. We're having a bit of a sticky patch at the moment and I can't raise him. I was wondering if he was in work and if I could speak to him, just for a moment."

"I'm not telling you anything," said Vass. "I was warned about you. You're lucky I don't call the police. We've been inundated by people like you all week. We have important work to be getting on with, and the last thing we need is for a load of reporters to be trying to get information from my staff. Or me for that matter!.

"Hey," Helen shouted loudly. "You're not listening Prof. We're not journalists. Geri here is Matt's girlfriend and she's trying to patch things up. All we need to know is where he is."

"Why the hell should I help her or any of you out?" Vass said bitterly. "That bloody intern has brought utter disgrace and shame to my department, to my staff. Do you know that ever since that article appeared in the newspapers we've been getting abuse regularly on the phones, crank calls. I came in this morning to a load of hate mail, about a dozen of them death threats. And that's not even including all the online abuse my workers are getting. That bloody article, the one that he went to the papers about, the public are blaming *us* for the missing bodies."

"Well, aren't they right?" asked Geri. "Don't they have a point? From what Matt said there's something rotten at the core of this place. And if my sisters are correct, you're at the head of it all."

Vass looked about them. Her anger quickly turned to fear.

"What on earth are you trying to suggest here? That I have something to do with those missing cadavers?"

"You're the chief pathologist are you not?" asked Martha. "You're in charge of the whole forensic operation here. Surely the buck stops with you? There are dozens of families out there with missing relatives, ourselves included. Matt told us that there were forged documents coming through to him and when he raised it, nothing was done, he was dismissed."

"What?" asked Vass. "What are you talking about? Forged documents, that's absurd. You can't forge documents, these are bodies, human beings, they're not lost luggage."

Geri stepped forward from the others.

"What do you mean?" she asked.

Vass looked flushed. She sneered, thinking about staying quiet. Then she caught sight of the death glare Geri was giving her.

"Professor," said the youngest Parker. "What do you mean you can't forge documents?"

"It's not possible," said Vass. "The way the system works, everyone has an identity file. I don't know how much you know about identifying human remains, but it's a fairly rigid process. Dental records and fingerprints are taken, usually as soon as they come in to us. These are put on files on the computer system. They stay on there until a person is identified, usually by a next of kin or relative. In order for something like that to be forged, they'd have to be altered *in* the system, *after* those records are made."

"Who has access to that sort of admin?" asked Martha.

"The office staff," said Vass. "And the interns of course."

"Like Matt?" asked Geri.

"Yes, he would have had that sort of access. The interns help with the filing, they do a lot of the admin work as we're utterly swamped. He would have access to all the information on somebody's identity as it would all be logged on the system."

"And what happens with those bodies that can't be identified for various reasons?" asked Martha. "They become property of the state?"

"Not the terminology I would use," said Vass. "They are handed over for a funeral service and cremation at the cost of the state."

"And who carries that out?" asked Helen.

"What do you mean?" asked Vass, confused. "Nobody carries it out. It's all done here. We have a facility in the basement for cremation."

Martha instinctively turned to Geri. The youngest Parker was perfectly calm and collected.

"So let me get this straight," said Helen. "There's no agency, no company that comes to collect bodies that have been turned over to the state? They're *all* kept here for cremation."

"Yes, that's correct," said Vass.

Martha had that familiar, nauseating feeling in the pit of her stomach. It was the one she always got when something big turned up during a case. She had to ignore it for now. She had to think of Geri and look after her.

"Professor Vass," she said, almost touching her face with her own. "You have to tell me where Matt is right now."

"I don't know where he is," said Vass. "I've not seen him in a month."

Another gut punch. Martha stepped forward, taking Geri by the hand.

"Pardon?" she asked, barely able to hide her surprise now.

"Take it easy Geri," said Martha. "Stay calm."

"Matt's not been here at work in about a month," said Vass. "I haven't seen him since before all that business with the wall and the stolen bodies. I spoke to the HR department, they say he's on some sort of unpaid leave, away in the Middle East to see his parents or something."

Everything was falling apart, thought Martha. Suddenly the warmth and happiness she had felt that morning had gone. Vanished in only a few words.

"Middle East you say?" asked Geri. "His parents?"

"Yes, that's right. Francis in HR said he'd been desperate to get away. Apparently one of them is gravely ill, his mother I think he said. I can't be sure."

That was enough for Geri. She turned suddenly and ran off, sprinting back up the way they had come from the reception area.

"Helen, get after her," Martha shouted.

She did as she was told. Martha grabbed Vass' arm.

"Professor, I need you to be very clear and very helpful," she said, calmly and coolly. "I need you to tell me what address you have on your system for Matthew. And I need it right away. It's vitally important. Do you understand?"

Vass' confusion subsided, just for the moment. She could see the emotion, the panic, the fear in Martha's face. She nodded.

"Of course," she said. "I've got it right here."

Twenty-eight

"WE NEED TO stay calm and collected," said Helen. "We can't jump to any silly conclusions at this stage. We need evidence. That's how it's always been."

"Are you kidding me?" asked Geri. "Since when did we ever need hard evidence and watertight theories to prove our suspicions? Name me one time where that's happened, Helen. Go on, I'll wait."

"Take it easy Geri, she's only trying to help," said Martha.

She didn't blame Geri for snapping. In fact, she couldn't really blame her for anything. This whole affair had been messy, perhaps worse than anything they had ever tackled before. Emotions had been running high from the start. And they hadn't always been as together as they were in the past. This latest twist in the tale had taken the wind out of all of them. The sooner they started to get answers the better.

"I just need to speak with him," said Geri. "I just need to sit down with Matt and get things out in the open. He needs to know he can trust me, can trust us. That's all."

"I agree," said Helen.

"You do?" asked Geri, turning around from the front of the cab. "You *never* agree with me."

"Well, I'm agreeing this time."

"Oh, okay then. Good."

"Don't sound so surprised, Geri," she said. "It makes perfect sense. And it's *exactly* what I was saying before you jumped down my throat. We have to keep cool heads and not assume anything sinister. For all we know there's a perfectly reasonable explanation for all of this."

Martha wasn't so sure that she shared her sister's optimism. Not this time at least. She always liked to think the best of people. But the evidence was mounting up against Matt that something fishy was going on. Lies were never a good place to start. And it seemed he had been lying through his teeth for a long time.

The city peeled away outside the cab and everything grew more remote and rural. Suddenly there were rolling fields, the grass white with frost, despite the weak sun sitting low in the sky above. Martha hadn't recognised the address Vass had given them. They'd simply handed it to the cab driver and they'd taken off.

"It's lovely out here," said Helen, gazing out the window. "It's amazing how there's such beautiful countryside right on your doorstep and you don't ever think to go and visit it. It's a bit of a shame actually."

"When do we ever have the time for that?" asked Martha. "Between work and family life we're lucky if we get five minutes to read a newspaper."

"Please," said Geri from the front. "Can we not talk about newspapers. Not just yet, it's all still a bit too raw for me. Thank you."

Martha bit her bottom lip. The healing process was clearly on hold until they had uncovered the truth with Matt. She was looking forward to it starting again. She thought about the future, their future. Perhaps it was time to close Parkers Investigations for a while, maybe take an extended leave of absence, to give everyone time to think and breathe and enjoy their own room.

It sounded wonderful. Not that Martha didn't want to spend time with her family, with her sisters. This case had brought out the very worst and the very best in their relationships with each other. They needed some time to get their heads together. All of them.

"Here we are," said the taxi driver, interrupting her thoughts.

The cab pulled off the main road into a small siding. It was remote, nothing about for miles but rolling fields and untouched countryside. There was a gate at the head of a dirt path that weaved its way through a meadow, leading all the way up to what looked like the ruins of a church.

"Are you sure?" Helen asked the driver. "This is the middle of nowhere."

"That's what the sat nav says," he pointed at the map. "I think that place is being done up or something. I don't know. It's the postcode you gave me anyway."

Helen looked at the others. Geri wasn't hanging around. She climbed out of the cab and was heading for the gate before Martha and Helen could react.

"Bloody hell," said Martha. "We need to watch her, Helen. She's going to do something she'll regret."

"Not as much as we'll regret it I'll bet."

They got out of the cab, Martha paying the driver.

"Hey, do you want me to hang around?" the driver called after her.

"That's very kind of you, but I think we'll be okay," she said. "I have a feeling this might run on and on."

"Are you sure? It's a bit exposed up here."

Martha had a sudden urge to hug the driver. It was about as kind a gesture as she had received in a long while. Or what felt like a long while at least.

"Thank you very much," she said. "We'll be fine."

The cabbie gave her a smile and reversed out of the siding. He pulled off down the main road and vanished over the crest of a hill heading back to the city. Martha turned back towards the gate, Geri and Helen already making their way up the path towards the church. This was it, she thought. Time to get answers. She had been in this position before, of course. It wasn't her first rodeo, so to speak. It was the same for Helen and Geri too. Only this time it felt different. This time it felt like there was so much more on the line. Everything was so deeply personal.

She pushed through the gate and hurried along the path to catch up with the others. As they neared the church they saw that the cabbie had been right. A skeletal frame of scaffolding was supporting the eastern facade. The old stonework of the building had been brushed and polished, making it seem like a bright beacon against the gloomy wintry backdrop. Modern double glazing took up the ancient windows, giving the whole building a sense of being completely out of time.

"This is his house?" asked Helen. "Bloody hell, Geri, you know how to pick 'em."

"Easy now Helen," said Martha.

They approached the church cautiously, not really sure what to expect. The path spread out into a wide porch outside the old arched doors. There were tracks in the dirt, deep, thick lines where some vehicle had been.

"Are those tracks new?" asked Helen.

"I'm not sure," said Geri. "They look pretty recent. Maybe the last few hours. I can't be sure."

"I agree," said Martha. "Not recent, recent. But it could have been last night. Or the early hours of this morning."

"Do we think it was Matt?" asked Helen.

"No idea," said Martha. "It's his place though, that's what Vass said. At least, it's the address he's given his place of work."

"When he bothers going there, that is."

"Right, I'm getting sick of this," said Geri. "Skulking about in the cold looking at mud. If you want answers you just need to ask questions."

"Geri, take it easy," said Martha.

She didn't listen to her sister. She marched up towards the main entrance of the church and banged on the doors. They gave a heavy sounding thud, metallic in nature. Martha was surprised, she had assumed they were wooden.

There was no answer. It was becoming a worrying trend for Geri when she knocked on doors. She stepped back and looked up at the imposing church that loomed over them all.

"Maybe he's out," said Helen. "Maybe it was him in the car that left those tracks."

"I'm not leaving until we've spoken to him," said Geri.

She started off around the side of the church. Martha's heart leapt. Her youngest sister was getting angry, she could see that from a mile away. But she was getting reckless too. She was far too involved in all of this.

"Geri. Wait. Helen, come on, we've got to stop her."

They chased her around the side of the church. The forest of scaffolding rose up to meet them. Geri was weaving in and out between the pipes, searching for something. She came to a stop short of the back of the building.

"Found it," she said.

"Found what?" asked Helen.

Geri reached down and pulled with all of her might. A heavy door opened from the ground, yawning as the hinges were brought back to life. She let it drop away and it landed with a bang, the poles and pipes of the scaffolding shivering as she did so.

"It's a church right? So it's got to have a crypt," said Geri. "Look, there are steps down here."

"A crypt? You've got to be kidding me," said Helen. "First we break into a morgue, now we're sneaking into a crypt? What the heck is wrong with us? Since when did we become so ghoulish? Did I miss the memo or something that we were becoming the Burbs?"

"I don't know what the Burbs is," said Martha. "But if it involves breaking and entering, which this absolutely *is,* then I can't say I approve of it."

"It does actually," said Geri, dusting off her hands. "But that's a film and this is real life. And I'm going in."

"Geri!"

Again, she was gone before Martha could do anything to stop her. She looked at Helen who shrugged.

"We've come this far, Martha. And no amount of protesting on our part is going to change her mind, is it?"

Helen was right. She usually was with these sorts of things. She had an indefatigable knack for cutting through the nonsense when she wanted to. Albeit, usually it was *her* nonsense in the first place.

"Come on then," said Martha, with a sigh.

They climbed down the ancient, slippery steps that led to the crypt. Everything was dark, save for a beacon of light up ahead from Geri's phone. The steps went down and down and down, taking them further and further from the surface. The walls were slimy with damp and offered little support as Martha tried to navigate each step one at a time. When they reached the bottom she was relieved.

The crypt was cold and damp. She produced her phone, as did Helen, and they turned on their torches. Vaulted ceilings above them were intricately carved, despite seeing no light of day. There was an ancient and forgotten feel to this place, like they were the first people to step foot there in hundreds of years.

"Now what?" asked Helen, her voice strangely close in the depths of the church.

"We need to find a way upstairs again," said Geri. "Although watch your footing, it's pretty wet down here."

She sloshed about in the dark, everything obscure beyond the cone of light coming from the back of her phone. Martha could feel the ice cold water or whatever it was seeping in through the sides of her shoes. Then she thought about Helen in her sandals.

"Aren't your socks sodden?" she asked her.

"What do you think?" came the snippy reply. "I'll probably get trench foot at this rate and that's literally the last thing anyone needs. In fact, I think I can already—"

Helen let out a yelp of pain. Then there was a thud and a splash.

"Helen," Martha shouted.

She turned her torch downwards and caught sight of Helen's backside poking up into the air. She wriggled her legs and pushed herself up, face filthy with dirty water, hair hanging in long, damp strands about her ears.

"Bloody hell, do you two want to make any more noise?" asked Geri, stepping over to them.

"I'm trying to find a way out of here and you're stomping about... all over the..."

She trailed off. Their torches had fallen on the long, rectangular object Helen had bumped into. It was different to the rest of the crypt, modern, made of wood. A thick plastic cover was wrapped all about it, the surface of the box devoid of any markings or writing. It was difficult to tell the full size of the thing in the darkness but Martha reckoned it was over six foot long. The more she looked at it though, the more she was filled with dread.

"Wait a minute," she said. "Wait a minute."

Her eyes were adjusting to the darkness now. She could make out at least some of the details about the crypt. There were more of these things dotted around the place. She panned her torch around and counted at least six more boxes, all sat on the flooded floor, all wrapped in plastic and all without markings. All except the last one she found.

The light from the torch started to shake as she grew more worried. Thick, black writing was stencilled on the top of the box at the far side of the crypt. Martha waded through the water, her feet squelching in her boots. She weaved in and out of the others, dreading what she was about to read. Although somehow, she already knew. She knew what she was going to see on top of the box. She knew that nothing was going to be the same, ever again.

The light fell on the box and the words stared back at her.

"What is it Martha?" asked Geri.

She had to choke back tears, her stomach churning as the sickening inevitability sank in.

"Human remains," she said. "It's bodies. They're coffins. The boxes are coffins."

A loud bang echoed down from the stairwell. They were trapped in the crypt.

Twenty-nine

GERI WAS PANICKING now. Up until that point she thought she had been handling everything rather well. Especially given the circumstances. She had been put through the emotional ringer over the past few days and weeks. Everything that she had believed in, in one shape or another, was unravelling right in front of her. Yes she had been headstrong in breaking into Matt's home. And yes she had been angry and upset with how it had all unfolded. But she had been justified, hadn't she? She had the right to feel scorned, to feel betrayed, to feel unloved.

The sisters were trapped in a crypt surrounded by dead bodies. Whoever had closed the entrance doors now knew where they were. And they could keep them there at their own leisure. Geri wasn't afraid of dying, not here, not now. She was frightened of what would happen to Martha and Helen.

"This can't be happening," said Helen, over and over again. "I mean, we've been in some scrapes in our time. But this is a whole new level of bloody morbidity. Stuck in a church's crypt up to our necks in water and surrounded by a load of missing corpses. You couldn't write it."

"Stay calm everyone," said Martha. "The trick is to try and stay calm. Does anyone have any phone signal?"

"No," said Helen. "And I've barely got any battery—"

Just as she said it, her torch went out. She hit the side of her phone but nothing.

"Make that *no* battery left."

"What about you Geri?" asked Martha.

"Nothing," she said. "These walls are ten, maybe twelve inches thick. If they've stood for hundreds of years against the bracing Scottish weather, they're not going to let something as trivial as phone signal through."

"Me neither," said Martha.

They all stood in silence for a moment, thinking about how they got here, to this point. It didn't make for happy thinking, Geri admitted. She looked about at the coffins, wondering the unmentionable. Then Helen went wading in as she always did.

"Do you think one of these is Mum?" she asked.

Neither Martha nor Geri wanted to answer that question. The anonymity of the coffins, as undignified as it was, actually helped their situation. They didn't have to deal with the tragedy that surrounded them. Not yet anyway.

"I don't know," Martha finally said. "I don't think I want to know. I want to know why they're here and what Matt has been up to."

"I have a feeling we won't have to wait very long to find out."

Right on cue and with more than a flavour of the dramatic, a door nearby was flung open, flooding the crypt with light. The Parkers all recoiled, shielding their eyes from the sudden brightness. Geri peered through her fingers as a silhouette made its way down a set of stairs not far from them. She didn't need to see any details, she knew who it was already.

"Well, well, well," said Matt. "Three for the price of one. Incredible."

Geri thought she would have been angrier to see him at last. She had thought about all the different ways she would greet him when they finally caught up with him. Most of them involved violence of some description, beating him to a pulp and standing on his head. Now that the moment had come, she found herself disappointingly static.

"I suppose I should offer to show you around the place," he said, starting back up the stairs. "Unless you want to stay in the crypt all day. Although I wouldn't recommend it, you'll get trench foot."

"I told you," muttered Helen.

Both Martha and Geri darted her unsavoury looks. The three of them waded and sloshed through the water and started up the stairs behind Matt. He waited until they were all out on the landing before closing the door and locking it.

Upstairs everything was sleek and modern. It didn't look like a church at all, or even a ruin. There was a new roof and flooring and the walls were a brilliant white. The outer shell of the church was intact but inside it had been completely renovated. At an extensive cost, thought Geri.

"Can I get you guys something?" he asked. "Tea, coffee? Something a bit stronger? I don't imagine being down there did anything for your nerves."

He sauntered casually down the hallway. There was something different about him, something confident that Geri didn't recognise. He was like a changed man, a completely different personality. Even the way he walked seemed new and odd to her.

"We know, Matt," she shouted after him. "We know everything."

"I very much doubt that Geri," he laughed. "Come on in, and we can have a proper talk about it all. Please."

Geri felt Martha and Helen's eyes fall on her. They were letting her take the lead. She was in charge. She looked back at them.

"Stay calm," said Helen. "We've got this."

"She's right," whispered Martha. "Just keep your head. We have to remember that Mum's body could be downstairs. We can't risk losing her again, or losing any of those remains for that matter. It's people's relatives Geri, there's more on the line here than just us."

"Okay," she said. "I'll do my best."

She led her sisters down the hallway, following Matt. A huge, expansive room opened up ahead of them. The main hall of the ancient church had been turned into a broad, spacious living area. The high beams of the ceiling had been lovingly restored and oozed a warmth and subtlety that made them a spectacular view above their heads. A huge fire pit took up most of the middle of the room, flame crackling and sparking as thick wooden logs were consumed.

Matt eased himself down onto one of the huge, circular sofas that surrounded the fire pit. He winced and held his ribs.

"Not quite healed up yet," he said. "Not as young and fit as I used to be."

"Wait until you get to Martha's age," said Helen. "Then you'll really know all about it."

"Helen," said Martha quietly.

"How did you get those injuries then?" asked Geri. "Professor Vass tells us that you've not been at work for weeks."

Matt smiled. He wagged a finger at Geri.

"I knew you were onto me," he said. "I thought my performance the other night was a bit over the top. Hammed it up as they say, chewed the scenery. I stopped short of tears though. I thought that might have been a bit of overkill."

"Hey, not cool man," said Helen. "We get that you're a liar but you don't need to be an arsehole, too."

"It's okay Helen," said Geri, patting her away. "You knew we were onto you? How did you come to that conclusion?"

"Just a hunch," said Matt, shrugging his shoulders. "When you do business like I do, you start to trust your instincts more and more. You have to, otherwise you'll wake up at the bottom of a river with your feet tied to a very heavy weight."

"I've heard that term 'business' before Matt," said Martha, stepping forward. "And I didn't like it. So you better start explaining what you mean very quickly before we call the police."

"Call them all you like, your signal won't get through the walls," he laughed. "I heard about your trip to Edinburgh, Martha. You got to meet the big boss lady. I'm impressed."

"Your boss perhaps?" she asked.

"Oh no, not at all," he sucked in air through his teeth. "No, no, she's too small-minded for what I've got planned. No, I don't deal with the monkeys, I'm more of an organ grinder sort of guy."

Geri was growing angrier and angrier. It was taking all of her effort not to leap across the sofa and strangle Matt where he sat. But she knew she needed to keep him talking, keep getting answers.

"Everything you told me, then," she said. "It was all rubbish, cobblers?"

"Pretty much, yeah," he said, with an arrogant smile. "I mean there were *some* truths in it. My mum and dad did die when I was young and I did drop out of boarding school. I've got the emotional scars to show for it too. I'll take you through them if you've got a spare evening."

"No thanks," snorted Helen.

"The bodies, in the crypt," said Geri. "Are they the ones that the police are looking for?"

"They are," said Matt. "Well, what's left of the ones I haven't shipped out of here, yet."

"Yet? You mean there's more."

"Oh God yes," he laughed. "I've been doing this for about a year now. Maybe longer? I don't know, I forget. You know how it is, when you're running an international export service—it's hard to keep a track of time, what with the different zones and all of that."

"International?" asked Martha.

Matt got up from the sofa. He hobbled over towards a long bar that stretched out from the open plan kitchen. He reached into a cupboard and produced a bottle of wine and a glass.

"Care to join me in some plonk?" he asked. "Come on, it's Christmas!"

"International exports?" Geri shouted at him, stomping towards the kitchen. "What the hell are you talking about Matt?"

He opened the bottle, the cork popping with a satisfying suck. He poured a large glass of the stuff and took a long, deep drink.

"Now *that* is good plonk," he said. "Not that supermarket bilge water you insisted we drank Geri. Honestly, no matter what I've done, I didn't deserve to be punished with that rubbish. It was like drinking something from a sewer. Ghastly."

"Matt, you need to start explaining yourself," said Geri. "Or so help me, I'm going to do something I'll go to jail for."

"Scary," he tilted his head. "You're always very cute when you get angry. Still, it's nice to see you're back together with your sisters, the gang reunited and all of that. You used to get *so* angry when you were talking about them. Seriously, it was like they'd slapped you in the face. Although I know how that feels, especially when they go running to the press with everything I've said. Naughty, naughty, naughty."

"What are those bodies doing in the crypt, Matt?" asked Martha. "We won't ask again."

He took another large drink. Licking his lips, he smiled.

"They're products," he said. "Assets, objects. Whatever you want to call them. They're my stock."

"They're human beings," Geri screamed. "They're not boxes of crisps or German cars. They're dead *people*."

"Blah, blah, blah, I've heard it all before, Geri," he said, mocking her. "Do you think *they* care what they are? Of course they don't, they're *dead*."

"That's not for you to decide," Helen jumped in. "Just because they're dead, doesn't mean they don't have families, loved ones, like us, who still care about them. What do you think it's been like not being able to say goodbye to our own mum? Did you ever consider that?"

"Geri, Helen, calm down," said Martha.

"Listen to your big sister, ladies," said Matt, pointing at her. "She's about the only one out of the three of you who talks any sense anyway."

Martha was angrier than she had ever been in her whole life. But she knew that it was no use being mad if they didn't find out what was going on. Matt was clearly relishing the attention, the self-praise for being the smartest person in the room. She had to play to his ego.

"It can't have been easy," she started. "Shifting a body isn't exactly light work. Even for a big man like you, Matt. How did you get them here? Were you alone?"

Matt smiled. He recognised how clever she was.

"Yes, very good," he said. "Geri told me all about how you could turn conversations around, Martha. Praise the villain, make him feel like he's the most important man in the world. I like it. You're very good at it. You almost had me."

"You can't blame me for trying," she smiled.

"No, of course not," he said, walking back towards the sofa.

Before he sat down, he pulled one of the cushions up and unzipped it. Tipping it upside down, a pile of used, tightly bound notes spilled out onto the floor.

"Blimey," said Helen. "Look at all that cash."

"Good, isn't it?" he said. "Now multiply that by however many cushions I've got in these sofas. And the ones upstairs and in the beds."

"A lot of money," said Martha. "But not Sterling, I notice."

Matt smiled. He bent down and picked up a pile of notes and threw it over towards her. She caught and flicked through the wad.

"Dirhams," she said. "From Dubai."

"Spot on," he said, throwing another pile at Helen.

"Lira," she said, looking at the money in her hand.

"Bingo," said Matt, throwing a final stack of bills at Geri.

She caught it but didn't look at it.

"Go on," he said. "Count it. They're Hong Kong dollars. In fact, I could be doing with a few more of those. Demand is getting quite high."

"Demand?" asked Geri. "Demand for what?"

"Ghost spouses," said Helen.

Martha and Geri looked at her, their jaws slack. She was still busy flicking through the lira and didn't meet their gaze. Then they turned to Matt who smiled, shrugged, and stretched his arms out.

"Got it in one," he said.

"Ghost spouses?" said Geri.

"As in ghost marriages," said Martha. "That thing you were harping on about, Helen?"

"Yeah," she said casually. "I told you both that's what I thought was going on, but you didn't believe me. In fact, you didn't even acknowledge me, if memory serves correctly. Matt here is selling bodies to markets who are marrying them off to single people who don't want to be alone in the afterlife. It's a huge business. As you can see."

Martha was dumbfounded.

"Is this true?" she asked Matt.

"It is. Every word of it," he laughed. "Geri told me you guys were good and I always sort of believed it. But it's not until you see it unfold in front of you, that you truly understand it. Well done. You wouldn't believe the amount of money you can get for a dead body on the black market these days. Thousands, tens of thousands if it fills a specific desire."

Martha was struggling. This was all getting too much for her. She decided to go on the offensive.

"So how does it work then?" she asked.

"Surprisingly easily," said Matt nonchalantly. "I take orders through the dark web, contacted through agents or what have you, somebody in Turkey or Hong Kong, Beijing or Kolkata who is looking for service and I'll ship the body to them via a courier service. Nobody asks any questions, you see? Not when you have a grieving relative on either end of the line. Death, it has a strange effect on people, I've found. Certainly did for me."

"But why?" asked Geri. "Why all of the lies, why all of this?"

"Money," said Matt flatly. "Cold, hard cash Geri. It was a business opportunity, a way of standing on my own two feet. My parents died when I was young and I was left destitute, without a penny. Those bastards didn't leave me a thing, they'd been too wrapped up in their careers and themselves to think about providing for me, the 'inconvenience' as my mother used to call me, to my face no less. So when I was old enough to do what I wanted, when I was out of care, free of any nanny holding my hand or orphanage officer trying to tell me what to do, I set about making my fortune. And here I am."

"But you're exposed now," said Helen. "We're onto you, we've caught you out."

"Hello?" Matt shouted, his hands spread out over all the money on the floor near the fire pit. "I've got more money than I can count Helen, I can do what I like, go where I like. There are dead people all over the world. This isn't even my first stop off. I started in Saudi Arabia but the heat there was a bit too much. The bodies didn't last as long as I wanted, couldn't get the storage facilities. I'll be sad to see this place go though, I liked Scotland and Glasgow. Even if things got a bit too… personal."

He looked at Geri. She didn't look back, disgusted to her core.

"So you were behind the robbery the other night," said Martha. "It wasn't gangsters, like Nicola Wu said."

"Ah yes, the robbery, what a laugh that was," he chuckled. "It's amazing how a business can grow and grow, evolve even. When I started all of this, it was just a case of bunging any old body in a box and shipping it out to the customer. Sometimes they didn't even care if it was a man or a woman. Now, I offer a full bespoke service. You can have what you want, for a price. A woman, no problem. Specific age, naturally. I'll even make sure the hair and eye colour is what a customer wants. What can I say? I'm generous."

"You're vile is what you are," said Helen.

"I'm a businessman," he snapped, suddenly angered. "I'm providing a service at a cost."

"You're stealing people's loved ones from under their noses and selling them to someone else on the other side of the planet," Geri screamed. "How is that, in any way, shape or form business?"

Martha was sure she was going to be sick. She kept swallowing, hoping that this nightmare would end soon. Then the thought hit her, like a bullet straight between her eyes.

"No," she said. "No, no, no. No, it can't be. You didn't. Please tell me you didn't."

"What's wrong Martha?" said Helen, grabbing her sister.

"Martha?" asked Geri.

Matt smiled across the room at her. He nodded slowly.

"He did it," she said. "He killed mum."

Thirty

"THIS CAN'T BE happening. It just can't," said Geri, pulling at her hair. "I can't believe what I'm hearing here."

"You better believe it," said Martha. "Because it's the truth. He murdered our mother. Matt was the hit-and-run driver."

"No, it can't be, it just can't be," she said.

"He just admitted it, Geri," Helen said.

She walked around the living room, around and around the firepit, like a demented puppy who had lost its way. She didn't know where to go, what to do, what to say. Here she was, in the middle of the biggest crisis of her life and every bit of information was making the situation worse and worse.

"Why?" she asked. "Why are you doing this to us?"

"It's just business," he said, with no hint of shame.

"Stop saying that," she cried. "Stop bloody saying the same thing over and over. Why Matt? Why are you doing this to me, to us, to our family?"

"He was fulfilling an order," said Martha.

Geri stopped pacing about the room. Helen looked over to her too.

"Isn't that right, Matt?" she asked him.

"Again, bravo," he clapped at her. "Actually really fascinating to see how this sort of thing gets unravelled. I didn't get the chance to see the consequences in Saudi. Not this time though. This time I've got a front row seat."

"I don't follow you, either of you," said Geri. "What the hell has this got to do with mum?"

"He said that the business has evolved," said Martha. "That he's now fulfilling orders that meet certain specifics. I can only assume that our mum filled the requirements needed for one of these orders. Does that sound about right?"

"Spot on," he said. "There's a client in Shanghai who is nearing the end of his life. A lifelong bachelor—he's riddled with cancer by all accounts. Not long left and doesn't want to spend an eternity in the next world on his own. So, he was looking for a more mature woman, who would, by all accounts, have been his wife in the living world too. And who do I get introduced to, not the day after the order came in, but the lovely Mrs Parker senior. It was just a shame it wasn't quite as clean as I had hoped it would be. Much like you three, she was tougher than she looked. I had to get out of there sharpish before anyone saw me and leave her behind."

"You son of a—"

Geri pounced forward, hands like claws ready to tear into her ex-boyfriend. Matt was too fast for her though. He ducked and rolled, grabbing a metal poker from the fireplace set beside the pit. He brought it down hard on Geri's back and she hit the floor with a meaty thud, writhing in agony.

Martha and Helen raced over to be with her. They tried to console her as Matt got to his feet, the poker still in hand.

"Easy now ladies," he said. "Let's not get violent."

"So you broke into your own morgue? Is that it?" asked Martha. "Why didn't you just fiddle with the system, the way you always did?"

"Takes too long," said Matt. "I needed your mother's body pretty much overnight in order to get it to the customer. So I decided to take matters into my own hands. I rented a digger, which is surprisingly easy if you grease the hand of the owners, and drove it into the side of the morgue. I knew where your mum and that man were being kept so I took them both, into the big scoop in the front and off I went. Just like that."

"So what happened to your face then?" asked Helen. "I thought you were injured in the break-in."

"Ah yes, my face," he laughed. "Well, I had to get rid of the van after your mother didn't play ball and die at the side of the road. Only I'm no explosives expert you see. I figured you could just set fire to the fuel tank and it would slowly burn up. Bloody thing blew up in my face didn't it? Had to walk for miles to the hospital to get treated. Still, it worked out alright in the end. Geri there didn't know the difference. And like I said, the client didn't have all that long left, or doesn't. I don't know, hopefully he was satisfied, I got my money at least. Fifteen grand as it happens, a bargain."

Martha felt her face contorting into the fiercest grimace she had ever pulled. The blood was pumping, thumping in her ears. She felt so angry her eyes might pop.

"So she's gone then," said Martha. "To Shanghai?"

"I certainly hope so," said Matt. "She was put on the plane and had a tracking number and everything."

Geri let out a groan. She tried to get up but was struggling. Helen helped her, propping her up on her elbows so she could see what was going on.

"You're a monster Matt, you know that? A complete and total monster with absolutely no moral compass. You disgust me," she said.

"And me," said Helen.

"That makes three of us," said Martha.

"Well, I'm truly humbled," he said. "To have reunited the famous Parker sisters in communal hatred for the one person. That's quite a feat."

His watch bleeped. He checked it and threw the poker down on the ground.

"But alas ladies, our time is up," he said. "You know what they say, time is money and all of that. And I have a basement full of assets that I have to shift. So, if you don't mind, I'll be asking you to take your places back down in the crypt for now. Only until I can find someone online who wants to buy three gobby sisters to marry off to their relatives."

"Good one," laughed Helen. "If you think we're going to just walk down there then you've got another think—"

Matt reached under the hood of the firepit. He pulled out a pistol and levelled it at the sisters.

"Oh right," said Helen. "I see. I didn't think… I didn't think he had a gun," she said to Martha.

"Get her on her feet and let's get on with this shall we?" he said. "I've got a flight to catch."

Martha and Helen helped Geri up from the floor. Matt nudged them back down the corridor towards the door that led to the crypt. He pulled it open.

"Down. Go," he barked.

None of them moved. He reached out and grabbed Geri by the wrist. Pulling her violently, he threw her down the stairs. Helen screamed and raced after her.

"Last but not least," he smiled at Martha.

She stepped over to the doorway and looked down. Helen had Geri at the bottom of the stairs, the pair of them covered in the filthy water that had flooded the crypt. Martha knew that if she went down there it was over. There would be no escape.

They'd be in the dark, hurt and alone. She had to do something and it had to be now. Otherwise they were finished.

She clenched her fists, ready to lash out when the sound of a doorbell filled the corridor. She looked around at Matt who's face flushed red. Grabbing Martha by the back of the neck, he hauled her away from the door. He jammed the gun into her side and pushed her along the hallway. She hit the front door hard as he looked out through the peephole.

The doorbell rang again. He cursed under his breath. Forcing Martha against one of the doors, he kept the pistol trained on her. He pulled the door open beside her but she couldn't see out, obscured from view.

"Hi," said Matt. "Can I help you?"

"Yeah, I was just driving by and thought I'd stop for a minute."

Martha recognised the voice. It was the taxi driver, the Good Samaritan who had asked if he should stay.

"Oh yeah?" said Matt. "What's that got to do with me?"

"Nothing, nothing at all," said the cabbie. "Only, I dropped these three women off here maybe about half an hour ago, an hour maybe. I just wanted to make sure they were okay, that's all. It's a bit remote and the light is getting on. You know what it's like these days, you read it in the news don't you, about bad things happening to people. Don't think I could live with it on my conscience if something happened."

"Don't know what you're talking about, mate," said Matt.

He was getting angrier, Martha could tell. His grip on her was tightening and she could feel the barrel of the gun digging deeper into her back.

"I reckon you should clear off before I call the cops," he said.

"Hey, no need to be like that," said the cabbie. "I was only checking to see if everything was alright."

"It's fine, everything's fine," said Matt. "Now clear off, before I have you locked up for trespassing."

"I was only trying to help," said the driver.

"Well go help somebody else. I don't need to be disturbed. Why the hell do you think I live out here in the middle of nowhere. To get away from peasants like you."

"Peasants?"

"Bloody taxi driver. You're a leech on society, bleeding people dry."

"Steady on mate, I was only asking—"

"Taking money from folk for giving them a lift. I know your type, working class, chip on the shoulder. Well, let me tell you something pal, other people have problems too you know. Other people have *real* problems and they don't need some tinpot, half-arsed, modern-day-saint come knocking on their doors putting their nose in where it doesn't belong."

Martha didn't see the punch but she certainly heard it. There was a distinctive crack as something in Matt's face broke with the force. The pressure on her back was instantly relieved as he tumbled backwards. She spun around as the taxi driver pushed his way in through the open door. He stood over Matt who was totally confused.

"Bloody hell," said the cabbie. "What is going on here?"

"Get the gun, quick!" Martha shouted.

Matt came to his senses. He coughed and sputtered, but reached his pistol before Martha could. He went to shoot her but she kicked his hand. The bullet pinged off the ceiling as the gun spun away.

Matt turned over and scrambled to his feet. He made off down the corridor.

"Stop him!" Martha shouted at the cabbie, the pair of them dazed by the gunshot. "Stop him. He needs to be arrested."

Matt bolted down the hallway, arms pumping, pushing him onwards. He was about to reach the living room when a foot tripped him up. He went flying through the air, screaming as he did so. Then he landed with a hard thump, his head hitting the rim of the firepit. Just like that he was out cold.

Martha and the cabbie raced after him. Helen and Geri were at the door that led to the crypt, the pair of them soaked to the skin.

"Blimey, what a trip," said the cabbie laughing. "That was worth a red card at least."

"Hey, you're the taxi driver," said Helen, helping Geri up the last of the steps and into the hall. "What are you doing here?"

"As I said to your big friend over there, I thought there might have been something wrong," he said. "Glad I came back now. Otherwise you ladies might have been in a bit of bother. Although I can see you can handle yourselves no problem."

Geri let out a groan as she slumped to the floor. The others helped her down as the cabbie called for an ambulance. Martha pushed Geri's hair from her face, cradling her head in her crossed legs.

"You're going to be okay now," she said. "It's over. It's all over."

"Matt," she said. "Is he…"

"No, I don't think so," said Martha. "He's alive. And he's going to pay for what he did to us, did to Mum. We'll get her back Geri, I promise you."

"I'm sorry," she said, eyelids getting heavier. "I'm sorry I didn't listen to you Martha. I should always listen to you."

Martha started to cry as Geri passed out. She breathed gently in her hands, just as she had done as a baby all those years ago. Funny how things come back around, thought Martha. Life had a bit of a habit of that sort of thing.

Thirty-one

THE CLOUDS HAD cleared away to reveal a brilliant blue sky. It was cold though—hat, scarves and gloves weather. Martha didn't mind. It felt like a fresh start, a new dawn, a wonderful way to begin the new year. Or at least as wonderful as a funeral could be.

Once again she found herself in a cemetery. Once again she found she was staring down into a grave. This had played out far too often over the last few years.

She stood looking down at her mother's grave, but she wasn't sad. Not anymore. She was relieved to have her mum back and to put her where she belonged, beside her husband. The congregation was filtering away, the service over. Soon the gravediggers would come along to fill in the hole and that would be that. Martha didn't mind though. Not after everything they had been through to get this far.

"We got you back, Mum," she said, looking at her mother's coffin. "It almost killed us, but we got you back. I told you we would. We couldn't have you remarrying after dad was gone, could we?"

She laughed at her own joke. Sniffing, she could feel the sting of tears starting behind her nose.

"I wanted to tell you that I love you, just one more time," she continued. "It wasn't your fault what happened. And I hope that you didn't suffer in the end. I guess how we got you back in the end was about all me, Helen and Geri could do for you. We thought about you every day of the ordeal. We thought about very little else to be perfectly honest. How could we? You are our mother. We weren't just going to sit back and let you be taken from us without putting up a fight. In the end I broke some rules to get you back. But it was worth it to have you back home. I hope the flight wasn't too bumpy and the cargo people packed you away neatly and tidily. I know how you used to love flying first class. Maybe freight is the way to go. Lots more room I imagine. Anyway, I'm rambling. I'm rambling because I don't want this conversation to ever end. I'll miss you mum, more than words could ever describe. I hope we did you proud, that's all. I hope that you can and were proud of your children. And that you knew we would go to the ends of the earth to make sure you were safe."

Martha wiped away the tears from her eyes. She felt stupid, embarrassed, talking to a box in a hole in the ground. Only it wasn't just that, it wasn't that simple. This, she realised, was the first chance she'd been given to properly grieve the death of her mother. Everything else had gotten in the way. Only now, standing on the edge of her grave, could she properly say goodbye.

Footsteps made her shiver. She wiped the tears clear from her face and tried her best to look normal. Helen and Geri sidled up beside her, one on each side.

"You okay, Mart?" asked Geri.

"Yes, fine," said Martha. "Just saying my goodbyes. Did you both get a chance to do the same?"

"Yes, I did earlier," said Helen. "Before the service".

"What about you?" Martha asked the youngest Parker.

"No, not really," she said, shaking her head.

"Why not?" asked Martha. "Would you like a moment just now?"

"No, it's okay," she said. "Mum knows that I love her. She doesn't need to hear it, not now. Not after everything that's happened. I can feel her, right here, on my shoulder, watching out for me. She's never really gone, not when you think about it like that. Talking to her coffin, I think that would take that away from me Mart. And I don't want it to go."

Martha squeezed Geri's arm. She was so proud of her, and Helen. They were stronger than her, more resilient, more independent. They were a credit to their mother and to her. She knew that she would be proud of them. Always.

The three Parkers stepped away from the grave's edge and headed for the row of cars parked up on the gravel path that ran through the cemetery. There weren't many there, only a select few who had braved the ice and the cold of a Glasgow January to see off Parker senior. DI Pope stood skulking at the back of the procession. Martha nodded at her as they made their way to the cars.

Matt had been arrested, Pope leading the investigation. He was due for trial in a few weeks and everyone expected him to be jailed. He was facing countless charges from all over the world and various countries were lining up to have him extradited. Even the papers hadn't held back, calling his crimes the 'worst of the century'. Justice, it seemed, caught up with everyone in the end.

Martha didn't want to think about it, not today. She would be in court when he was sentenced and she would celebrate then. Right now, it was all about her mother.

The sisters made their way to the lead car at the head of the procession. Martha opened the door and helped Geri in, followed by Helen. She was about to join them when someone caught her eye.

"You guys carry on," she said to them.

"What? Where are you going?" asked Helen.

"You're not going to another funeral are you?" asked Geri.

"I'll catch another car. Go on just now, I won't be long. I have to speak to somebody really quickly."

She closed the door and the car rolled gently down the path. The rest of the mourners all began to disappear too, all except the three figures standing beneath the spartan branches of a tree a few yards from the grave. Martha walked over, the nerves building in her stomach.

"Thank you for coming, Ms Wu," she said, as she approached them.

Nicola Wu took her expensive sunglasses off. Her flame-red hair was the only dash of colour about her, everything else either black or white. The two goons on either side of her were similarly dressed for the occasion —crisp suits and stylish black ties.

"I hear it was the boyfriend in the end," she said. "Can't say I'm surprised. Men are so utterly unreliable. That's why I steer well clear of them. Keeps me focussed and sharp. Still, they have their uses, as these two prove."

She smirked at her bodyguards. Martha bowed her head.

"You didn't need to come," she said. "In fact, I was rather surprised to see you here."

"Yes, well, I must be getting sympathetic in my old age," said Wu. "Something about a bit of closure, it can drive a woman insane. This Matthew character, he's facing life behind bars I take it?"

"I assume so," said Martha. "Once the trial is complete."

"Yes, I suspected as much. I'm sure I'll be able to find all kinds of unpleasantness for him to be put through when he's handed over to the Crown. I don't like rogue agents Martha, they make me very nervous. And if there's one thing I don't like to be, it's nervous. Isn't that right boys?"

"Yes ma'am," said one goon.

"Don't like to be nervous ma'am. Not you," said the other.

"See, they have their uses," Wu grinned. "It's nice to get answers though. And for that I'm grateful to you, Martha. I know you're strictly legitimate. But you saw your word through with the police and uncovered what was going on. I don't like to let something like that go without reward."

Martha's chest tightened. The last thing she wanted was a reward from Wu.

"Oh no, please," she said. "I can't accept anything from you Ms Wu, please. Not that I'm not appreciative. I just don't want to put you to any bother. Or expense."

"What are you talking about, Martha?" she said, tipping her sunglasses forward. "You've already had your reward from me. I'm not buying you something else."

"Pardon me?" asked Martha.

"How many taxi drivers do you know who could floor another man with one punch?" asked Wu.

Martha needed a moment to understand what she was being told. She shook her head.

"No, I don't get it," she said. "The cabbie, he was only there to check on what we were doing."

"And who do you think owns the taxi firm?" she asked. "And who do you think wanted to get to the bottom of who was causing such a ruckus among my friends in the, shall we say, less than legitimate business world, eh? Come on Martha, you're a smart cookie."

Martha wasn't sure how to react. She was grateful of course, why wouldn't she be? If the driver hadn't turned up at that moment then there was no telling what trouble they would have been in. The idea that Nicola Wu had been so directly involved in her life, in *saving* her life, however, didn't feel right.

"Sleeping dogs lie," said Wu. "I think we'll just scratch it all up to experience and move on. How does that sound?"

She snapped her fingers. A large, black Range Rover roared out of nowhere. The goons opened the back doors and Nicola Wu climbed in. She blew Martha a kiss before driving off, leaving her alone in the cemetery.

"Bloody hell," she said aloud. "I've got to start hanging around with a better crowd."

Thirty-two

THE FRONT DOOR opened with a creak. The noise seemed to wake everything up. The early morning light seeped in, chasing away the shadows. Martha Parker stood in the doorway and looked about her kingdom.

The office was hers, the business was hers. This was where she made her money but more than that, it was where she helped others. She liked to think that in her own small way she was making a difference. Even if it came in bad circumstances.

Everything was exactly as she had left it the night they had gone to the club in Glasgow's leafy west end. There was even a mug of ice cold tea collecting mould sitting on her desk where she had forgotten to clean it out. That had been two months ago now, but it felt much longer than that. So much had happened since that night. Too much to properly comprehend. In time, she thought, she would look back on it all and try to get her head around it. But that was for another day.

Today, she had a purpose. She wandered over to the back of the office and turned on the heater. Its bright red bars gently glowed into life and the heat was instant. She held out her hands and rubbed them together, chasing away the cold.

She had decided to reopen Parkers Investigations for business. At least on a part-time basis to start off with. Any lingering casework would be completed and then she would pick and choose which jobs she wanted to take. There was, after all, only so many Parkers to go about the place. Things would be different, everything would be different now. But she wanted to try and get as much normality back into her life as was possible. It didn't take long, thankfully, for that normality to come breezing in the door.

"How the hell can you say that Home Alone two is better than the first one. That's utterly absurd," Geri said.

"I'm not saying it's better, I'm just saying that it's got better *bits* in it," Helen fired back.

"But they're practically the same film?"

"Oh, now who's being absurd?"

The younger two Parker sisters brought with them a bit of life and energy to the office. It wasn't just the office though, it was Martha's whole existence. They were her family, the loves of her life. She couldn't be without either of them. If the last case had proven anything, it had been that. She would do anything to keep them both happy and safe. All they had to do was ask.

"Morning Mart," said Helen, stuffing a half-eaten doughnut into her mouth.

"Yeah, morning Martha," said Geri, sinking into her chair at her desk. "Can you have a word with her please. She's lost the plot already and it's not even nine o'clock."

"It's actually ten o'clock smarty pants," said Helen. "And you're late."

"You were late, too."

"I had to get breakfast."

"And how many breakfasts is that?"

"None of your business."

Martha started to laugh. She leaned back in her chair as her sisters continued to argue for a few more minutes, until they realised her hilarity.

"What's so funny?" asked Helen.

"Are we just clowns to you? Is that it?" asked Geri.

Martha calmed down. She got up from her chair and walked over to the others. Stretching out her arms, she beckoned both of her sisters in. They looked at each other and then back to her.

"Are you feeling okay?" asked Helen.

"You're not dying or something are you?" asked Geri. "I don't think I could handle another trip to the cemetery so soon after everything else."

"No I'm not dying," said Martha. "And I'm feeling just fine. I just wanted a hug is all. Is that such a terrible thing for a sister to want?"

Helen and Geri very carefully got up and wandered over to Martha. They all wrapped their arms around each other and she gave them each a kiss on the forehead.

"I love you both dearly," she said. "And I consider myself to be the luckiest person alive to spend each and every day with both of you. You're both amazing individuals and you work even better as a team. And I want to thank you for keeping an old fossil like me hanging around in your company. It means the world."

"Oh stop," said Helen.

"You're making me feel quite sick," said Geri.

They hugged for a few more minutes and Martha was happy, truly happy. She could have stayed there until the world came to an end. As it happened though, there were unhappy spouses and cheating partners who needed answers.

No sooner had the clock hit one minute past ten when the phone rang. Martha let Helen and Geri go, and picked it up.

"Parkers Investigations," she said. "How can I help you?"

ACKNOWLEDGEMENTS

As this is a book about siblings, I feel it's only appropriate that I thank my own for starters. My brother Adam and sister-in-law Kirsty have been avid supporters and followers of not only this series but my whole writing career to date. They're always the first to champion me when I'm not there, and to give me the usual familial joshing when I AM about. I'm grateful for everything they've done so far. And I can only thank them again here.

The inspiration for this series came from my wife's family. And so without my in-laws, there probably wouldn't BE any Parker sisters.

My thanks also go to the Caledonia Crime Collective. I'm proud to call myself a member of this eclectic group who are ALWAYS on hand with answers to the most bizarre of questions.

I'd also like to make a special mention of thanks to my agent Hannah. She's been an endless supply of insight, advice and solidarity to me. The Virgil to my Dante and for that I will always be in her debt.

A special thanks and shout out too to Sean at Red Dog, not only for the boundless energy and talent he shows on a daily basis, but for the faith he's shown me and the three snooping sisters you've just read about.

Being a writer can be a lonely business but I've always felt part of this community. And for that, I will always be your humble servant.

Milton Keynes UK
Ingram Content Group UK Ltd.
UKHW012006131223
434291UK00004B/292